THE CASTLE
IN CASSIOPEIA

THE CASTLE IN CASSIOPEIA

DEAD ENDERS BOOK THREE

MIKE RESNICK

an imprint of Prometheus Books
Amherst, NY

Published 2017 by Pyr®, an imprint of Prometheus Books

Cover illustration © Dave Seeley
Cover design by Liz Mills
Cover design © Prometheus Books

Inquiries should be addressed to
Pyr
59 John Glenn Drive
Amherst, New York 14228
VOICE: 716–691–0133
FAX: 716–691–0137
WWW.PYRSF.COM

21 20 19 18 17   5 4 3 2 1

Library of Congress Cataloging-in-Publication Data

Names: Resnick, Michael D., author.
Title: The castle in Cassiopeia / by Mike Resnick.
Description: Amherst, NY : Pyr, an imprint of Prometheus Books, 2017. |
    Series: Dead Enders ; 3
Identifiers: LCCN 2017003048 (print) | LCCN 2017007936 (ebook) |
    ISBN 9781633882317 (paperback) | ISBN 9781633882324 (ebook)
Subjects: LCSH: Imaginary wars and battles—Fiction. | Space warfare—Fiction. |
    Human-alien encounters—Fiction. | BISAC: FICTION / Science Fiction /
    Military. | FICTION / Science Fiction / Space Opera. | GSAFD: Science fiction.
Classification: LCC PS3568.E698 C37 2017 (print) | LCC PS3568.E698 (ebook) |
    DDC 813/.54—dc23
LC record available at https://lccn.loc.gov/2017003048

Printed in the United States of America

To Carol, as always,
And to twenty-two young men and women who are going to be
shaping the field of science fiction for years to come:

Nick DiChario	*Tina Gower*
Ron Collins	*Marina J. Lostetter*
Alex Shvartsman	*Andrea Stewart*
Lou J. Berger	*Kary English*
Larry Hodges	*Sharon Joss*
Martin L. Shoemaker	*Lezli Robyn*
Alvaro Zinos-Amaro	*Leena Likitalo*
Robert T. Jeschonek	*Laurie Tom*
Ken Liu	*Liz Colter*
Brennan Harvey	*Jennifer Campbell-Hicks*
Brad R. Torgersen	*Sylvia Spruck Wrigley*

PROLOGUE

"**H**ow soon can you and your Dead Enders be ready for another assignment?" asked General Cooper. "An urgent one?"

"It depends on what the problem is," said Nathan Pretorius, as he entered the office and sat down opposite the general's desk.

"Do you remember the Michkag clone, the ringer you installed in Orion last year?"

Pretorius frowned. "Oh, shit!" he muttered. "They discovered what he was and killed him?"

"Nice guess," said Cooper. "I only wish it was that easy."

"Oh?" said Pretorius, arching an eyebrow.

"The bastard has turned!"

"Turned?"

"He decided he *likes* being the most powerful general the Coalition's got," growled Cooper, "and he's not going to help us defeat his own race. He's a brilliant strategist, and thanks to being raised here he knows more about our equipment, and about how we think and react, than any other alien in the whole Coalition. It turns out he's been feeding us false data for months."

"Does he know that we know?" asked Pretorius.

Cooper nodded his head. "He does now. We had the bastard surrounded out by the Bellermaine system. Had him outnumbered twenty-to-one."

"And he escaped?"

Cooper grimaced. "He didn't even *try* to escape. He destroyed every last one of our ships. Nothing survived, not even any records of how the hell he did it."

"I'm impressed," said Pretorius.

"We've got to eliminate him," continued Cooper. "Kill him, capture him, whatever it takes."

"You had a shot at him," said Pretorius. "You blew it."

"And that operation began *before* he knew we were onto him," growled Cooper. "He's currently the best-protected being, human or alien, in the whole Coalition, probably in the whole damned galaxy. We're not going to get him with sheer force; they'll spot us coming, and if they don't think they can beat us they'll move him before we start getting too close."

"Somehow I can intuit what's coming next," said Pretorius dryly.

"You and your Dead Enders are going to have to take him out before he costs us this goddamned war!"

"Where is he?" asked Pretorius.

Cooper waved his hand in a gesture that encompassed roughly half the galaxy. "Out there somewhere," he said. "All we know is that he's not in Orion anymore. He's probably not even in Coalition territory."

Pretorius frowned. "That's not much to go on."

"It's all we've got."

"And I have to point out that my team isn't exactly up to speed. We lost Felix and Circe on the Antares mission."

"What, exactly, have you got left?"

"Three women and an alien. And me."

"And what do you need?"

"I won't know until—"

"You attack him?" interrupted Cooper.

Pretorius shook his head. "Until I figure out, first, how we're going to find him, and second, how we're going to get to him once we know where he is. In that order. There's no sense hunting for weaknesses in his defense until we know where to find him."

"How soon can you be ready to go?"

"It'll take a couple of days to gather my team, and then as long as it takes to get actionable intelligence on Michkag's whereabouts."

"If we *had* any actionable information, I'd have given it to you weeks ago."

"I know," said Pretorius.

"Then what makes you think can come up with anything at all, regardless of the time frame?" demanded Cooper.

The ghost of a smile crossed Pretorius's face. "I don't go to the standard military sources."

"All right," said Cooper. "Let's get this show on the road. How much money will you need?"

Pretorius shrugged. "Beats the hell out of me."

Cooper nodded. "Okay. I'll give you an open line of credit for—"

"Forget it," said Pretorius. "We have to assume he's not in the Democracy, at least not yet. And lines of credit to Democracy banks aren't going to honored almost anywhere else. So we'll want every form of human and alien cash."

"And if you need more?"

"Pick a neutral planet, stick a box of various currencies there—"

"Under heavy guard," said Cooper.

"Under *unobtrusive* guard," Pretorius corrected him.

Cooper nodded his head. "And what else?"

Pretorius shrugged. "I probably won't know until we need it."

"And that's all?" demanded Cooper.

"You've already proven that outnumbering him isn't the key to stopping him," said Pretorius. "But if you'd rather try again . . ."

"Shut up," said Cooper irritably.

"You're sure you wouldn't prefer to——?"

"Shut up and get out!" snapped Cooper. As Pretorius walked to the door of the general's office, he added, "And bring me back the head of that goddamned clone!"

1

"**I** get so damned tired of bailing you out," complained Pretorius, as the robot accompanied Snake to the front desk.

"Hi, Nathan," she replied. "Somehow I doubt that you're using your own money."

"Hell, you've been jailed so many times I couldn't afford your bail."

"We now remand Sally Kowalski into your custody," said the robot in a grating monotone.

"I have no idea how this goddamned system works," growled Pretorius. "You've been caught so often your bail ought to be much higher."

She smiled and shook her head. "I get caught because no one else can do what I do. They take one look at the results, know it was me, and come get me, and none of them has to work very hard. I have *never* been arrested *during* a theft."

"Then why the hell don't you pull a heist that *anyone* can do?"

"Because I'm an artiste," said Snake.

"I suppose we'll put that on your tombstone," replied Pretorius as he led the small, wiry woman out onto a slidewalk.

"Unless you've moved from that fortress you laughably call an apartment we're heading the wrong way."

"No, we're not."

"But there's nothing up ahead except the military prison."

Pretorius smiled. "You should be used to prisons by now."

"Which of the team members are you bailing out of there?" she asked.

"We're just visiting."

"Right," she said. "And you paid thirty thousand credits to bail me out so I could visit another jail."

"Another prisoner, anyway," said Pretorius.

"And it's one of our Dead Enders?"

Pretorius shook his head.

"Okay, I give up. Why am I going to be thirty thousand credits worth of fascinated to meet whoever it is?"

"Circe was our empath," replied Pretorius. "With her dead, I have no one who can read minds or emotions. I'm hoping you're just criminal enough to tell me what he's thinking and whether you think he's lying?"

"What *who* is thinking or lying?"

"Michkag."

"'Our' Michkag? I thought he was out in Orion somewhere, leading the Coalition into one trap after another."

Pretorius shook his head. "The original Michkag."

"What's *he* doing—leading some kind of prison revolt?"

"As far as I know, he's obeying the rules and minding his own business," answered Pretorius.

"I haven't seen him since we captured him and delivered him here," said Snake.

"Neither have I."

She frowned and stepped off the slidewalk. "Okay, this is as far as I go until you tell me what the hell this is about."

Pretorius also got off, and stared down at her.

"It's the clone," he began.

"Shit!" said Snake. "He got himself killed, and now you're wondering if it's safe to make a deal with the original and put him back."

"I wish it was that easy," said Pretorius.

"Oh?"

He nodded. "Let's get to the prison. I don't want anyone to overhear what I say next."

She stared at him, frowning. "It's *that* big?"

"Just get back on the slidewalk."

She got onto it with no further argument and was silent for the last half mile, until they got off and entered the prison.

The instant they were inside she took his arm and led him to a corner of the lobby.

"Okay," she said. "*Now* I want to know what's going on."

"The clone has turned."

"He's on *their* side now?"

"That's right."

"So what's the problem?" she asked. "We got to the real one. Surely we can get to the phony."

"He's *not* a phony," replied Pretorius. "He's a clone."

"Same thing. He's an imitation Michkag."

"Michkag was the best general—hell, the best *anything*—that the enemy had. We tell the public that he fought us to a draw, but the truth of the matter is that he was beating the shit out of us."

"I know."

"So we found ourselves a turncoat, paid him to come over to our side with a skin scraping, and cloned the original Michkag."

"I know," she said irritably. "I was there, remember?"

"Right, you were there," he said as they approached the prison. "And you and the rest of my Dead Enders sneaked him out to the fortress in Orion and made the switch."

"So tell me something I *don't* know."

"What you don't know is that the clone is every bit as bright as the original, and that he's decided he likes being the general of an army and navy numbering more than five billion. Because he was raised within the Democracy, he had years to study us, to look for weaknesses, and because he was the property of the military he learned how the military thinks. How *our* military thinks. And of course he was trained to know how the Coalition military thinks, because he had to pass as the real Michkag." Pretorius stared down at her. "You beginning to understand the problem?"

"What do you think you can learn from the original?" asked Snake, as they continued through the heavily guarded building. "And why should he tell you a damned thing? If they were winning with him in charge, then surely they're winning with an even brighter, better-trained version of him in command."

"I don't know what we can learn," admitted Pretorius.

"Then why are we here?" demanded Snake.

"I don't care how brilliant you are, how exceptional your comprehension of military tactics is, how cleverly you improvise under pressure, if you rise to the position Michkag had you've also got to be more than a little bit of an egomaniac." He paused. "Maybe he'll be jealous of another Michkag capturing all the glory."

"Jealous enough to help us?" asked Snake dubiously.

Pretorius shrugged. "I don't know. I'll tell you one thing, though."

"What?"

"We'll never know if we don't give him a chance."

A uniformed guard approached them. "Your purpose, sir?"

"I'm here to speak with the prisoner Michkag. My name is Pretorius; General Cooper will clear me."

"And her?" asked the guard, indicating Snake.

"Sally Kowalski," said Pretorius. "He'll okay her too."

"One moment, sir," said the guard, heading off to a different room.

He returned a moment later. "Follow me, sir and ma'am."

Pretorius hoped that Snake wouldn't make a fuss about being called "ma'am," and fell into step behind the guard.

They entered an airlift, floated up three levels, and emerged into a narrow corridor. They proceeded down the length of it to the end, past a number of barred doors, until they came to what seemed like a completely open room.

"See that line on the floor?" said the guard. "No farther."

"Force field?" asked Pretorius.

The guard nodded his head. "Of course."

"Overpowering or lethal?"

"Lethal," was the answer. "We don't play guessing games with how much an alien can take."

"Okay, thanks," said Pretorius.

"I'll be at the far end of the corridor, where we stepped out of the lift," said the guard, pulling out his burner and setting it to lethal.

Pretorius turned to look into the cell. A large, powerful-looking member of the Kabori race was seated on a chair that was clearly built to handle his size and weight. He was a little over six feet tall, with a prehensile nose, more like that of a proboscis monkey than an elephant. He had two very wideset eyes, earholes but no ears, and a sharply pointed chin. His arms were the length of a gorilla's, and just as heavily muscled. His feet were almost circular. His head and body were devoid of hair, and his color, top to bottom, was a dull red. He stared expressionlessly at the two humans.

"Hi, Michkag," said Pretorius. "Remember us?"

"You and the rest of your motley crew dominate my every waking thought," said Michkag bitterly.

"I'm sorry to hear that."

"Someday I will escape and reclaim my empire. Then you will know the meaning of the word 'sorry.'"

"Not gonna happen," said Snake.

Michkag glared at her for a long moment. "You think *you* can stop me?"

"I don't have to," she said with a smile. "You've already been stopped."

"You mean these walls and this force field?" said Michkag, waving his arm contemptuously around at his surroundings. "Sooner or later my forces will come and set me free."

"First they have to know you're here," said Snake.

"They will find me."

She shook her head. "They won't even come looking for you."

Michkag considered what she had said, then shook his head as if to clear it, and frowned. "Did you come here just to speak nonsense to me?"

"No," said Snake. "I came here to gloat after *he*"—she jerked her thumb in Pretorius's direction—"lays the news on you."

Michkag turned to Pretorius and stared at him for a long moment.

"Well?" he said at last.

"No one's looking for you because they're perfectly happy with the Michkag they have," said Pretorius.

"What are you talking about?" growled Michkag. "*I* am Michkag."

Pretorius shook his head. "You're *a* Michkag. The clone we replaced you with is still running things for the Coalition."

"Then why are you . . . ?" began Michkag. Then, suddenly, he froze, and after a few seconds the equivalent of a smile gradually played across his lips. "You no longer control him."

"That's right."

"Then he is a true clone. He carries my genes and my thoughts."

"Not for long," said Pretorius.

Michkag uttered a harsh laugh. "You can't lie to me! You have no idea how to combat him, and you have come to me for advice." He paused. "You will die of old age, or torture—or preferably a painful and disfiguring disease—before I tell you anything useful."

"You haven't heard my offer yet," said Pretorius.

"You're going to sneak me back into Orion and pull off the same switch that got me here in the first place?" said Michkag contemptuously.

"No, you're too dangerous ever to be allowed loose again."

"Then what can you possibly offer?"

"You've spent more than a year in this one small cell," replied Pretorius. "We'll never set you free, but if you'll agree to help us I can arrange for you to be transferred to a heavily guarded villa on a few acres of ground. Except for the guards you'll be the only one on the whole planet, and no ship will land except to bring replacement guards, but it'll be a hell of a lot more pleasant way to spend the rest of your life than being cooped up here."

Pretorius couldn't read Michkag's expression, but he could tell from Snake's face and demeanor that she thought they were wasting their time.

"Well?" he said after a couple of minutes had passed.

"I shall borrow an expression I have heard from Men on those occasions when I have been in their company."

Michkag fell silent for another thirty seconds.

"I'm still waiting for your answer."

Michkag walked across his small cell until he was just a few inches from the force field, and looked Pretorius full in the eye.

"Go to hell," he said.

2

The Dead Enders were comfortably sprawled on the leather furniture of the elegant penthouse suite of the plain-looking building that housed the military's headquarters.

"And then he told the boss to go to hell!" said Snake with an amused laugh. "But of course, once we're back in the Orion Cluster we're gonna wish *we* were in hell instead."

"I've never been to Orion," said a young redheaded woman. "Can it really be that bad?"

"Worse," said Snake.

"We may not even go there," said Pretorius. "Our information is that the Michkag clone knows we're onto him, and he's left Orion well behind him."

"But why?" asked Irish, the redhead. "He's surrounded by his military there."

"*I* can tell you why," said Pandora, a middle-aged woman, the team's computer expert.

"Please," said Irish.

"If *we* could find out he's a clone, and of course we could, there's every likelihood some of his lieutenants could find it out too. And a few of them have to think that this isn't the Michkag they swore their allegiance to, that this one was working for the Democracy until a year and a half ago, and who knows where his loyalties lie?"

Snake shook her head. "If he made them even stronger, produced even more victories for them, why would anyone believe that?"

Pretorius couldn't suppress a chuckle. "Snake, you've got a prison record as long as your arm. How many times have you fed the police or the courts, all of whom are aware of your history, some bullshit story and gotten off scot-free—and how many times were you jailed for the same story? We can't be sure what they'll believe, especially once they know it's not the Michkag who recruited them."

Snake shrugged. "Okay, point taken."

"Anyway, we'll try Orion first, or at least check it out," continued Pretorius, "but my guess is that he's elsewhere."

"Where?" asked Irish.

"It's a big galaxy," answered Pretorius. "Half the job is finding him."

"And the other half is killing or capturing him when he's surrounded by maybe fifty thousand warships," added Pandora.

"Against four of us," said Snake.

"More than that," said Pretorius.

"We already lost Felix and Circe on that mission to Antares," said Snake irritably. "Who the hell is left?"

"You're about to lean on him," said Pretorius with a smile.

"Proto?" she said, jumping back from the cushion that was next to her.

"Gzychurlyx at your service," replied the cushion.

"If you want to be at our service," said Pretorius, "use a name we can all pronounce."

"If it's up to *me* to choose, why did you name me Proto?"

"It's short for protoplasm, and that's the closest word I could come on the spur of the moment to imply that you're a shape-changer."

"I'm not, you know."

"Okay, a shape-projector," said Pretorius. "Big difference."

"There certainly is," said Proto. "They always shoot a few feet too high."

"So we're a man, three women, and a footstool or whatever the hell he chooses to look like tomorrow," said Snake. "And Michkag's got what, eighty billion soldiers in uniform and God knows how many lurking in bars and drug dens and planetary capitols." She turned to Pretorius. "I sure admire your notion of fair odds, Nate."

"We captured the real Michkag and put this one in his place with just about the same crew," replied Pretorius.

"And we rescued Edgar Nmumba from that prison in Antares with the same crew that's sitting here right now," added Pandora. "And one of us"—she jerked a thumb toward Irish—"was a neophyte on her first assignment."

"Oh, we're good," replied Snake. "*Real* good. Maybe the best there ever was. But why do we always have to face odds of three or four billion to one?"

"Because we're good," said Pandora with a smile. "Maybe the best there ever was."

"So what's our first step?" asked Irish.

"We took it this afternoon," answered Pretorius. "I visited the original Michkag, and brought Snake along with me to see if she could spot any inconsistencies that I missed."

"And did she?"

"Nope," said Snake. "Probably the first time in his life he went five whole minutes without lying."

"So now we have to figure out where the clone is and how to get to him."

"Same thing we did with the real one," said Pandora.

"This'll be harder," said Pretorius.

"Why? They're the same guy, at least genetically."

"The first one had never been threatened or captured. *This* one knows that we were able to get to the best-protected being in the galaxy and actually kidnap him. He'll be even better protected—and he knows who we are and what we look and sound like."

Pandora frowned and emitted a sigh. "Yeah, well, there *is* that."

"So where do we look for him?" asked Irish.

"We don't," said Pretorius. "Or at least, not without some help. It's a big galaxy; he could be anywhere. My guess is that he doesn't have such a large army with him that it'll stand out on a small undeveloped world or system. So first we have to pinpoint his location, and then we'll dope out what it takes to get to him."

"Well, it's got to be easier than last time," said Proto. "This time all we have to do is kill him, not capture and secretly replace him."

"I don't know about that," replied Pandora. "Last time he thought he was untouchable, that his fortress was impregnable. This time he knows better."

"You make it sound like we're after the same Michkag," said Proto.

"It a way we are," responded Pandora. "Physically identical, in charge of the same military machine, probably no brighter or dumber than the last one. Doubtless attacks problems and enemies in the same way as the original."

"So I repeat," said Irish. "Where do we start?"

Snake and Pandora both smiled. "Where we always do."

Irish frowned. "Where is that?"

"You've been on a mission with us, so you should know," said Pandora.

"One mission," said Irish. "So I don't know what's routine yet. Where do we begin our search?"

"At the boss's favorite whorehouse," replied Snake.

3

They were three days reaching McPherson's World, most of it spent traversing the Fitzgibbon Wormhole. They emerged in the Neutral Zone, populated with ships from the Democracy, the Coalition, and half a dozen other planetary or military conglomerations. They homed in on the Tradertown of McPherson and set the ship down in a spaceport that seemed larger than the little town needed but which was ninety percent full. By the time they climbed down the stairs to the ground, Proto had assumed the shape of a totally nondescript human male, and they soon were walking across the flat dusty surface to the largest building in town, one that appeared to any outsider to be a very large, very plain, white frame farmhouse.

"I almost hate to ask how you discovered this place," said Irish.

"It's got a sterling reputation," replied Pretorius with a grin.

"I can imagine!" replied Irish.

Pretorius chuckled. "Yeah, it's got a pretty fair reputation for *that*, too. But two-thirds of the clientele aren't here for sex—or, at least, not *only* for sex. If it's happening anywhere in the galaxy, Madam Methuselah will know about it if anyone does. She doesn't play sides, and she doesn't allow any confrontations on her property."

"Her property?" repeated Irish. "You mean the house and the surrounding yard?"

"I mean the whole planet," answered Pretorius.

"Oh, come on!" said Irish. "No one owns a planet!"

"*She* does," said Pandora.

"She's had enough time to populate it with people she wants as neighbors, living in houses she designed, on property she defined," added Snake.

"I *saw* her last time," protested Irish. "She can't be thirty years old! Maybe thirty-five at the outside. She hasn't had *time* to do all that!"

Pretorius chuckled. "She's about eight hundred years old."

"I don't believe it!"

"One thing McPherson has besides a whorehouse is a weekly newspaper," said Pretorius. "The files go back six or seven centuries. And there are holos of her in almost every issue, looking exactly the way she looks today."

"What's her secret?" asked Irish.

"Beats me," said Pretorius.

"But if she sold it, she could buy half the goddamned galaxy instead one grubby little world in the Neutral Zone," added Snake.

And grubby it was, eighty percent dirt and the rest dust. Almost all the water was underground, or at least out of sight. The town consisted of the spaceport (which in truth was simply a landing field, with no customs to pass through), a pair of boarding houses, a message-forwarding station, a spare-parts shop for the more popular types of smaller spaceships, a general store that sold everything from dry goods to medicine to antique weaponry . . . and then there was Madam Methuselah's, which had a fame far out of proportion to both its size and clientele.

"Here we are," said Snake, pointing to a frame building that was clearly the largest structure in the town, but seemed unexceptional in all other respects.

"I can't get over how famous a grubby little whorehouse on an even grubbier little planet is," said Irish, shaking her head.

"It's not that little," said Pandora. "There must be seventy or eighty rooms beneath ground level, as well as all the ones you'll be aware of once you enter."

"And, as you know from last time," added Pretorius, "about two-thirds of her clientele have more important business here than the exchanging of bodily fluids."

They climbed the three faux wooden stairs to the large veranda. The door sensed their presence and slid into a wall, and then they were inside. Females of more than a dozen races lounged in the main rooms, and another thirty or forty were probably busy working at the moment. The walls were covered with erotic paintings, holographs, and etchings from dozens of worlds, which meant most of them should have been turnoffs to ninety percent of the clientele, but somehow they were almost *all* erotic. Just ahead of them was a huge, elegant bar made of an alien hardwood that constantly fluctuated in color from a brilliant gold to a deep, rich mahogany.

"There she is," whispered Pandora, staring at a beautiful blonde woman who was standing at the bar, speaking to one of the alien bartenders.

Pretorius briefly studied his crew.

"Okay," he said. "Irish, come with me. The rest of you, try to make yourselves inconspicuous, which I realize is a tall order in a whorehouse. And if some man or alien approaches you, talk to him, see where he's from, and find out if the Coalition's made any inroads on his system. Proto, I'd tell you to go to the bar and have a drink, but why show everyone that you're maybe eighteen inches tall when you're not projecting this image. No sense losing the elements of secrecy and surprise in case we ever need them around here." Pretorius lowered his head in thought for a few second. "You come with Irish and me."

"Whatever you say, Nathan," replied the image of the well-built six-foot-tall man.

Pretorius turned back to Snake. "I know you," he said. "Any man lays a hand on you, you're as likely to cut it off as step away. You make a commotion while I'm talking to Madam Methuselah and I'll leave you here."

While Snake was coming up with a reply, Pretorius caught Madam Methuselah's eye. She smiled at him and pointed toward the narrow corridor that led to her office, and he began walking, followed by Irish and Proto. Once there, they found themselves in a room that was even more lavishly furnished than the one atop military headquarters.

"Welcome back, Nathan," said the stunning blonde with the ancient eyes. "You've been well, I trust."

He shrugged. "I'm here, anyway."

"I'll take that as a positive," she replied. She turned to Irish. "I remember you from last time. I hope Nathan is treating you well."

"No complaints," said Irish.

"Except for getting shot at and starved and—" added Pretorius with a smile.

"You travel with Nathan, you have to expect these little inconveniences," she said with a smile. "I don't recognize your other friend."

"Who's your favorite murderball player?" asked Pretorius.

"Jaboxtin Tchakyan of the Bellarma race," replied Madam Methuselah. "Why?"

"Proto?" said Pretorius.

Instantly Proto became the perfect image of Jaboxtin Tchakyan, right down to the well-worn golden boots that were his trademark.

"Well, I'll be damned!" exclaimed Madam Methuselah. "You know, not much impresses me after all these centuries in this business and location, but your friend certainly does! That's just remarkable!"

"Surely you've had shape-changers before," said Pretorius.

"Yes, but they're usually limited. If you're a boy, you can become a girl. If you're a Teelarben, you may become a Jaxtil. But to not only change who you are, but to perfectly change into someone I had suggested, someone you've probably never met before, that is truly unique!"

"Shake his hand," suggested Pretorius.

She walked over to Proto and extended her hand. It passed right through his hand, arm, and body.

"Is he there at all?" she asked, stepping back.

"Oh, yes," Pretorius assured her. "Show her, Proto."

Proto let her see him as he really was, then reverted to human form.

"That's remarkable!" she exclaimed. "Where do you come from?"

"Elsewhere," answered Proto.

"What the hell kind of answer is that?" demanded Madam Methuselah.

"An essential one," explained Proto. "As you see, my race can't reach anything that's two feet above the ground, and has no fingers for firing a weapon—so when one of us leaves our home planet, we are sworn to secrecy."

"And now to business," said Pretorius.

"All right," she said, walking back to her desk with obvious reluctance and sitting down on the luxurious chair that immediate changed its shape to accommodate her as comfortably as possible.

"Can you keep a secret?"

"You say that once more, Nathan, and you can march right out of here and never come back," said Madam Methuselah.

"No offense intended," said Pretorius.

"All right," she said. "Now what secret do you wish to confide in me."

"One I hope you know already."

She merely stared at him curiously.

"About a year and a half ago you helped my team by pinpointing where we could find Michkag."

"I know," she answered. "I wish things had turned out more favorably."

"They turned out just fine—*that* time."

She frowned. "What am I not understanding, Nathan? You went to Orion to eliminate Michkag. He was there until perhaps fifty days ago, so clearly your mission failed."

"My mission was a success," said Pretorius. "Until," he added with a bitter smile, "perhaps fifty days ago."

"I like guessing games as well as the next eight-hundred-year-old madam, Nathan, but why don't you tell me what the hell you're talking about?"

"Your information was good," said Pretorius. "We got to Michkag's headquarters and took him back into the Democracy with us."

She frowned. "You *took* him? Why didn't you kill him?"

"I have no idea why Cooper and the others didn't kill him when we got him back home," said Pretorius. "I certainly would have."

"I'm confused, Nathan," she said, irritation creeping into her voice. "Why would you kill him there, but not in Orion?"

"Because we didn't want anyone to know he was dead."

"I'm still confused."

"We didn't want anyone to know he was dead because we had managed to clone him from a skin scraping we got some years back. The clone was raised in the Democracy, trained in the Democracy, and pointed toward one goal: to replace the real Michkag and subtly weaken his empire until they were finally willing to make peace with the rest of the galaxy."

Madam Methuselah considered what she'd been told for a long minute, then nodded her head. "I see," she said at last. "Yes, you couldn't possibly kill him where anyone might find out. They'd just anoint a new leader and nothing would change. But to replace him with *your* puppet, a clone who was loyal to *you* . . . I call that goddamned brilliant."

"Thank you."

"And of course the clone remained true to his breeding and not his training, or you wouldn't be here."

Pretorius nodded. "He decided he liked running an empire more than he liked being responsible and loyal to us."

"Well, that explains it," she said.

"It?" said Irish, her first contribution to the conversation.

Madam Methuselah turned to her and nodded. "He's gone, of course. He must have known that if he disobeyed a few orders, or won a couple of battles he was supposed to lose, that the Democracy would figure he'd turned, and once they figured that, then Orion was the most dangerous place in the galaxy for him to be."

"So do you know where he is?" asked Pretorius.

Madam Methuselah shook her head. "To be honest, I didn't know for sure that he was alive until you just told me the situation. I know he's not in Orion any longer, but he could have been assassinated by one of his underlings."

Pretorius shook his head. "He takes a lot of killing."

"If he's still alive, and it seems that he is, then my guess is that he's totally out of the Coalition's territory."

"That's almost a fifth of the galaxy!" said Pretorius.

"And the Democracy controls a quarter of the galaxy," she answered. "Do you realize how much galaxy is left for the taking, Nathan?"

"There are other political entities, other kingdoms," said Pretorius, frowning.

"Could any of them withstand an attack by the Coalition?"

"No," he admitted. "But they couldn't withstand the Democracy either."

"Oh?" said Madam Methuselah, arching an eyebrow in mock amusement. "And do you plan on absorbing the rest of the galaxy any time soon?"

"Of course not."

"That's probably why he didn't have, or won't have, much trouble establishing himself there. Remember: he's not seeking a war of conquest. That would spread his forces too thin. He's offering a smaller, weaker kingdom a chance to join the Coalition and by doing so become a part of a political and military entity that will soon be unrivaled in the galaxy, even by the Democracy."

"It makes sense," agreed Irish.

"And you've no idea where to begin looking for him?" asked Pretorius.

"Until a few minutes ago, I thought he was probably dead," agreed Madam Methuselah. "I know this breaks most of the laws of science and statistics, but I've been breaking them for centuries. I plan on living at least another five hundred years, and I do not want to live in a universe ruled by Michkag or his clone, or where my remaining customers are all Kaboris like Michkag." She stared long and hard at Pretorius for a few seconds. "By tomorrow I will have gotten word to *all* my sources to drop whatever they're doing and concentrate on pinpointing Michkag."

"Thank you, Madam Methuselah," said Pretorius.

She stood up. "I never take sides, Nathan, you know that—but I'm on your side on this one."

"And I deeply appreciate it."

"You'll be leaving now," she said. "Keep in touch with me daily, so I can let you know of any information that comes in."

Pretorius frowned in thought for a moment. "I could use another favor, too," he said. "I should have thought of it before we even set out on this mission."

"What is it?"

"A ship and a pilot."

She frowned. "Don't you have a ship here?"

He nodded. "Yes, and we'll be boarding it and leaving momentarily. What I need now is a ship that can take Proto back to headquarters."

"Why?" asked Proto and Madam Methuselah in unison.

"We don't even know what sector of the galaxy Michkag's in, let alone what world. I don't know what it may take to assassinate or capture him. I've got a team member—" he pointed to Proto "—who can look so much like him that Michkag's own mother couldn't tell them apart . . . until he opens his mouth. I should have thought of this sooner, but we've got a turncoat Kabori back in the Democracy, a scientist named Djibmet who actually got the skin fragment that we got Michkag's DNA from and spent a few years of his life training the clone. I want him to teach Proto to speak in Kabori, in case he has to impersonate Michkag somewhere up the road."

"Not gonna work," said Madam Methuselah. "He can *look* like Michkag, but unless he's hiding a Kabori's jaw structure in that sluglike body, he'll never be able to pronounce the words properly. One or two sentences and he'll give himself away."

"You're sure?" asked Pretorius.

"Proto, become Michkag for a minute."

Proto did as she said.

"Now pronounce these five common Kabori words," she said, uttering them.

He tried.

"You see?" she said, turning to Pretorius. "*I've* got an accent. *He's* got a speech impediment."

"Oh, well, it was a thought," said Pretorius. "And this saves him a trip back to headquarters." He got to his feet, signaling Irish to do the same. He frowned. "I just wish I knew where to start."

"I think I can help you," said Madam Methuselah.

"Oh?"

"If you don't mind traveling with a notorious thief and smuggler."

A small smile crept across Pretorius's face. "I've traveled with worse."

"I doubt it," she said, returning his smile. "His name is Apollo;

he's wanted in the Coalition, the Democracy, and three other galactic conglomerations. If anything out of the ordinary is happening anywhere, he's the man who can get you to wherever the clone doesn't want you to go."

"Sounds good to me," said Pretorius.

"He'll want to meet you alone first," said Madam Methuselah. "An awful lot of worlds have put prices on his head, and he won't want to be surrounded by your crew until he knows he can trust you and you can control them."

"Not a problem. Have him contact me and name the time and place."

"I should warn you," she added. "He's not cheap."

"You get what you pay for," replied Pretorius. "No one ever said the galaxy would be cheap in terms of blood *or* treasure."

And with that, he, Irish, and Proto left the room, picked up their companions, and returned to their ship.

4

"**S**o where to now?" asked Pandora, who was sitting at the ship's control panel.

"Nowhere in particular," replied Pretorius.

"Makes sense," said Snake. "I always knew we should look nowhere in particular."

"He'll contact us," said Pretorius.

"Michkag?" said Snake. "I hardly think so."

"No, Apollo."

"Who the hell is Apollo?" demanded Snake.

"You'll like him," said Pretorius, allowing himself the luxury of an amused smile. "He's broken even more laws than you have."

"Impossible!" scoffed Snake.

"I'll admit it's hard to believe," said Pretorius.

"I hate to interrupt," said Pandora, "but I'd like the coordinates to Nowhere in Particular. I would hate to take us to Elsewhere by mistake."

"Find the least populated area—that's the least populated by planets, not by inhabitants—within a dozen light years, then create a small orbit of maybe half a light year or so, and just stick to it until I know where I'm meeting Apollo."

Pandora shrugged and began manipulating the controls. "You're the boss."

"It's comforting that *someone* remembers that," replied Pretorius.

"Do you know anything about this Apollo, other than the fact that Snake is already jealous of him?" asked Proto.

Snake picked up a cushion and hurled it at what appeared to be Proto's midsection in his nondescript human guise. Of course it went right through the image and bounced off the back of his chair.

"Thank you," said Proto. "But I didn't really need another cushion."

"Next time I'll stomp on your foot," she growled. "I guarantee you'll feel *that*."

They traveled in silence for a few moments. Then Pandora turned away from the panel to face her companions.

"I just ran a check on Apollo," she announced.

"Aren't you supposed to be piloting the ship?" said Snake.

"It's been on automatic for the past five minutes," said Pandora. She turned to Pretorius. "Your soon-to-be-friend Apollo is a very interesting man, Nate."

"So I've been told," he answered. "But only in broad, general terms. I assume you've got some specifics."

She nodded her head. "Some. And I imagine for every one I've got, there are two or three that nobody knows about yet. Well, nobody who's still alive, anyway."

"Okay, lay it on us," said Pretorius.

"He's wanted for murder on seven planets," said Pandora. "That's not *one* murder."

"Seven," said Snake.

Pandora shook her head. "Eleven."

"Guy's got a temper," said Snake.

"Interesting thing, though," continued Pandora. "Every victim—five men, two women, and four non-humans—had records longer than his."

"A falling-out among thieves?" suggested Proto.

Pretorius grimaced. "One falling-out I could buy," he said. "Maybe two. But *eleven?*"

"A telling point," said Irish.

"Okay," said Pretorius. "What else have you got?"

"Suspected of espionage on three worlds," said Pandora, checking her screen for the statistics. "Robbed banks on at least four worlds. Poaching."

"Poaching?" said Pretorius, frowning.

"Very rare dragonlike creature from the jungle on Matera VI. Some part of it is worth a small fortune, though I'm not clear whether it's an eyeball, which looks in the illustration like a goddamned diamond, or the tusks, which dwarf just about anything I've ever seen illustrated."

"What else?" asked Pretorius.

"About two dozen disturbing the peace convictions on frontier worlds."

"And you know how hard it is to get charged with disturbing the peace on one of those planets," said Snake.

"Sounds like a real charmer," said Pretorius. "Anything else?"

Pandora smiled. "Yes, one more thing."

"Must be really interesting to amuse you that much."

"Two Medals of Courage from the Democracy," she replied. "That's the highest single honor the Democracy can bestow on anyone in or out of the military."

"And which was he?" asked Pretorius. "In or out?"

"Once each."

"Sounds like he's fit for just about anything," said Pretorius.

"Except maybe crocheting," said Snake with a smile.

"I don't know," said Proto. "Give a man like that a crochet needle and there's no telling what he might do with it."

"Point taken," said Pretorius, repressing a smile. "Snake, you see him with crocheting equipment, you report it to me immediately."

"You don't seem especially worried about a man with those credentials," noted Pandora.

"Madam Methuselah vouches for him," answered Pretorius. "She's never steered me wrong."

"I hate to think our fate depends on the word of an eight-hundred-year-old hooker," said Snake.

"Unlike the word of a contortionist thief that I have to bail out every year or so?" said Pretorius with a smile. "I'll bet good money *she's* never been convicted of anything."

"Oops!" said Pandora. "Incoming."

"Holo," ordered Pretorius.

A few seconds later the image of a tall burly man with a thick beard and flaming red hair appeared on the middle of the desk. He wore two burners, a screecher, a pistol of indeterminate properties, and there was a wicked-looking knife stuck in one of his boots.

"Pretorius?" he said in a deep, hoarse voice.

"Nate," said Pretorius, holding up a hand.

The man nodded. "Figures, given what's traveling with you. I'm Apollo. Merilee said you wanted to talk to me."

"Merilee?" repeated Pretorius. "So that's her name?"

Apollo shrugged. "Beats me. But I wasn't going to keep calling her Madam Methuselah, so I decided Merilee fit her."

Pretorius grinned. "I wish I'd thought of that a few years back."

"So what can I do for you?" asked Apollo.

"I suppose saying 'Help us save the galaxy' is a little trite," answered Pretorius. "How about 'Help us save the Democracy and work up from there'?"

"I've never saved a galaxy, or even just the Democracy, before. What's the job entail, and what does it pay?"

"How soon can—?" began Pretorius.

"Just a minute," said Apollo, holding up a hand. "My mistake."

"Your mistake?" said Pretorius, puzzled.

"I'm sure you're talking from a military ship, but I'm in a kind of sleazy hotel, and there's no guarantee that we can keep this conversation confidential."

"Not a problem," said Pretorius. "I'll be happy to meet you at a location of your choosing."

"Okay," said Apollo. "There's a world not too far from me, Prateep II. I'm sure it's in your star charts."

"I need more than just a world's name to locate you," said Pretorius.

"Marumbu," was the reply. "City on the equator, named after the man who mapped the planet and settled there. I'll be at a bar called the Crippled Worm."

Pretorius frowned. "The Crippled Worm?"

"Yeah," said Apollo. "Ain't you ever seen a crippled worm?"

"No."

Apollo chuckled. "Nobody else has either. On the other hand, I'll bet there's not another joint called the Crippled Worm anywhere in the galaxy."

"You're probably right," said Pretorius.

"Come armed," continued Apollo. "This planet's right in the middle of No Man's Land—or it would be if they called the damned area No Man's Land. Got a lot of critters from the Sett Empire and the Coalition, and some of 'em take exception to anyone that looks like they come from the Democracy."

"Got it," said Pretorius.

"What's your favorite drink?"

"Anything wet."

Apollo threw back his head and laughed. "By God, I like you already!"

"That's a comfort, given your muscles and your weaponry," said Pretorius.

"The weapons are just to make me feel safe."

"Right—and the muscles come from digging in your garden."

"So how soon can you be there?"

Pretorius looked at Pandora, who held up two fingers. "Two days," he answered.

"Okay, I'll have a five or six-hour head start on the alcohol," said Apollo. "And Nate?"

"Yeah?"

"One more thing."

"What is it?" asked Pretorius.

"If your ship is flying with any insignia, lose it before you land."

Pretorius smiled. "We lost it before we took off."

Apollo smiled again. "Good! I hate dealing with amateurs!"

5

Prateep II wasn't much of a planet, a dusty little backwater with three Tradertowns and a few unimpressive farms. Marumbu was an even less impressive settlement, housing three cheap boarding houses, a drug den, a pair of bars, and a restaurant that had been serving the same single item every day for more than a decade.

By the time Pandora set the ship down in what passed for a spaceport a mile out of town, Proto and Irish had already used the computer to learn the basics of the Kabori language. Pretorius opened the hatch, climbed down to the ground, and decided that walking into town was probably less dangerous than riding in the beat-up vehicle that was provided.

It wasn't hard to spot the Crippled Worm, since it had a bright pink ten-meter-long facsimile of its name at the front edge of its roof. He studied it for a moment, for no logical reason that he could discern but simply because it seemed truly unique on such a commonplace world, and then entered.

There were a pair of Beldonians at the end of the bar nearest the door, then a Malator, a trio of purple-skinned beings of a race that was unfamiliar to him, and finally a huge, heavily muscled, thickbearded, redheaded man. Pretorius walked right up to him.

"You Nate?" he asked, studying Pretorius.

"Yes."

"And I'm Apollo. Barkeep!" he yelled. "Bring my friend a wormsblood!"

"A wormsblood?" repeated Pretorius, frowning. "What the hell is that?"

"Mostly it's wet," said Apollo with a smile.

"What the hell," said Pretorius with a shrug, taking the glass that the mildly reptilian bartender brought over. "Might as well give it a try."

"Well?" said Apollo, studying him as he took a swallow and made a face.

"Well, I'm not going to have to see a medic anytime soon," said Pretorius. "This'll kill any germs I've picked up along the way—even the ones that are beneficial to me."

Apollo laughed and slapped Pretorius on the back. "We're going to be great friends, Nate!"

"That's a comfort," replied Pretorius. "I'd hate to have three hundred pounds of bearded muscle decide to be my enemy."

Apollo picked up his glass and headed off toward a table in the far corner of the bar. "Come on, Nate. No reason why anyone else should be privy to whatever the hell it is we're talking about."

"Sounds good to me," said Pretorius, following Apollo and sitting down opposite him.

Apollo signaled to the bartender, who promptly brought a bottle to the table and left it there.

"Same stuff?" asked Pretorius.

"Nah," said Apollo. "But don't spill it."

Pretorius looked at him questioningly.

"It eats away at my beard," explained Apollo. "Who the hell knows what it'll do to a naked chin?"

"Too bad we can't draft your stomach," said Pretorius. "If the stuff you pour into it in this tavern doesn't kill you, nothing can."

Apollo laughed again. "So do you want to tell me why you're here, other than to let me buy you booze?"

"Madam Methuselah thinks very highly of you," said Pretorius. "I'm sorry, but I know absolutely nothing about you."

Apollo smiled. "Nobody does—and especially not the authorities. That's why she thinks so highly of me." He learned forward. "So what's the problem?"

"You ever deal with Michkag?"

"The head honcho of the Coalition, right?" said Apollo.

Pretorius nodded.

"Yeah, I graced one of his prison cells for a week or two," continued Apollo.

"Ever meet him personally?"

"I sure as hell hope not," said Apollo. "I hate to think I missed the opportunity to break that bastard in half."

"Maybe you'll have that opportunity yet," said Pretorius, carefully sipping his drink.

"Oh?" said Apollo. "Suddenly this is getting very interesting."

"Before I go into any details, I need two things."

"And what are they?"

"First, a private room where no one can hear what I'm about to tell you."

"No one can hear you now," said Apollo.

"This joint is all windows," said Pretorius. "Someone with the right equipment could read my lips from across the street."

"No problem," replied Apollo. "I've got a room at the boarding house about fifty meters to the east of here." He stood up, and dropped a bill on the table. "Thank goodness they honor the Democracy credit at this joint. Let's go."

They walked out the door, turned east, and walked in silence until they reached the boarding house. Apollo entered first, waved to the desk clerk, who was the same race as the bartender, then led Pretorius to a room at the back. He opened the door, revealing four windowless walls, a bed, two chairs, and not much else, not even a sink. Pretorius sat down, and then Apollo closed the door and sat down opposite him.

"Okay, here's your private room," said Apollo. "Now what's the second thing you need?"

Pretorius stared at him for a long moment. "The truth," he said at last.

"What particular truth did you have in mind?" asked Apollo, seemingly amused.

"You're more than just a big strong guy who likes to drink," said Pretorius. "Madam Methuselah could have directed me to a robot or an android that could outfight you and wouldn't rack up a bar tab."

Apollo stared back at him for an equally long moment, and then smiled. "Damn!" he said. "You're good! Nineteen out of twenty people buy my act without a single question."

"I'm flattered," said Pretorius dryly. "So what else can you do beside whip twice your weight in alien monsters?"

"I've got a doctorate in alien physiology, another one in alien languages, I'm a licensed surgeon, and I hold five patents for different hand weapons and one for medication on low-gravity worlds." Apollo smiled. "Other than that, I just eat and drink a lot, and beat the shit out of people and aliens who annoy me."

"I'm impressed," said Pretorius.

"You damned well ought to be," said Apollo with a laugh.

"You've got excellent protective coloration."

"My fists and my weapons are all I need ninety-eight percent of the time."

"How the hell old are you?" asked Pretorius. "You look in your early thirties."

"I keep fit," answered Apollo, "but the truth of it is that I'm fifty-four years old." Suddenly he grinned. "But a young fifty-four."

"You're not going to stay fit if you keep drinking that shit we had in the bar."

"I wholeheartedly agree with you," said Apollo. He reached beneath his shirt, made a quick adjustment, and brought out a small transparent plastic pouch. "My drinks," he explained.

"Well, I'll be damned!" exclaimed Pretorius.

"But I'm almost as friendly as I pretended to be."

"I'm glad you're on our side!"

"But am I?" said Apollo. "I still don't know what the job is, or what it pays."

"It's Michkag," answered Pretorius. "In a way."

Apollo frowned. "In what way?"

"This gets a little complicated," said Pretorius. "Seven or eight years ago Michkag tripped and skinned his elbow—and he bled."

Apollo sat perfect still for a moment. Suddenly a huge smile spread across his face. "Sonuvabitch!" he exclaimed. "Someone cloned the bastard!"

Pretorius nodded. "A countryman of his managed to get hold of a skin scraping. He deserted the Coalition and came to the Democracy with it."

"And that was his price for safe passage, of course?"

"Right. We cloned Michkag, and Djibmet—the countryman—

spent the next few years educating the clone, teaching him to love our side and be willing to betray the Coalition."

"So when you killed the real Michkag you had to do it secretly so you could replace him with the clone," said Apollo.

"Not quite."

Apollo stared at him for a moment, then grinned again. "You kidnapped the original!"

"Yes. And the clone, who'd spent his whole brief life learning to talk and act and react like Michkag, was put in his place."

"Fascinating," said Apollo enthusiastically. "And now I know what your problem is and why you've sought me out."

"Do you?"

"Of course. The new Michkag *likes* being Michkag, and if he was raised by your military, he probably knows a hell of a lot more about how to fight us than the original ever did."

"That's it in a nutshell," said Pretorius.

"The original won't help?"

"Would you?" asked Pretorius.

Apollo shook his head. "You got to him once. If he helps kill or capture the clone, you'll essentially have gotten to him twice."

"That's the situation. The original's back in the most secure jail in the Democracy. My team's mission is to eliminate the clone."

"Yeah, I can see there'd be no point in capturing him," said Apollo. "His unique knowledge of the Coalition probably covers less than two years, and since he knows that he can be kidnapped (since the original was), then probably half his defenses are to prevent kidnapping rather than assassination."

"You're quick on the uptake when you stop pretending to be a big burly bear," said Pretorius.

"Hell, I *am* a big burly bear," replied Apollo with a laugh. "I just happen to be a bright one."

"So . . . are you with us?"

"How much does the job pay?"

"Plenty."

"How many zeroes go after the plenty?"

"Do you know Wilbur Cooper?"

"The general?" said Apollo. "Yeah, I met him once, when we captured Tsandori IV."

"Good. You can argue price with him."

"That won't do," replied Apollo. "You're in charge of this mission. You name the price, and I say yes or no. Simple as that."

"Tell you what," said Pretorius. "*You* name the price, and *I'll* say yes or no."

Apollo looked around the room, saw a book sitting on the bed-table, walked over, picked it up, opened it, pulled a pen out of his pocket, and jotted a number down on the endpaper, then handed it to Pretorius.

Pretorius stared at it for a moment, then closed the book and handed it back to Apollo.

"Welcome to the team," he said.

6

Pretorius and his new team member took some ancient public transportation to the Marumbu spaceport, where they boarded the ship and he introduced Apollo to the rest of the crew.

"Nice to meet you all," he said. "And with no insult intended, I can see where you'd need a big, burly weightlifter like me."

"We had one," said Snake. "Felix Ortega. Ever hear of him?"

"Can't say that I have," replied Apollo.

"Neither will anyone else," she said. "He got killed on our last mission."

"Careless?"

Snake shook her head and grinned. "Biggest target."

Apollo threw back his head and laughed. "By God, I'm glad Merilee recommended me! I'm going to enjoy working with your ladies, Nate!"

"Just remember that when the shooting starts and we all hide behind you," said Snake.

"So," said Pandora, "now that we're all brothers and sisters, where do we find Michkag?"

"The clone?" asked Apollo.

"We all know where the original is," replied Pandora. "Let's assume from this point on that any time any of us mentions Michkag we're talking about the clone unless we say otherwise."

"Fair enough," said Apollo. He rubbed his chin for a moment. "Well, he's sure as hell not in the Coalition."

"Why not?" asked Irish.

"He knows he's got to be number one on the Democracy's hit list," answered Apollo. "If he's not surrounded by his army, then he's not in the Coalition."

"Maybe he's in hiding?" suggested Irish.

"For a few months, when he's got a few billion soldiers doing nothing besides guarding him and carrying out his orders?" Apollo shot back.

"If they're all out on missions, what's the difference where he hides?" persisted Irish. "Why stay in the one place when he knows we're looking for him?"

"*Are* they all out on missions?" asked Apollo. "According to my sources, they haven't attacked anything in a few months."

"Our sources agree with that," put in Pretorius.

"I don't have many facts at my fingertips . . . *yet*," continued Apollo, "but I think he's more likely to be making alliances to help him against the Democracy than to be conquering minor kingdoms or empires. I mean, hell, he's already ruling the second-biggest conglomeration in the galaxy, the Coalition and the Democracy have been fighting to a standstill since long before he came on the scene, so if you're a power-hungry bloodthirsty bastard like Michkag who's tired of fighting to a draw, what's your next step?"

Pandora nodded her agreement. "You form alliances to help you."

"And you make sure they know that there's a very painful and expensive penalty if they refuse."

"But eventually he's going to go back to Orion," said Snake.

"Why?" asked Apollo.

Snake frowned in confusion. "It's his home."

Apollo shook his head. "Michkag was born on Sylvatti V. That's four hundred light years away from the Orion Cluster. The Coalition's been around for three centuries. They know the chain of command. They've recruited just about as many troops as they can feed and supply. It functions smoothly, despite the fact that your team managed to kidnap the real Michkag. And since it functions pretty much the way it should, why shouldn't he set up shop somewhere else for the next ten or twenty or fifty years until it's a mirror image of the Coalition?"

"He'll be an old man—well, an old *alien*—by then," said Irish.

Apollo smiled. "Tell her, Nate."

Pretorius looked puzzled. "Tell her *what*?"

Apollo sighed deeply. "I agreed to my salary too soon." He turned to Irish. "A Kabori's life expectancy is about three hundred Standard years. According to the best estimates I've encountered, Michkag—the *real* Michkag—is forty-one years old. We have to assume the clone's physiology is the same, even if he himself is just six or seven."

Snake frowned. "How do you know all this?"

"Seriously?" asked Apollo.

"Of course seriously."

"I'm brilliant," said Apollo.

"And modest," said Irish with a smile.

"Absolutely," said Apollo, returning her smile. "Almost beyond calculation."

"By the way," said Snake, "have you got a last name?"

"Dozens of 'em," answered Apollo. "Which one do you want?"

Snake smiled. "The one with the biggest reward attached to it, of course."

"Pretorius," said Apollo.

"If you're all through playing games," said Pretorius, "let's get some dinner in the galley, get a good night's sleep, and spend tomorrow figuring out where to start looking for Michkag."

"Well, of course, if you *want* to eat and sleep first, fine," said Apollo. "I'm just the new kid on the block."

"You think you know where he is right now?" said Pretorius.

"No," admitted Apollo, "but since I'm already on the payroll, I thought I might as well get started. But there is absolutely no way I can locate the best-hidden being in the galaxy before dinner."

"Somehow I find that comforting," said Pandora.

"I probably won't know before tomorrow morning," continued Apollo. Then he shrugged his massive shoulders. "Unless I get lucky."

Pretorius stared at him. *If you can actually deliver, I'm glad you're on our side*, he thought. *In fact, you're making me wonder if Michkag really* is *the most dangerous thing in the galaxy.*

7

By the time Pretorius awoke and emerged from his compartment, which he simply was unable to think of as a cabin despite the fact that that was what it was labeled, Apollo was already working at the computer while Pandora watched him and the machine with a proprietary interest. Snake and Irish sat at a table in the galley, eating what passed for their breakfast, while Proto, in his true shape, surrounded and covered a bowl containing whatever it was he had told the galley prepare for him.

"Making any progress?" asked Pretorius.

"Some," answered Apollo.

"How long before you know what section of the galaxy he's in, or likely to be?"

"I knew that an hour ago," replied Apollo. "I'm trying to pinpoint him now."

"You did?" said Pretorius, surprised. "An hour ago?"

"Yeah."

Pretorius turned to Pandora. "Is what he's doing making sense to you?"

"That's a meaningless question, Nate," she replied.

"Meaningless?" he said, frowning.

"He's feeding in data and asking for data in codes that are meaningless to me," said Pandora. "If I asked you to compute a baseball player's batting average, you could do it. But if I asked a Bellarban to do it on the same machine with the same figures, and he didn't know what a hit was or an out, or that walks don't compute, could *he* do it? Apollo seems to have spent most of his adult life beyond the Democracy, and he certainly seems to have a profound knowledge of unsavory characters and events. I know my computer inside out, so if I had his knowledge I'm sure I could come up with an answer as quickly as he will."

"Seems a shame," said Pretorius. "All that strength and all that brainpower in one person."

"Oh, I have my weaknesses," said Apollo.

"Yeah?" said Pretorius. "What are they?"

"If I told you, then they'd be *our* weaknesses," was the reply.

"Go back to work," said Pretorius, heading off to the galley for a cup of black coffee.

"Watch your step!" snapped Proto, scurrying out of the way.

"Sorry," said Pretorius. "It's early in the day."

"It's noon, ship's time," said Snake.

"Okay, it's early in *my* day."

"I have a question," said Irish.

"Shoot," said Pretorius, taking a sip of his coffee and seating himself on an empty chair.

"This is only my second mission with the Dead Enders," she said, "and I freely admit my inexperience in these things . . . but we're a crew of six, and he's probably surrounded by a billion or more armed, highly trained men."

"Kaboris," Snake corrected her.

"Whatever," said Irish. "My question is: once we know where he is, what next? I mean, whether you want to kill him or kidnap him, those are tremendously high odds against us."

"Snake's worth any two of them," replied Pretorius with a smile. "When she's sober, anyway."

Snake made a face at him, but Irish simply looked worried. "I'm being serious, sir. I know last time all we had to do was break Nmumba out of a prison cell. That was hard enough, and it was basically an unpopulated prison planet. But now you're talking about killing or kidnapping what is probably the best-guarded being in the galaxy, and he won't be on some little backwater prison planet."

"We managed to exchange this one for the original on a world that was just as heavily protected, maybe even more so, than wherever he's at now—and we did it with a team of six. You don't accomplish things like this by spending hundreds of millions of lives on each side. Even if you pull it off, there's not much left worth governing or ruling on either side when it's over."

"Man's got a point," said Apollo, still manipulating the computer.

"So what have you got so far?" asked Pretorius.

"He's not in the Democracy."

"Big surprise."

"Not in the Coalition's territory either."

"Ditto."

"Believe it or not, he's set up shop in what's left of the Sett Empire."

"The Sett Empire?" repeated Pretorius. "We beat the shit out of them centuries ago."

"At great cost to the Republic," added Pandora, referring to the Democracy's predecessor.

"Right," agreed Apollo. "Not a bad idea, really. They've got a few thousand planets with structures already built, they're closer to the worlds of the Coalition than to the Democracy, they haven't been a military threat or power for a couple of millennia, and of course there's every chance some of the locals still bear a grudge against us."

"After this long?" said Snake, frowning.

"You just have to explain it in terms they understand," said Apollo. She looked at him questioningly. "If you don't pledge your loyalty to us and let us use your worlds and recruit your people, we'll destroy half a dozen Democracy planets using your depleted military, and of course they'll be quick to take their unequal and bloody revenge. On the flip side: the Democracy's had nothing to do with you for a couple of millennia, since it was the Republic, and it has almost no trading agreements with you. They're already enmeshed in half a dozen military actions, which is a euphemism for war. Do you really think they're going to send a major force to your aid if you annoy us by refusing us?"

"Shit!" said Snake. "You're right." A brief pause. "I *hate* being wrong."

"Okay," said Pretorius, "so they're in the old Sett Empire. But *where* in it?"

"Soon," said Apollo, uttering a number of rapid commands in a language that only Pandora and the computer understood.

"Damn!" said Pandora after another minute had passed. "That's a fascinating chain of connections. I never thought of that!"

Apollo shot her a grin and said, "I'm flattered!" then turned back and uttered more commands. And finally, after three more minutes, he exhaled deeply, deactivated the computer, and turned to face Pretorius and Pandora.

"I can't pinpoint the exact planet. They've got too many defenses up, too much electronic camouflage. We're going to have get over there and do a little reconnoitering."

"Get over *where?*" demanded Pretorius.

"Oh, didn't I say? Michkag's set up shop somewhere in the Cassiopeia Sector."

"How hard can it be to spot a couple of billion soldiers and ships?" said Snake from the galley.

"Harder than you think," replied Pretorius and Apollo in unison.

8

"So should we start approaching Cassiopeia?" asked Pandora, moving to the pilot's chair as Apollo got up and wandered over to the galley.

Pretorius shook his head. "No sense telling them we're here until we know where *they* are."

"What the hell?" growled Apollo.

"What's wrong?" asked Pretorius.

"No beer!"

"The galley was outfitted by the military," said Pretorius.

"And nobody in the whole fucking military drinks beer?" demanded Apollo.

"Oh, shut up," said Snake. "If you're *that* desperate, I've got some."

"I liked you from the start," said Apollo with a smile, "even if you do barely come up to my belt."

"It's not a gift," said Snake. "Five credits for a container."

"Five credits!" demanded Apollo. "They're only two credits, tops, in any bar in the Democracy."

"Okay," replied Snake with a shrug. "Go buy from a Democracy bar."

Irish and Proto were already laughing when Apollo reached into a pocket, pulled out a bill, and threw it at her. She held it up to the light, examining it, smiled, and returned it. "He does very good work," she said. "Now give me a real one—and the price is up to six credits."

Apollo threw back his head and laughed, then reached into his pocket again, pulled out a ten-credit note, and handed it to her.

"You want change?" she asked.

"Keep it. You've been four credits worth of fun."

"You think *that's* fun?" said Snake. "I could slit your belly open, top to bottom, for another fifty credits."

"I'll bet you could, too!" said Apollo, still smiling. He turned to Pretorius. "I'm starting to like our crew more and more."

"Might as well," said Irish. "You're stuck with us."

"*You're* stuck with *me*," said Apollo. "A lot of people might find that more uncomfortable."

"A lot of people aren't facing a billion-to-one odds," replied Irish.

"Yeah, well, there *is* that," agreed Apollo.

"Yeah," put in Pandora. "Having him on our side probably lowers the odds to nine hundred and eighty million to one."

Apollo turned to Proto, who had projected the shape of a rather nondescript man to make his shipmates feel more comfortable. "Ain't you going to pile on too? Everybody else seems to enjoy it."

"I've been piled on enough times myself," answered Proto. "I don't enjoy it, so why should you?"

"Ah!" was the reply. "But I learned to do something about it."

"You're more than eighteen inches tall," said Proto.

"Hell, even your name sounds heroic," added Irish.

An amused smile crossed Apollo's face. "You think so, do you?"

"Apollo is the god of art, poetry, music, medicine, and a bunch of other stuff, depending on which source you read," said Irish. "Damned right I think so."

"Good," said Apollo. "I chose well."

"You didn't choose me at all," said Irish. "I come with the ship."

He chuckled and shook his head. "I mean I chose my *name* well."

"You *chose* it?" she said, frowning.

"Yes. You want to build muscles and learn to defend yourself? Grow up—if they'll let you—with the name of Frothingham S. Platt," said Apollo grimly. "I don't know which I hated more, Frothingham or Splatt. You learn to defend yourself or you die young." He grimaced. "So after I'd defended myself from a few hundred bullies and left the planet and went out on my own, I decided to come up with a name that, even if no one envied or even cared for it, wouldn't invite almost daily attacks. I'm Apollo now, and I'll kill or cripple anyone who says I'm not."

"They gave you degrees in your specialties without a last name?" asked Pandora.

"They didn't *give* me anything," said Apollo. "I *earned* everything I've got."

"You know what I mean," persisted Pandora. "What the name on your degrees?"

"Apollo Zeus."

"Figures," said Pretorius with a smile.

"Zeus was Apollo's dad," replied Apollo. "And I'll fight anyone who says different."

"Still, an interesting choice," said Pretorius. "If I'd had your size and muscles, I think I'd have chosen Hercules."

"They've already got three or four guys called Hercules out on the Frontier," answered Apollo. "I'm the only one of me I know." He paused. "I'd love to go up against Michkag, mano a mano."

"Mano a thingo," said Snake. "He's no Man."

"And we're not here to wrestle or box him," added Pretorius. "Our job is to assassinate him."

Apollo made a face.

"What's wrong?"

"Assassinate," replied Apollo. "It sounds so . . . *secretive*. Let's just walk up to him, kill the bastard, and be done with it."

"As long as he's just as dead at the end of it, you can use any verb you want," said Pretorius.

"But first," said Pandora, "getting back to the business at hand, we have to locate him."

"Shouldn't be that hard," answered Apollo. "He breathes what we breathe, and there are only seventeen oxygen worlds in the Cassiopeia Sector. He'll want some freedom of action for himself and his troops; that eliminates five worlds with uncomfortably high gravity. They won't want to import water; that knocks out three more. And you've contacted them or intercepted signals, so we know they're still there and still alive. That knocks Benodi VI out of consideration."

"Why?"

"Damned planet's got some disease-carrying germs and insects that wiped out the whole population about twenty Standard years ago. According to a report I pulled up half an hour ago, the place is still teeming with them."

"Okay, that leaves eight worlds that might house him and his military," said Pandora. "How do we narrow it down further—without using the ship for bait, that is?"

"Send out an SOS," suggested Proto, "and see where help comes from."

"And if help comes in the form of eight or ten enemy ships, what then?" said Pandora.

"Okay, bad idea," admitted Proto. "But how about determining which of those eight possible worlds have a lot of transmissions going to and from them?"

"Makes sense," agreed Apollo.

"You don't think the signals will be disguised and rerouted?" said Pandora.

"Of course they will be!" said Apollo, still grinning.

"Then I don't follow you," said Pandora, frowning.

"That's *good*," said Pretorius. "I should have thought of it myself."

"Will someone please explain what you two are talking about?" said Proto.

"You want to tell 'em?" said Apollo.

"Sure," said Pretorius. "We've got eight populated worlds in the sector. We know, or think we know, that one of them is Michkag's headquarters. He's only had a few months to move here, set it up, put in all his defenses, reset his various alliances. He's capable of defending his world against attack, but he's really not ready for a major war for another couple of years, at least not anywhere nearly as ready as he was in Orion."

"We all know that," said Snake. "What do you and Apollo know that we *don't* know?"

"So far we've narrowed down his location to eight worlds just through logic, observation, and a little brainpower," answered Pretorius. "He has to assume anyone could do that, could intuit what we know right now. So how does he convince us to pinpoint one of the seven worlds that *isn't* his headquarters?"

"Oh, shit!" exclaimed Snake. "Of course. He'll have ten times as many messages coming and going from the other seven worlds, all in some code that translates out as gibberish and drives us crazy trying to dope it out."

"And each of the other seven worlds will have a few military ships in orbit," added Irish, "guarding it against attacks that will only come if the attackers guess wrong, while the world we want will have no visible defenses at all." She smiled. "But when we use our instruments, we'll find that it's far and away the best-guarded of them all."

"How do you like our crew now, Apollo?" asked Pretorius.

"They learn quick," he said approvingly.

"So what's next?" asked Snake.

"We study the sector for a couple of days, see what they're trying to direct our attention away from, and then . . ." Pretorius stifled a chuckle. "I almost said 'then we attack,' but of course we don't. Then we sneak in, eliminate our target, and hope we can sneak back out again."

"That easily?" asked Proto.

"Is anything ever that easy?" Pretorius shot back.

"Not in this life," said Apollo. "But from my observations, I figure you know that better than most."

"Oh?"

Apollo smiled. "Nate, you're a walking spare parts shop. I don't know what's *in* you, but you've got a prosthetic left foot, an artificial right knee, a replacement eye (and I hope it sees into the infrared or the ultraviolet or both), and that left ear doesn't look quite real."

"Not bad," said Pretorius.

"What did I miss?"

"Spleen, left lung, and just about all my teeth."

"Yeah," said Apollo, staring at him, "those teeth are a little too perfect. My mistake."

"Could have been worse," said Pretorius.

"Oh?"

Pretorius nodded. "Could have happened four or five thousand years ago, before they could fix or replace all these things."

"I don't know about the rest of you," said Apollo, "but I like working with an optimist." He turned to Pandora, who was working the computer. "What are you doing?"

"Setting it up to eliminate seven of the eight worlds within two to three Standard days," she replied. "We're now keeping a log on every signal coming and going from each world, plus every ship taking off, orbiting, and landing. And it may not even take that long."

"Why not?" asked Pretorius.

"They've put a stealth code on most of the messages that a ten-year-old could break," she explained. "They *want* it to look like they're hiding things, but they're making it awfully easy to see what they're sending and receiving." She paused and checked the codes moving across her screen. "Same thing with the ships. They want us to think they're protecting themselves from observation with a stealth code, but like I said, any kid could break it."

"Good!" said Pretorius. "So we'll know where we have to go in a day or two."

"If not quite how we're going to get there," added Apollo.

"Oh?" said Irish.

"They're trying to direct us away from their planet," said Pretorius, "but I assure you they'll know we're not one of their own as we approach, even if we capture one of their decoy ships from one of the other seven worlds. If we use a valid cloaking code, and they've got their entire planetary defense geared to spot such a thing, they'll identify us before we even enter the atmosphere."

"And if we simply approach them in the open," added Apollo,

"because this ship carries no military insignia, even so they'll be able to determine that we've got weapons, and more to the point, that we're carrying a mostly human crew."

"So how *do* we land, once we've identified the planet we want to land on?" asked Irish.

"Indirectly, that's for damned sure," said Apollo with an amused smile.

"You want to define 'indirectly' in this situation?" said Snake.

"We'll have to capture one of their ships—one built for humans or oxygen-breathers who are relatively human in structure—and learn the codes we'll need to land on the planet we want."

"And it won't be easy," added Pretorius, "because the proxies are there as disguise and bait. The last thing they'll be allowed to do is land on the planet we're after."

"But if he's feeding a billion soldiers, they *have* to transport food in," said Pandora.

"Unless it's an agricultural planet," replied Pretorius.

Pandora frowned. "Even so, it couldn't be producing enough food to feed a billion soldiers of Michkag's size."

"Unless they had a couple of billion citizens living there, and Michkag's army wiped them out," said Pretorius. He grimaced. "You've got to remember who and what we're going after."

"So what do we do now?" asked Snake.

"Pandora and Apollo will spell each other at the controls and the computer," said Pretorius.

"And the rest of us?"

"I should have thought that would be obvious," he answered.

"Oh?" she said.

Pretorius smiled grimly. "We wait."

9

And wait they did. Four hours passed, then five more, and Apollo was able to eliminate only one planet.

"Damn!" he muttered, glaring balefully at the viewscreen. "This is the most boring war I've ever participated in."

"Beats getting shot at," offered Snake.

"Not if you know who to shoot back at," he replied irritably. He got to his feet and turned to Pandora. "Here," he said. "*You* try to spot the real planet. I'm gonna get something to drink."

"Limit it to water or coffee," said Pretorius. "We've only got two beers left, and they're both mine."

"You had the ship make them up especially for you?" demanded Apollo pugnaciously.

"I bought a dozen on Bereimus III," answered Pretorius. "They're what's left."

Apollo stared at him for a long moment. "Okay," he said. "What the hell. If they're yours, they're yours."

Pretorius chuckled.

"What's so damned funny?" said Apollo.

"If you hadn't acknowledged my ownership of them, I'd have fought you before giving you one. But since you're being a gentleman, or as close to a gentleman as I suspect you ever get, what the hell, have one and bring the other over to me."

"You've got qualities, Nate," said Apollo, taking the last two containers from the galley and handing one to Pretorius. "Sometimes they're a little hard to see, but you've got qualities."

"One of them is clearheadedness," replied Pretorius with a smile. "I figure it might be a little bothersome trying to drink a beer right after you knocked half my teeth down my throat."

The line broke what minimum tension had arisen, and everyone laughed.

Except Snake.

"He's not the only one who'd like a beer," she said to Pretorius.

"Are you going to fight me for the other one?" he asked in amused tones.

"No, of course not."

"Good."

"Some night when you're sleeping, I'll just walk up and slit your throat," she continued.

Pretorius handed her his container. "You'd do it, too, wouldn't you?"

"You wouldn't be the first," replied Snake.

"Then who'd bail you out of jail the next time?"

"When General Cooper needs me bad enough, he'll find someone," she said with a confident smile.

Apollo tossed her his container. "Remember this the next time you've got a spare."

"I hate to interrupt this love-and-beer feast," announced Pandora, staring at the screen. "But I've got something interesting here."

"Oh?" said Pretorius.

"Ship just approached one of the two planets that haven't had anyone land on them since we've been watching."

"So that eliminates it?"

"No, I don't think so," she said. "Take a look." She tripled the size of the screen, and had it project the image in three dimensions.

"There's nothing there at all," said Snake, staring at the planet.

"But there *was*," answered Pandora with a smile. "And three ships took off from the planet and escorted it away." She maneuvered the controls. "See? There they are, basically herding the ship to"—she checked the identification at the bottom of the screen—"the Colteipa system."

"And the planet that didn't want any visitors?" asked Pretorius.

"I don't know about '*any*' visitors yet," said Pandora, "but they sure as hell didn't want this one."

"Okay," continued Pretorius, "has it got a name?"

She uttered a couple of words in code, and the machine answered: "Garsype III."

"That's it," said Pandora. "I'm sure that's not what the natives call it, always assuming there *are* natives, and I can't imagine Michkag hasn't given it a Kabori name—"

"Probably Michkag III," interjected Snake.

"It wouldn't surprise me," agreed Pandora. "But all we know right now is that it's officially Garsype III and was named by whoever first mapped the Sagittarius region."

"Native population?" asked Pretorius.

"Close to two billion during the last census, which was . . . let me see . . . seventeen years ago."

"All right," said Pretorius. "Snake, you and Irish get out your computers and help her. I want to know if the damned world has produced an outstanding athlete, painter, sculptor, surgeon, *anything* that a reporter from beyond the sector might want to interview, which would clearly be to the credit and glory of Garsype III."

"You think it'll work?" asked Snake dubiously.

"Probably not," admitted Pretorius. "It's a first step, and it's better than saying, 'Hey, please tell us if you guys are hiding Michkag and his navy so we know whether to attack or not.'"

"Yeah, well, there *is* that," agreed Snake.

"Got one!" said Irish.

"Who is it, and what did he or she do?" asked Pretorius.

"A female track star named Travii," answered Irish. "Seems to have set sector records in sprint races at three different distances. She'd be about forty Standard years old now."

"Okay," said Pretorius. "Five of us can't hide the fact that we're the race of Man, so I guess you're elected, Proto."

"What do you want me to do?" he asked.

"We know that if you're projecting a false image, our cameras can't capture it and pass it on, so just be your normal eighteen-inch-high self. We'll go audio. And Pandora, run a close-up of the *real* him—the image we can actually capture and transmit—and fill the frame so that he looks bigger and no one can see any part of anyone else."

"Proto?" she said.

Suddenly he became his true self for all to see.

"Okay, got him," she said. "Now what?"

"Now you keep the camera on him. Proto, move your mouth as if you're speaking. Apollo, you'll do his talking for him. Pandora, the camera stays on Proto and no one else."

"I need a name," said Proto.

Pandora scanned her screen for a few seconds. "As far as I can tell, they've never had any business and meeting with Pysonobs. Let me find a name." A brief pause. "Proto, you're now Rekorpa."

"No first name?"

"Not if you're a Pysonob."

"I suppose we should all go to our cabins and watch on the intership screens," said Irish.

"No need to," said Pretorius. "The camera's on Proto and nowhere else."

"Okay," said Pandora to Proto. "I'm contacting them now." The bridge emptied out. "I just hope they can't identify our ship as part of the Democracy."

"Not to worry," said Pretorius. "It was built especially *not* to be identified by its structure or the elements used to construct it."

Pandora turned the camera onto Proto, and made it a close-up so almost none of the desk was visible. "Okay," she whispered some ten seconds later. "You're on."

"Greetings," said Apollo, as Proto moved his lips.

"Identify yourself," said a voice, and Pretorius realized that either there was no camera at the other end, or that it was at least deactivated.

"Certainly," said Apollo. "I am Rekorpa. Perhaps somebody in Customs remembers me?"

"Why would we?" asked the voice suspiciously.

"I am a holo-journalist," he said. "I interviewed the magnificent Travii some years ago, and told her that someday I would be back to do a follow-up feature for her admiring public."

"Go away."

"But—"

"She is not available for interviews."

"At least tell me that she's alive and in good health, so I can pass the word to my viewers."

"She is alive and in good health," was the answer. "Now please leave the system or we will send ships to escort you out of it."

And with that, the line of communication was severed.

"Well, that didn't help much," said Pandora.

"It helped more than you think," said Apollo with a huge grin.

"Oh?" said Pretorius.

Apollo nodded. "After you hit upon Travii as the excuse for Proto getting in touch with them, I did a little more research on her, just in case one of us had to feed some facts to him."

"And?"

"She was murdered in what I think you'd call the winner's circle of a track meet on Jankoza II ten years ago. It was actually the cause of a brief military action between Garsype and Jankoza." He grinned again. "They must have been pointing a burner or a screecher at the head of the poor critter that told you she was alive and well. Given the circumstances of her death and its aftermath, I can't believe there's a single native of any planet in this system who doesn't know that she's dead and exactly how she died."

"It makes sense," agreed Pretorius.

"So we can assume Michkag is there?"

"We could be wrong," said Apollo, "but if I was a betting man, I'd give plenty of ten-to-one that we're not."

"Well, *if* he's there," said Pandora, "we've still got a hell of a major problem. We're in a ship that clearly wasn't created in this system, or even this sector. If we try to land, they'll open fire before we get within twenty miles of the ground. And if we go to the neighboring systems and swipe one of their ships, we'll just be escorted away, gently (I hope) but firmly, as we can assume they do to other relatively local ships."

"I think better on a full stomach," said Apollo.

"Actually, so do I," said Snake, joining him. "Of course, it takes a hell of a lot less to fill mine."

"You look troubled," said Irish to Pretorius.

"Do I?"

She nodded her head. "Yes."

He sighed deeply. "That's because I am."

"You don't know how we're ever going to land on the planet, right?" she suggested.

"Oh, I know exactly how," he said. He flashed her a bittersweet smile. "That's probably why I look troubled."

10

"So what's the plan?" asked Snake, when they had all finished eating and the entire crew was gathered on the bridge.

"It probably starts on Colteipa II," suggested Apollo.

"That's the next star system over, right?" said Snake.

"Right," said Pretorius. "Actually, it probably starts a few hundred miles *above* Colteipa II."

"Of course," said Apollo. "I just assumed everyone would figure that much out."

"One of us has no idea what the hell you're talking about," said Snake.

"Make that almost all of us," added Irish.

"We're going to capture a Colteipa II ship," said Pretorius.

"And then what?" asked Pandora.

"Then we're going to approach Garsype until they send a couple of ships out to stop us."

"If you're going to blow them out of the ether," said Proto, "why not stay in this ship, which is probably far better armed?"

"We're not blowing anyone anywhere," said Apollo with an amused smile. "Do you really want to take on three or four of their ships with a Colteipa II ship *or* this vessel?"

"No, of course not," said Proto. "But Nate just said we're going to approach the planet until they try to stop us."

"Right," said Apollo, still smiling. "And then what?"

"If I knew, I wouldn't be asking questions," said Proto irritably.

"Then we land on Colteipa III or IV, or one of II's moons," said Pretorius.

"Then we're farther away than we are now," said Snake, frowning. "How does that help us?"

"It's such an unusual thing to do with a ship that is clearly not in any trouble, that's operating smoothly, I think they'll leave at least one ship in orbit to try to find out what the hell's going on."

"Okay, they land," said Snake. "Now what?"

"Now we demand that they surrender their ship to us, of course," said Apollo.

"That's the stupidest thing I've heard since we left headquarters," said Snake. "Why the hell would they do that?"

"To save Michkag, of course," said Pretorius.

"Michkag's safely ensconced in his headquarters on Garsype," said Pandora, frowning. "Surely they know that."

"After we fire a shot or two into their subspace sending mechanism, they'll have to take it on faith," said Apollo.

"And they will," said Pandora.

"Until we transmit an image from our ship to theirs."

"And they're gonna look at the six of us and immediately surrender?" said Snake contemptuously.

"No, we're only going to let them see two of us," said Pretorius. Snake frowned. "Just two?"

"Yes," replied Pretorius. "You can be one of the two if you like."

"What the hell am I missing here?" said Snake.

"The other one they'll see isn't here yet . . . exactly," said Apollo.

"I give up," said Snake. "I still don't know what you two are talking about."

"Proto," said Pretorius. "You've seen Michkag when we kidnapped him back at Orion. You spent a couple of weeks in the ship with him. Let's see you become him."

The change was instant. In less than a second it seemed that Michkag himself was standing menacingly on the bridge.

"Very good," said Pretorius.

"I've never seen Michkag," said Apollo. "Are there any scars, any birthmarks (always assuming they get born), anything at all different from what we're looking at?"

"I've never seen him either," added Irish.

"Yeah, he looks right," said Snake, and Pandora nodded her agreement.

"Snake, go into the galley and grab as big a knife as you can find there," said Pretorius.

She walked to the galley and was back a moment later.

"Proto, just to be certain: despite what we see, you're still eighteen or nineteen inches high, right?" said Pretorius.

"That's right."

"Okay, Snake. Cut his arm off."

She swung the knife like a sword, and the arm rolled down to the floor, always in touch with the rest of the illusion.

"Not bad," said Pretorius. "But next time remember to gush some blood out of the wound."

"Right," said Proto.

"There you have it," said Pretorius. "We demand their ship and codes, or we kill Michkag, who was here on a secret mission."

"Too bad," said Pandora.

"What's too bad?" asked Pretorius.

"It's a lovely ruse," she said. "But it won't work."

"Why don't you think so?"

"You seem to have forgotten: the sensors in the camera show the real Proto, not the image he's producing."

Pretorius lowered his head in thought for a moment, then looked up. "It'll still work," he said. "It'll just take a little more effort."

"How?" demanded Snake.

"We simply find a way to make them enter our ship," replied Pretorius. "We can't fool their cameras—though we could if Apollo and Pandora had a fully equipped lab and maybe two Standard days to come up with a countermeasure—but we can still fool their eyeballs."

"So how do we make them come aboard?" asked Irish.

Apollo chuckled.

"You've figured it out," stated Pretorius. "*You* tell them."

"The mind boggles with possibilities," began Apollo. "Do any of them know of Nate and his accomplishments? Let them know he's commanding this ship and they'll want to present him to Michkag for the reward, if any, and the glory. Or if they don't know who the hell he is, assume they're as greedy as any other sentient species. So just tell them you don't want any trouble, you didn't know Garsype was off limits, you're new to the area, you're escaping from someone or something in the Democracy or the Coalition, there's a price on your head, so as soon as you get the ship working again you'll be on your way, and I guarantee they'll figure they can capture you whenever they want and turn you in for the reward."

"You're a devious son of a bitch, and I admire that in a teammate," said Snake, "but if they buy that, they'll never believe that Michkag's on board."

"How long does it take for the four of us to disarm them while

Snake and Proto are doing their little live-action pantomime? Five seconds? Ten? I guarantee it'll freeze them for that long. Remember, they've never seen anyone who can do what Proto does."

"Do you really think it'll work?" Pandora asked Pretorius.

"I sure as hell hope so," he responded. "Because if we don't come up with a better idea by the time we've stolen a Colteipa ship, that's what we'll do."

And when they neared the outskirts of the Colteipa system, Pandora looked up from the control panel.

"We're in luck," she announced.

"Nearby ship?" asked Pretorius.

"So to speak," she said. "They seem to have created some small of colonies on the eighth and ninth planets. They're all enclosed, of course; there's nothing to breathe there if you don't thrive on ammonia. But it means their ships are parked outside, which makes sense. You could poison the whole colony if you opened the doors wide enough and long enough to let one of the ships in or out."

"That makes getting a Colteipan ship the easiest part of this job," said Snake.

"Too bad we can't capture a pilot as well," said Irish.

"It'd be nice," agreed Pretorius. "But it's not essential for this stage of the mission. Where we may need one is after we've taken over one of Michkag's ships and want to put it down on Garsype." He exhaled deeply and shrugged. "We'll worry about that when we come to it. Pandora, is there just one contained structure on each planet?"

"There's just one on Colteipa VIII," she replied. "Colteipa IX has four, all little ones, that I spotted, and there may be some on the far side."

"Which of the little ones on Colteipa IX has the fewest ships?"

She had the system create a holographic map above the controls. "This one," she said. "Four ships left. One just took off."

"Numbers aren't always indicative," said Pretorius, "but unless something happens in the next few minutes to change our minds, we'll land there, make sure we can handle one of the ships, and then disable all the rest, including the one we're leaving behind."

It took them half an hour to reach and land on the planet, considerably less than a minute for both Pandora and Apollo to state that they knew the make of the ships if not the model and should have no trouble piloting one, and another minute to board it with sirens blaring and mildly humanoid bipeds racing out of the enclosed mini-city. Apollo got to the firing mechanism and quickly disabled all four ships that were on the ground—three from Colteipa and their own from the Coalition.

"Get us to Garsype quick!" Pretorius told Pandora. "I don't want to fight our way through any Colteipan ships from around the sector that are being notified that we've stolen this one."

"Same wormhole as before," she replied. "We'll enter it in just under an hour. Can't get there any faster than that."

"Proto?" said Pretorius.

"Yes?"

"In case we do try to pull off this Michkag imitation, how long can you have a spill of blood stay on the floor?"

"As long as it's attached to the rest of the image," answered Proto. "The only limit is how long I maintain the image."

"Okay," said Pretorius. "If it takes more than a minute to disable them, we're screwed anyway."

"I take it everyone here has seen and interacted with Michkag," said Apollo. "What's he like?"

"I never saw him," said Irish. "I'm the rookie on the team."

"Now *I* am," said Apollo.

She shook her head. "There's nothing rookie about you. You're more like some all-star we traded for."

"I'm flattered," he said with a smile. "And I still don't know what Michkag's like. Although I imagine he has a lot in common with history's other great tyrants."

"He's bright," said Pretorius. "And creative. And merciless, of course. He never bites off more than he can chew."

"Until he ran up against you," suggested Apollo.

"Not quite," answered Pretorius. "He was holding his own against the Democracy. We didn't outgun him; we *tricked* him. I mean, who the hell ever thought we could find a turncoat who actually could supply us with an identical Michkag, or that we could pull off the switch inside the most heavily guarded fortress in the whole damned galaxy?" He paused. "It was a confluence of circumstances that'll never happen again. This is not an enemy we can underestimate. *Especially* this enemy. Don't forget; he was created and tutored inside the Democracy."

"I'm surprised you volunteered to go up against him again," said Apollo.

Pretorius smiled. "I don't recall the word 'volunteer' in any of my discussions with General Cooper."

Apollo chuckled. "Nevertheless, someday you must join me as a freelancer."

"Who has a freelancer's back?" asked Snake.

Apollo offered her a mock frown. "Why do *you* always ask the tough questions?"

"Got a Colteipa II ship coming this way," announced Pandora.

"Armed?" asked Pretorius.

She shook her head. "Looks like a passenger ship," she answered. "A big one."

"Then if they're just bringing a load of passengers back they probably don't know this ship is stolen—and even if they do, they're not going to endanger all those passengers. Just send them the equivalent of a friendly wave and keep on going."

"Right," said Pandora, and a few second later uttered a deep sigh. "It worked."

"Okay," said Pretorius. "How long until we're within the Michkag's system?"

"Three hours, maybe three and a half."

"We can assume they'll have ships out to the edge of it, not just around Garsype. In fact, *especially* not around Garsype."

"Seems reasonable."

"Then we'll initiate contact out at the edge, where we'll face even odds, or at worst two-to-one."

"Makes sense," agreed Pandora.

"Apollo," said Pretorius, "I'm putting you in charge of the weaponry. Remember, we're going to do our damnedest not to damage whatever ship seeks us out, because if things go the way we plan, we're going to be approaching and landing on Garsype in that ship."

"Got it," said Apollo. "Anyone here speak Kabori?"

"I think I do," said Proto. "But I haven't tried yet."

"Ditto," added Pandora.

"And you haven't tried either?"

"That's right."

Apollo turned to Pretorius. "Let me guess," he said with a grin. "Whenever you bet, you always pick longshots."

11

They spent two hours maneuvering in deep space, making sure no one from the Colteipa system was following them, then headed slowly toward Garsype.

"They're going to contact and probably approach us as we reach the outskirts of the system," said Pretorius. "It's not inconceivable that the second they see Men onboard they'll start firing, and there's no sense having Proto take the form of Michkag since the holo won't show that."

"So what do I do?" asked Pandora. "Tell them that the camera's not working?"

"Would you buy that if you were expecting enemies to come after Michkag at any moment?" said Pretorius.

"No," she replied. "No, I wouldn't."

"So we've got to show them *some*thing," he said. "And the only thing we can show them that's not a Man is Proto."

"You've already admitted that won't work," said Snake.

"No he didn't," said Apollo with an amused smile.

"Of course he did," persisted Snake. "Train the camera on him when he's being Michkag and all we get is the *real* Proto."

"Right," said Apollo, still grinning at her.

She stared back at him, then at Proto. And suddenly she clapped her hands once and emitted an amused laugh. "Son of a bitch! It'll actually work better this time! They would certainly question what the hell Michkag was doing aboard our ship, but not a . . . a whatever-the-hell-you-are, Proto."

"Right," said Pretorius. "And you'll speak to them in Terran. I guarantee that if the Democracy is your major enemy, every means of communication you have will recognize and translate Terran."

"There's another advantage," added Irish. "Since he has no facial features as such, he won't look nervous when he's speaking to them."

"So when they contact us, and it won't be long," said Pretorius, "we'll turn the camera on Proto."

"But what shall I say?" asked Proto nervously.

"Don't worry about it," answered Pretorius. "I'll do the speaking for you. Just move your mouth a little. They've almost certainly never seen a member of your race, so the mouth's movements won't have to match the words or pronunciations." He paused, then smiled. "Actually, I probably haven't been in your unadorned, undisguised company for ten hours in well over a year, and to tell you the truth, *I* don't know where the hell your mouth us."

"I guess that's a compliment," said Proto.

"It's more than a compliment," said Pretorius. "It could be a lifesaver."

"Times six," added Apollo.

"All right," said Proto. "Where shall I stand?"

Pandora pointed to a spot halfway across the bridge from her control panel. "Right there."

Proto undulated to where she indicated.

"Okay," said Pretorius. "How the hell many planets in this system?"

"Fourteen," answered Pandora. "Garsype's the third."

"Start approaching the fourteenth, circle it a few times, and if nobody stops or questions us, do the same to the thirteenth, and so on until we're stopped and contacted."

"You got it," she said, heading toward the outermost planet, one of half a dozen gas giants on the outer perimeter of the system.

They went through the same routine on the fourteenth and thirteenth planets. Then, as they approached the twelfth, they received a radio signal.

"Halt where you are!" said a hoarse voice in Kabori.

Three small ships showed up on the viewscreen.

"Name, race, and purpose of this intrusion," demanded the voice.

"I am sorry," said Pretorius in Terran. "I do not mean to trespass. I mean no disrespect."

"Name!" insisted the voice, and it was obvious that the ship had no intention of showing any of its crew to its camera.

"Napoleon."

"What the hell kind of name is that?" said the voice.

"It is *my* name," said Pretorius. "I do not know from what it might have been derived."

"Race?"

"It will probably just translate as gibberish."

"Race!" repeated the voice.

What the hell do you look like when you're being yourself? thought Pretorius, staring at Proto. "Briefcase."

"Container?" demanded the voice.

"I told you it wouldn't translate very well."

"And why are you here?"

"I assure you this system was not my destination," said Pretorius. "My ship needs some minor repairs, and I am looking for a safe place to set it down while I am making them."

"You may not set it down in this system," said the voice sternly.

"But I *must!*" Pretorius said desperately. "It cannot reach the next system in its current condition. Please let me land."

"What is the matter with it?"

"I don't know!" said Pretorius desperately. "You can see me on your viewscreen: I am very small, I am unarmed, I cannot locomote with any speed or dexterity."

"It is against regulations," insisted the voice.

"If I can't land and effect repairs, I will die in space."

"That is hardly our concern," replied the voice.

"Let me make a counteroffer," said Pretorius. "I am an archaeologist. If you will let me land, you can land right beside me, watch me the entire time I effect repairs so you'll know I have no ulterior purpose, and to show you my gratitude you may take all the accumulated artifacts I have gathered from a dozen worlds, some of them quite valuable, plus all the food I have except for enough to see me through to the next star system."

"One moment," said the voice.

The transmission went dead.

"Well?" said Snake.

"It's working, or they wouldn't be conferring right now," said Apollo. "Five'll get you ten when they come back online they're willing to transmit their images."

No sooner had the words left his mouth than a typical member of the Kabori race appeared on the screen.

"All right," he said. "You may land and effect repairs. Are you a chlorine breather?"

"No," said Pretorius. "I breathe oxygen."

"Pure oxygen?"

"An oxygen-nitrogen compound."

"All right," said the Kabori. "Follow us to the seventh planet, which has a similar atmosphere. It almost certainly won't be what you're used to, but at least you'll be able to function in it for short-term repairs."

"Thank you," said Pretorius. "I shall always remember you for this."

"Just remember us long enough for us to relieve you of your artifacts."

They cut the transmission again and began heading for the seventh planet.

"What do we do when we get there?" asked Irish.

Apollo laughed. "It's obvious."

"Not to me, it isn't," she said.

"Those look like two-man ships," said Pretorius. "After we touch down, we hide in our cabins until Proto signals us that they're all inside our ship, and we kill them."

"What if they leave one or two behind?" asked Irish.

"We find which ships they're on and eliminate them. And if we're not sure, well, it's an oxygen world, so Proto will finally get a chance to play Michkag, or if I feel that's too far-fetched, then some high-ranking officer."

"Let's hope it doesn't come to that," said Pandora.

"I devoutly hope so," added Proto. "I hate being in the middle of any shooting."

"It'll all be going on over your head," said Apollo.

"Damned well better be," muttered Proto, returning to his human form.

They passed a few planets, followed the Garsype ships through a very small wormhole, and in less than thirty minutes they were in orbit around the seventh planet.

Pretorius turned to Pandora. "Anyone signal you where to set it down?"

Pandora shook her head. "Not a word, not a signal."

"Okay, choose a nice flat spot and land."

The ship touched down, and Pretorius immediately opened the hatch. "Instruments say we can breathe this stuff," he said. "Might as well find out if they're right."

"Smells bad, but it seems harmless enough," said Apollo.

"I agree," said Pretorius. "Good. That means if we've got to go outside, with or without our phony Michkag, we can do it."

"What now?"

"Get out of sight. They'll either all enter the ship, or they'll leave one or more behind. We kill whoever comes aboard, and improvise if there are less than six."

Snake, Irish, and Apollo made their way to their quarters.

"What if they signal first?" asked Proto. "I can't manipulate the controls, and we don't want Pandora out here where they'll see her the second they board us."

"Good question," said Pretorius. He turned to Pandora. "Send them a message, no image attached, that you think you damaged the camera when landing."

Pandora sent the message, finished just as two of the ships touched down, and closed the door to her sleeping compartment seconds before the third touched down.

Pretorius squatted down in the galley, out of sight to anyone entering through the hatch, and Proto stayed where he was to greet their visitors.

One of Michkag's soldiers entered the ship, then a second. A third followed a few seconds later and barked out a question.

"I do not understand," said Proto in Terran, "and my translating mechanism seems to have become disabled during the landing procedure."

Pretorius dared a quick peek. *Four . . . five . . . Where the hell is the sixth?*

The intruders began yelling at Proto, and when it seemed that the nearest was about to kick him Pretorius stood up, burner in hand, and killed the first two. Snake and Irish accounted for one apiece, and then Apollo, outsized and outweighed but not outmuscled, grabbed the fifth from behind and with a quick move snapped his neck.

"That was fast," said Pandora, emerging from her compartment, screecher in hand. "What about the sixth?"

"We're going to have to get to him before he either leaves the planet or reports that things aren't going smoothly here," said Pretorius.

"Hell, that's easy enough," said Apollo.

"Oh?"

Apollo nodded. "Proto, study this one I just killed."

"Oh, shit!" exclaimed Pretorius. "Of course!"

"Of course *what?*" demanded Snake. "What are you talking about?"

"He's not going to come *here* if he doesn't hear from his companions," said Pretorius. "But if I walk over to his ship with my hands in the air and Proto, disguised as this warrior here, is holding a burner to my back, I'm sure as hell going to get into his ship before he realizes anything's wrong."

"Good plan," agreed Apollo. "There's just one little change we need to make."

"Oh?"

Apollo grinned. "*I'll* be the prisoner. After all, I already killed one with my bare hands."

"He does have you by about sixty pounds of muscle, Nate," said Snake.

Pretorius stared at Apollo for a long moment, then shrugged. "Shit!" he muttered. "When you're right, you're right. Proto, I know you can't pick up one of their weapons, but try to hold the image of one in the image of your hand. Can't have him getting suspicious because you're carrying the wrong weapon."

"Right," said Proto, and a moment later they were staring at the mirror image of the fifth dead Kabori.

"Just a second," said Apollo, walking over to the galley. He returned a few seconds later with the knife they had discussed the night before.

"Just in case," he said, tucking it in the back of his belt. He turned to Proto. "Now remind me to take it out when we're done, or I'm gonna embarrass the hell out of some nurse who has to stop the bleeding."

"To say nothing of cutting off half your IQ," added Snake.

"Okay, let's go," said Apollo, walking to the hatch, climbing down to the ground, then raising his arms above his head, partially to show he was an unarmed prisoner, and partially to shield Proto as Pretorius lowered him to the ground on a thin cord.

"Which ship?" asked Proto as they neared the trio of ships.

"Makes no difference," said Apollo.

"Why not?"

"Because if we start entering the wrong one, he'll stick his head out and tell you. And he's got to be curious as all hell. What happened at our ship, why is only one of you coming back, who told you to take a prisoner and a Democracy prisoner at that, who—?"

"Okay, I get the picture," said Proto.

"Looks like you're not the only one," said Apollo, as a Kabori stuck his head out, yelled something in his native tongue, and vanished back inside his ship.

Apollo walked directly to the ship and climbed the stairs to the open hatch while Proto, who was incapable of climbing stairs in his true form, waited outside.

There was one loud bellow, three or four *thuds* as bodies crashed into the ship wall, and then the same loud *crack!* Proto had heard on their own ship when Apollo had snapped his opponent's neck. A few seconds later the corpse was hurled down to the ground. Then Pretorius, Snake, Irish, and Pandora made their way over to the ship and entered it.

"Can you run the damned thing?" Pretorius asked Pandora.

"Give me a few minutes to translate some of the commands and yes, I can do it," answered Pandora. She turned to Apollo. "How about you?"

"Yeah," he replied. "Same make-up as a Tabarinti ship. Just got to learn a couple of new words."

"Then let's get this show on the road," said Pretorius, and in less than ten minutes they were finally on their way to the world that had been taken over by the false Michkag.

12

"**T**he next step is gonna be a little bit harder," announced Pretorius as the ship neared Garsype.

"Oh?" said Irish.

Apollo chuckled. "By a magnitude of five hundred or so."

"I'm sure you're right, but can you explain, please?" she replied.

"You saw the difficulty we had just approaching an outer planet," said Pretorius. "Now try to imagine how much harder it's going to be to land on Garsype."

"But we're in a military ship!" Irish protested.

"Yeah," agreed Apollo. "But sooner or later, before we touch down, they're going to want to see who's piloting it, and what's he doing where he wasn't scheduled to be. For the first part, all we can show them is a Man or a briefcase, and for the second, I hope we've got a good storyteller on board. And for 'storyteller' read 'liar.'"

"Okay," said Irish grimly. "Now I understand."

Pretorius reached into a sack that he'd brought out of a storage area and began withdrawing small artificial leather packages. "Field kits," he announced, passing them out. "Each one's got a t-pack that can translate to and from all the major languages and dialects, though they're pretty slow working with Kabori. I'd be a lot happier if we had one legitimate Kabori speaker with us." He paused. "And each kit has condensed meals that taste almost as bad as they look but will keep you alive and healthy—"

"And foul-tempered," added Snake.

"And foul-tempered," he agreed. "Two medications, one for

wounds, one for fevers and diseases. Tiny oxygen mask that fits entirely over your nose and nowhere else, no straps, no nothing. Small blade that won't do much damage to anything over a meter tall, but will cut through any non-metallic bonds like paper. There *was* a suicide pill, but I got rid of it. Dead Enders don't give up. Ever." He continued listing the contents. "Infrared lenses. Ultraviolet lenses. And that's it. Hope you don't have to use them."

As they passed the outermost of Garsype's two moons, Pandora called Apollo over to the controls, made a few quick adjustments, then looked at him questioningly.

"Yeah, looks like pay dirt to me," he said.

"Out in the open like that?" said Pandora.

He shrugged. "Put yourself in Michkag's place," he said. "Maybe you're not well hidden, but on the other hand, you own the whole damned planet, and it sure as hell makes sneaking up on you difficult if not impossible."

"What are you talking about?" asked Pretorius.

"I think we've found his headquarters," said Pandora. "We'll have to get closer before I can be sure."

"It's in the open, in the middle of a huge, flat, featureless, miles-long and miles-wide field," added Apollo.

Pretorius frowned. "That makes it an easy target," he said. "Maybe too easy. Maybe it's just a city built by the locals."

"Oh, it was built by the locals, all right," replied Apollo. "No one builds a structure like that in the minimum amount of time Michkag's been here."

"Then why are you so sure Michkag's taken it over?" persisted Pretorius.

Apollo grinned. "Because it's got military ships coming and

going just about every sixty seconds, and it's got a huge fleet of battleships parked on the ground right at what seems to be the entrance to the place."

"There's a high wall around it," added Pandora, "maybe fifteen or twenty meters—and from what little I can tell, it seems to be unbroken. I'm sure there have to be a number of entrances and exits—I mean, after all, it's two or three kilometers across, and it's well over a kilometer front to back—but if I had to define it, I'd say it looks more like a castle than a city."

"A castle?" repeated Pretorius, frowning.

"A city-sized castle," added Apollo.

"Makes sense at that," said Pretorius after considering it for a moment.

"In what way?" asked Snake.

"He's a brand-new Michkag, even if only we know it, and he's in the business of establishing a brand-new empire," answered Pretorius. "They're not ready to go to war with the Democracy for a few years, or probably even with whoever's running the Coalition in his absence—and you can bet your ass that once he's turned it over to someone, it's not going to be returned willingly. He's got to consolidate his power, make sure he can trust his generals, and assure himself that the citizenry doesn't revolt against what I imagine will not be the most liberal ruler they've ever had. When you get right down to it, he can probably protect himself much better in a totally enclosed environment like a castle than anywhere else."

"It *does* tend to make it a little more bothersome for *us*," said Apollo.

"Put in for hazard pay," said Pretorius.

"If you live through it," added Snake.

"Well, they're certainly not going to let us land atop the castle or next to it," said Pandora. "And if I take up orbit around the planet, you can bet that *some*body's going to notice pretty damned quick. So what should I do?"

"Find a small outpost a thousand or more miles away from the castle," said Pretorius.

"I don't know," replied Pandora dubiously. "Even a small one's going to have armed ships."

"Yeah, but they're not going to fire on a Garsype military ship," said Pretorius. He paused for a moment, then added, "At least, not right away."

"Then what?" persisted Pandora. "They're certainly going to contact us."

"That all depends on the new kid," said Pretorius.

"The new kid?" she repeated, frowning.

"Apollo," said Pretorius, turning to him. "Madam Methuselah knew the problem we're facing, and you're the one she recommended. I hope to hell that means you can speak Kabori like a native. What passed for it on Colteipa or the seventh planet of this system may stand out like a sore thumb here."

"Of course I can," answered Apollo with a smile." And sixteen other languages, none of which you need. At least, not right away."

"Okay, one problem solved," said Pretorius. "They're going to ask you a bunch of questions, but I'm sure we all agree that you're creative enough to come up with a pack of believable lies, so I see no sense trying to coach you beforehand. You're coming with five human prisoners, two males and three females. One of them tried to disable the controls, got as far as fucking up the video, but hadn't gotten to the sound before you got to *him*."

"I couldn't have written it more believably myself," said Apollo. "Better perhaps, but no more believably."

Pretorius turned to Proto. "You're going to be our captor again. You'll have Apollo directly ahead of you, so until we're pretty close they won't be able to see your mouth." He paused, frowning, and turned to Apollo. "I suppose it's too much to hope that you're also a ventriloquist?"

"Way too much," said Apollo. "We'll have to do it the easy way."

"Nothing easy about it," replied Pretorius. "They're going to have to be awfully gullible."

"If they haven't seen much action they probably will be," answered Apollo. "And it sure doesn't look like Garsype has seen any action at all."

Pretorius sighed heavily. "Okay," he said. "I suppose it'll work." He paused. "It damned well better."

"I have no idea what you two are talking about," said Pandora, frowning in confusion.

"Apollo will be first in line, with his hands behind his back," explained Pretorius. "They'll assume that he's tied or cuffed, and he's big enough that they won't be able to see that Proto's lips aren't moving. The four of us will fall into line in front of Proto, each with our hands behind us."

"And a burner in each hand," added Apollo with a chuckle.

"I'll be directly in front of Proto," continued Pretorius, "and be his voice. It wouldn't do for a woman's voice to come out of one of those oversized Kabori."

"How can you or I answer their questions if we don't speak the language?" asked Proto.

"Apollo speaks it," answered Pretorius.

"But he's in front of me."

"I'll start jabbering the moment they see us," said Apollo. "As they get closer you'll yell at me in Terran, and I'll growl back and lower my voice until it's barely above a whisper. You and the Kaboris will be able to hear each other, and Nate will hear everything I say. Everything important, anyway. If I gesticulate wildly enough it should take their attention away from Nate's lips, which he'll be moving as little as possible anyway."

"It's always possible that you could annoy the shit out of them and they could shoot you dead," said Snake.

"Before they question me?" replied Apollo. "I hardly think so."

"Why the hell not?" she asked. "They'll still have four of us to question."

Apollo turned to Pretorius and the women. "Anyone got any medals they can loan me? The more impressive, the better."

A moment later he had pinned seven of them to the left side of his shirt.

"Okay," he said. "I don't have a uniform, and Nate's would split open the first time I took a breath or a step, but these *should* make it look like I'm more important than you are. I mean, hell, I'll be the only one with the hardware on my chest, and I'm the only one Proto feels a need to keep covered even though my hands are tied behind my back. Ain't nobody gonna shoot me before they find out who I am and what I've got to say, doubtless under what they call duress and we call torture."

"Do we *always* have to improvise plans on the spur of the moment?" muttered Snake.

"Get Cooper to give us ordinary assignments and we'll use ordinary plans to solve them," said Pretorius.

"Yeah?" she said pugnaciously. "Well, I can think of half a dozen reasons why this won't work."

"Only six?" said Apollo with a smile. "How uncreative. I can think of nine."

She muttered an obscenity at him and then fell silent.

"Okay," said Pandora a moment later. "Have you got a preference for hemisphere, polar cap, equator?"

"Any place that's out in the open," answered Pretorius, "where we can be pretty sure we know who and how many are waiting for us before we land."

"And if there's more than one ship or one encampment, make sure you land a little distance from it," added Apollo.

"Why?" asked Pandora.

"Because what little strategy we have requires us to be walking *toward* all our captors. If any are behind us, they're going to see that our hands aren't tied or cuffed."

"Damn!" said Pandora. "I never thought of that!"

Apollo chuckled. "That's because you're a pilot and a computer expert, whereas I am a lawbreaker of interstellar standing."

"Good thing our small-time friend here is so in love with himself," said Snake. "It wouldn't to do have any Kaboris recognize him."

"I like your spirit, Small One," said Apollo.

"Thanks, I suppose," replied Snake.

"I can't say much for your brain, but at least it's in a small head."

"Well," said Snake, "I suppose we should all be glad that you've got a belly like that or your ego wouldn't have any place that it could fit."

"Business now, love fest later," said Pretorius.

"Okay," said Pandora, "I think I've got a spot."

"First question," said Pretorius. "How far from the castle?"

"Halfway around Garsype. When it's noon here, it'll be midnight, or close to midnight, at the castle."

"So far so good. What's waiting for us?"

"Hard to tell," Pandora answered. "It's certainly not a city. It's a little big for a tented camp. If I had to guess, I'd say it's a permanent outpost consisting of seven or eight buildings. They've got three . . . no, four, ships on the ground."

"Too big?" asked Proto.

"We're just gonna fool 'em, not wipe 'em out," said Apollo.

"We *hope*," interjected Irish.

"I don't know why we don't take them out from up here," said Snake.

"Because if they don't check in when they're supposed to, the castle will know an enemy has landed on the planet," said Apollo. "That puts the odds of our getting safely inside the castle up from maybe ten-to-one against to maybe five-thousand-to-one."

"That's how to get rich, Nate," said Snake. "Every time Cooper sends us out on one of these idiot missions, describe the mission to some local bookie and bet your pay that you'll come back. If you get killed, you weren't gonna need your money anyway, and if you *do* survive, you'll be a millionaire."

"You'll forgive me if thoughts of becoming a millionaire are farthest from my mind at this moment," said Pretorius, walking over to the control panel and looking at the holographic map.

"That's it," said Pandora. "You want me to try another place?"

He shook his head. "They're half a world away from an overwhelming force, and there's no reason to think we'll find easier pickings north or south."

"We could look," said Irish.

"I'd rather not take the time," said Pretorius.

"Why?" persisted Irish. "No one's after us right now."

"That we're aware of," answered Pretorius. "But sooner or later someone over in the Colteipa system is going to notice those ships we destroyed, and we also left some ships and bodies on the seventh planet of this system. If they're not searching for us yet, they soon will be."

"So this is the outpost you want?" said Pandora.

"You just heard me explain it to Irish."

"I wanted to hear it once more, just to be sure."

"This is the spot. Take us down."

Pretorius turned to Apollo. "They're going to signal us any minute. You'll answer them."

"Of course."

"Remember: you're coming with prisoners, and one of them has damaged the video."

"Not a problem," said Apollo. "I'll tell them some of our controls have been compromised too."

"Yeah, good thinking," said Pretorius.

"Why?" asked Pandora, puzzled.

"We have to tell them before we land that all the Men are prisoners," said Apollo. "Otherwise they might fire as the first of us climbs down out of the hatch."

"And since they know we had a battle and that the video is damaged, they'll buy that the landing is compromised too," said Pretorius.

"I still don't understand," said Pandora. "Why is that important?"

"Because the notion of multiple prisoners who were active enough to damage some of the controls even after they were captured might make them think we're not quite as safe as we want them to believe—and if they move out to the landing coordinates they give you, I want you to be able to land a couple of kilometers to the east or west and give us time to get off the ship and Proto to change his image before they're close enough to see what's happening."

"Of course!" said Pandora. "Damn! I feel so dumb!"

"Don't," said Pretorius. "I've seen you commit espionage on computers that are so complex that I'll bet even Apollo couldn't handle them."

The ship began dropping down, and soon entered the atmosphere.

A voice spoke on the radio. No one but Apollo understood it.

It says, "X457Q3T, please answer," announced Apollo.

"Do you want to do the speaking?" asked Pandora.

"I'd rather type it," said Apollo, "but if I get any of the language wrong, or even correct but awkward, it could start them wondering. So yeah, I'd better speak."

"Okay," she said, swiveling away from the controls. "It's all yours."

Apollo spoke briefly, waited for the other end to utter a couple of sentences, and then spent a couple of minutes speaking again, clearly explaining what the soldiers on the ground would be facing when the ship landed.

Finally there were a couple of sharp commands, Apollo gave brief answers, and then communication ceased.

"Well?" said Pandora. "Where am I landing?"

"When we're at about ten thousand kilometers your instruments will be able to determine the exact make-up of the complex," replied Apollo. "I assured them that all the prisoners were placid and under control." He paused and frowned. "I didn't want to prime them for any kind of action by saying they'd also damaged our ability to land exactly where we want, so just touch down two kilometers to the west of the outpost. If we descend slowly enough and there are no weapons in evidence, I can't believe they're going to shoot one of their own ships out of the sky."

They began their descent, and when Pandora changed course with just four kilometers left to go there were some brief inquiries on the radio.

"Ignore them," said Pretorius.

There were no further messages, and no shots were fired, and ninety seconds later they touched down on Garsype, which had been their goal from the first minute of the mission.

13

"Any welcoming committee?" asked Pretorius as the ship touched down.

"Not so far," replied Pandora.

"There will be," said Apollo. "You can bet the farm on it—if any of you *has* a farm, that is."

"Here they come," said Pandora. "Seven—no, eight—of 'em—and they're not Kaboris."

"I recognize them," said Pretorius. "They're Janbottis—a race from the Coalition. Obviously they hired on here. Apollo, do you speak their language?"

"About as well as I speak Kabori," answered Apollo. "They make a couple of guttural sounds I can't match, but they'll figure out what I mean."

"They're sure as hell not natives," said Snake. "Every one of them is wearing a mask attached to canisters on their backs."

"And I'll bet not one of them is carrying a bouquet of flowers to greet us," said Apollo.

"Let's get moving!" said Pretorius. "I want Proto on the ground before they see how he gets there."

"Is there anything else I should do?" asked Pandora, as Proto changed his image to that of a heavily armed Janbotti, complete with facemask and air canister.

"Yeah, everybody grab an oxygen mask," said Pretorius.

"But the air checks out as fine!" protested Snake.

"You don't know what the air in their building is like," said

Pretorius. "Better to be prepared." He turned to Pandora. "I'd say to lock the controls and panel, but if we pull this off no one's coming inside the ship, and if we need to get back here and take off in a hurry, it'll take extra time if you've locked it down."

"You're sure?" she said. "I could at least lock the weapons system."

He shook his head. "If we need to escape or defend ourselves, the last thing we need is a weapons system we can't use for a vital minute or two."

She shrugged. "You're the boss."

Snake, Irish, and Apollo walked to the hatch, opened it, and were standing on the ground seconds later. Then Pretorius passed Proto down to them. Pandora got up and walked over to the hatch. Pretorius took one last look around the deck and followed her down.

The group of Janbottis was perhaps a kilometer away when Pretorius growled a curse.

"Goddamnit, Snake!" he snarled. "No weapons on display! You're a prisoner!"

"It's just a mini-screecher," she said. "It's only good for discouraging guys who think I'm an easy lay."

"You're not an easy anything," said Pretorius, "but you're damned well going to be an unarmed uneasy captive!"

"All right," she muttered. "You want it?"

"No, they're close enough to see if you hand me something. Stick it in your boot."

"And that's what you and Apollo have done?"

"That's what I've done," answered Pretorius. "Make sure it doesn't make a bulge."

"Better start lining up," said Apollo. "They're almost close enough to make us out as individuals."

Proto stood directly behind Apollo, the three women, and Pretorius, in that order.

"Don't forget your weapon, Proto," said Pretorius, and instantly the index finger on Proto's right hand morphed into a wicked-looking burner.

"If you're going to prod me with it at any time," said Pretorius, "give me a good hard push with your finger or hand so I'll know what you're doing."

"I can't," said Proto. "I don't really have a finger or a hand."

"Shit! I forgot," said Pretorius. "And nobody talks except Apollo. He's going to be feeding me lines that I have to say for Proto, in between all the bullshit he's yelling at the Janbottis and at Fate in general."

"They should be within earshot in another twenty seconds," announced Apollo. "I'd say thirty, but they've got awfully big ears and it's a pretty damned quiet planet, so far at least."

"From the look on their faces," said Snake, "it looks like all they really want to say is 'Die, Democracy swine!'"

"Enough," said Pretorius, lowering his voice to a harsh whisper. "From this point on, nobody talks except Apollo."

"And you, when you pretend I'm answering them," added Proto.

"Yes," agreed Pretorius. "But none of you will react to me, or give any indication that my lips are even moving."

The lead Janbotti yelled something.

"What was that?" asked Pretorius softly.

"He wants us to walk up to him and his pals," said Apollo. "No sense answering back. It's a direct order, and besides, if you make your voice loud enough to match him, he'll surely see that it's coming from you. He's a *big* bastard; probably even got thirty or forty pounds on *me*. That makes for a large lung capacity, and a hell of a loud voice." He paused briefly. "Okay, from this point on, pay no attention to what I say unless I'm translating. I've got to get them used to the fact that I never shut up."

"Until they shoot you," whispered Snake.

"No problem," said Apollo. "I'll just hold you up in front of me." He turned to face the largest of the Janbottis. "What do you think of *that*, meathead?"

When they were twenty yards apart the lead Janbotti spoke.

"I wouldn't marry you if they gave me half the Democracy for a wedding gift!" yelled Apollo. "How you can stand to look at that face in the mirror is beyond me!" He then, very softly, uttered a single sentence in Janbotti, and after that went back to insulting the speaker.

Pretorius whispered "Now, Proto" and began speaking while Proto's lips were moving. When he finished he made a very soft clicking noise, rather than be seen reaching out to touch his "captor" who wasn't standing there anyway, and Proto stopped mouthing words.

"So you captured them on Brondoke?" said the leader as his mask directed and amplified his voice.

Apollo frowned and translated between curses.

"What is Brondoke?" asked Pretorius, as Proto pretended to utter the words.

"The seventh planet, you ignorant fool!" said the leader. "Did they put up much of a fight?"

Apollo kept up his performance.

"I killed four of them," said Pretorius through Proto.

"I am sure the commander will be happy to reward you," said the leader.

"Who *is* the commander? I am a stranger to the Sett Empire."

"You certainly are!" cried the leader, with a laugh his companions all shared. "This is now the Cassiopeia Dominion, and our commander—the whole Dominion's commander—is the magnificent Michkag. Surely you have heard of him?"

"I thought he was the leader of the Coalition," said Pretorius, as Proto moved his lips once again.

"He still is," came the answer. "And now he has added the Dominion to it. Where do you hail from?"

Apollo uttered a few choice insults while transmitting the answer to Pretorius. Proto heard it, of course, as he had heard all the others. "I am from Matunite VI," he said without thinking.

Oh, shit! thought Pretorius. *You blew it! I was supposed to do the talking for you!*

The leader stared at Proto intently. "Say that again."

He was too close for Apollo to translate without being overheard. Proto merely stared at him.

"I will ask one more time: say that again."

"Matunite VI," repeated Proto.

"Not just the world," said the leader, "but the whole damned sentence."

Proto stared at him silently.

"I thought so!" said the leader. He pulled a dagger out of his belt and shoved it into what appeared to be Proto's belly—and of course nothing happened except that hand and weapon went right through the image. He took a swing at Proto's jaw, went through that image as well, and lost his balance. He fell atop the *real* Proto, and Pretorius kicked his head with all his strength, knocking him out.

Suddenly they were facing half a dozen burners and screechers, all set to lethal—and then, before anyone could fire at the little group of Men, there was a huge beast in their midst, much like a Tyrannosaur but fifty percent larger.

The Janbottis all turned their fire on the creature, which did it absolutely no harm.

"Well, I'll be a son of a—" began Apollo, pulling a burner out of his boot and firing at the nearest Janbotti. Less than a second later, Pretorius, Snake, Irish, and Pandora were firing their own weapons as well, and shortly after that they were facing a pile of Janbotti corpses.

"Goddamn, that was clever!" enthused Apollo. "You ever pull anything like that before?"

"I've never had to," replied Proto, once again appearing as a Kabori. "It was just an act of desperation."

"Well, it's one hell of an act!" said Apollo. "Put it in your resume. I'm sure we'll want an encore or two before this mission is over."

"Everyone all right?" asked Pretorius.

The three women all answered in the affirmative.

"So what do we do next?" asked Apollo.

"If they were watching closely, Proto's trick isn't going to work against them a second time," said Pretorius.

"It happened so fast," said Irish. "I'd almost bet that none of them can be sure that Proto himself didn't kill a couple of them while we were firing at the others."

"It just means they're not going to invite us in," replied Pretorius. "So we have two choices: break or shoot our way in, or try another outpost. Either way, it's going to be difficult to keep our presence a secret."

"We can't just stand out here all day," said Apollo. "They'll have locked the gates, of course, but we can blow them open."

"Why are we even doing this?" demanded Snake. "Our goal is halfway around the planet."

"We'd like to know how to approach it, what codes we need to signal them so they don't blow us out of the sky as we approach," answered Pretorius. "Also, only one of us can look like a Kabori. We'd like to find some diagram of that castle, as well as a signal that says we're friends and please don't shoot us as our ship approaches. We also want to know if there is some covert way of entering the castle, or at least some spot on that enormous building where we can get off the ship and into the place before we're spotted."

"Well, Nate, do we try to get in, go back to the ship, or just stand here talking?" asked Apollo.

"We go in like cowboys with our guns blazing," said Pretorius. He turned to Proto. "Stay right in the middle of us, and get ready to scare the shit out of them again if and when I tell you to."

"Right," said Proto.

"Okay," said Pretorius, "let's get started."

The six of them raced up to the gate through which the Janbotti party had exited. There was no camouflage about pretending to be prisoners or being unarmed. When they reached it, Apollo fired his burner at the lock, which melted as the door swung open.

The small dirt street in front of them was empty, and they prepared to enter the outpost.

"There's a roof over the whole damned complex," said Pretorius. "That means they're breathing *their* air, so put your oxygen masks on."

"They've got to have a few ships," said Snake. "I wonder where they're hiding them?"

"I don't know," said Pretorius. "Just look into each window and doorway, and assume someone's looking back even if you can't see him."

"Got it!" said Apollo, looking at something he held in his hand.

"Where?"

"See that fourth building on the left?"

"Looks like all the others," said Pretorius. "What makes it different?"

Apollo showed him a small device, about the size and depth of a poker chip.

"What is it?"

"It's an energy reader," answered Apollo. "And while everything looks alike, and everything looks deserted, that one building is consuming about eighty-five percent of all the power that this outpost is using."

"You're sure?"

"Damned right I'm sure. I invented it."

"Hope to hell you're as good as you think you are," said Pretorius, turning to the rest of his team. "Fourth building on the left. Proto, resume human form and go first."

"I thought *I* was going first," said Apollo, frowning.

"You really want to?"

"Hell, yes!"

"Okay, go first. But when they blow your head off with a shot that would have been about five feet above Proto, remember that you volunteered."

"Oh, shit!" growled Apollo. "Suddenly I could only think of him as a blob or a dinosaur. Okay, Proto, after you."

"What do I do if I make it to the door before anyone starts shooting?"

"You celebrate, because it means they're all dead or asleep," said Apollo.

"Seriously, damn it!" said Proto. "I can't reach out and push the damned thing open, even if you blow off the locks."

"If no one's tried to shoot you or stop you, just step aside," said Pretorius. "Once we start entering, come in second or third, so if you have to turn into a huge creepy-crawly, it'll block their vision of everyone who's behind you."

"Got it," said Proto. "Should I start now?"

Pretorius nodded his assent, and Apollo said, "Unless you got something better to do."

Proto began walking toward the fourth building on the left. The group expected to be fired upon any moment, but nothing upset the stillness of the afternoon air, and they soon saw why.

"Well, that's dumb!" said Apollo. "No windows."

"Damned place was probably built by whatever lived here before the Kaboris took over the planet and decided to stick the Janbottis out here," said Pretorius. "It's only been a year, a year and a half tops, and they've probably spent every spare minute and credit making the castle functional."

Proto reached the front entrance—it wasn't really a door—and then stepped aside. A moment later Apollo blew it away and sent it crashing against an interior wall.

"Why the hell didn't you melt it?" demanded Snake. "It wouldn't have made a sound."

"Look at the size of that thing," responded Apollo. "Did you really want to walk across two meters of hot melting metal?"

"Besides," added Pretorius, "it's not as if they don't know we're here."

Proto entered the compound, waiting for a shot that never came, and was followed a few seconds later by the five Men.

"What now?" he asked.

"No sense waiting to be picked off one by one," said Pretorius. "Let's draw their fire and see where they are."

"That's suicidal!" snapped Snake.

"For you or me, yes," replied Pretorius. "But not for Proto."

"A dinosaur again?" said Proto.

"No, I think they'd hide from that." Pretorius paused in thought for a few seconds. "Come up with something about two-thirds the size of a Man. Cover him with scales, and give him a sling that holds a rifle—laser, projectile, sonic, I don't care. But make it *big*. If they shoot first, I want them shooting at *you* before you can pull that weapon out of its sling and start shooting at them, or just at buildings in general. They've got to figure a gun like that'll shoot through a wall like a knife through warm butter."

"Okay," answered Proto. "Let me concentrate for a second."

"Gather around him so no one can see exactly what he's doing," ordered Pretorius.

And it took very little more than a few seconds for Proto to appear exactly as Pretorius had described him.

"I just saw some movement inside the building!" whispered Irish.

"Well, they had to be *some*where," said Snake.

Proto turned to Pretorius. "Now?"

Pretorius nodded his assent. "Now."

Proto took a tentative step inside the structure, then another, with Apollo directly behind him.

"Ready or not," said Apollo in a soft sing-song voice, "here we come!"

14

"**W**hat's going on?" demanded Apollo, staring at the empty corridor. "Proto's dinosaur couldn't have scared them *all* away."

"I agree," said Pretorius. "If there's one thing they're not, it's cowards."

"Okay, keep your eyes and ears open," said Apollo. "They have to be waiting somewhere that they think gives them the advantage."

They continued down the corridor, eyes and ears alert, weapons at the ready, but they couldn't see a living soul.

"There's some grinding noise behind this door," noted Apollo, pointing to his left.

"Push it open and let Proto walk in first," ordered Pretorius.

"Okay," said Proto. "I just hope they'd rather shoot me dead than in the foot so I can't run away."

"Don't think so much and just do what he tells you to do," said Snake.

Apollo gave the door a shove, and Proto entered the room. It seemed to be filled with machinery, but not any they were familiar with.

"It's sure as hell not a weapon, or an observation station," said Proto. "There's a computer over there controlling it, but it's a pretty simplistic one."

Apollo walked around the room, studying the various sections of the machine. Finally he smiled.

"You figured something out," said Irish.

"I think so," he said, still smiling. "And no, this room's not a weapon shop or an observation station. In fact, it's a hell of a lot more important that that—at least, it is if you're a Janbotti. You know what it is?"

"What?" asked Pandora.

"I'd say it's a climate control room, but that's too simplistic," answered Apollo. "What it really is is an *atmosphere* control room. It's providing them with the only stuff on the whole damned planet that they can breathe."

"You know, it makes sense," said Pretorius.

"Yes, it does," said Apollo. Suddenly he smiled again. "But it also tells us how to get from here to the castle without firing a shot or striking a blow."

"Oh?" said Pretorius.

"I *like* you!" said Snake suddenly. "You're even nastier than I am!"

"You figured it out before the boss did," said Apollo with a smile.

"Oh, I figured it out," said Pretorius. "I'm just not as delighted with wholesale slaughter as some of us are." Pretorius frowned, lost in thought for a few seconds, then looked first at the ceiling and then at the walls. "Okay, they're totally enclosed. No windows, no walls, not even a chimney that I could see. Should be a piece of cake."

"You know," said Pandora, "it makes sense. The castle was built the same way: no windows, no inner courtyards, nothing but a roof that covers every inch of it, with solid walls right down to the ground, so Michkag can give visitors whatever air and gravity they need without having to transport them to and from an outpost like this."

"We'll worry about the castle when we come to it," said Pretorius, pulling out a burner from one boot and a screecher from the other. "First things first. Time for target practice."

And so saying, he activated the burner and melted the computer that seemed to be the brain of the machine. Soon everyone but Proto, who of course could not lift or hold a weapon, was firing at the huge machine until it turned into a reeking pile of melted sludge.

"Now what?" asked Pandora.

"Now we wait until they have trouble breathing or functioning," answered Pretorius.

"We can speed that happy moment up a bit," said Apollo, walking back out into the corridor and blowing a huge hole in the ceiling and roof. "Might as well let that wonderful stuff escape into the atmosphere rather than give these bastards an extra few minutes of comfort."

They talked, and they waited, and after about half an hour they heard a pair of ships' engines starting to warm up.

Pretorius turned to Apollo and Snake. "Go outside and see to it that they don't take off to warn anyone about us."

"Jesus!" exclaimed Snake, when she and Apollo returned a moment later. "It was like shooting clay pigeons in a carnival back when I was a kid!"

"Do you suppose there's any left?" asked Pretorius.

"Not a chance," said Apollo. "No place else to put 'em where they couldn't be seen from overhead."

"Okay, what's next?" asked Snake.

"Next we walk through this whole compound and check into every room until we find what we're looking for," answered Pretorius.

"Not more Janbottis?" she said.

He shook his head. "You find any, kill 'em." He paused. "But the fresh air really should have wiped out any survivors already."

"Uh . . . do we *have* any plans?" asked Irish.

"We will soon," said Pretorius. "Spread out and search every room, every closet, every cubbyhole, until you find something, *any-thing*, that will show us the safest way to approach the castle, and to gain entrance to it once we've landed."

"That's gonna be a little harder than you think," said Apollo. "Unless we can set it down next to an unlocked and unprotected door in the middle of the night."

"First things first," said Pretorius. "First we have to find out what we're up against, what the obstacles are. *Then* we'll worry about how to get around them." He paused and looked around the room at his team. "And the first step is to comb through this place and find out everything we can about the castle. And remember, there may be a few Janbottis still lurking throughout the outpost. I doubt it, but there's no sense not being careful."

Apollo headed out the door and turned into the corridor. Proto was just a step behind him.

"No," said Pretorius firmly. "Apollo can take care of himself. Go with Pandora or Irish."

"That's almost an insult," said Irish.

"You ever kill anyone?" asked Pretorius.

She shook her head. "No."

"That puts you well behind Apollo and Snake. Just let him walk a step or two ahead of you as a target."

Snake walked to the door again.

"Damn it!" growled Pretorius.

"What now?" asked Irish.

"Proto, if you're going to be a decoy, stop being a lizard and become a Man. They're not going to shoot their first volley into anything else."

"Sorry," said Proto, who instantly assumed his human form and led Irish out of the room.

"Snake, you're next," said Pretorius.

"I hope there's one left," said Snake as she walked out the door.

"Me now?" said Pandora.

Pretorius shook his head. "You stay here."

"But—"

"I'm not playing favorites, and I'm not saying I don't think you're up to the task," he said. "But if Apollo gets himself shot, you're the only one with enough expertise to pilot a ship with Kabori controls or counter any spy systems we find once we reach the castle."

"So you and I stay here until someone returns or contacts us?"

Pretorius grimaced. "You're half right. *You* stay here. *I* go hunting for . . . hell, for whatever."

He turned and hurried out into the corridor. He assumed that Apollo and Snake would be checking the place out room by room in an orderly manner, so rather than inspect the same rooms that they had already cleared, he walked as far as he could, came to a left turn just before reaching what he thought of as the back wall, passed a pair of open rooms, and then came to a closed door.

Pretorius reached out to open it, only to find that it was locked. He didn't want to mess with molten metal, so instead of his burner he pulled out his screecher, turned it to full power, and shattered the lock and indeed the entire handle with a blast of solid sound.

As he was entering the room, a Janbotti wearing a breathing mask launched itself at him, knocking him back into the corridor. He was about to swing at the Janbotti's head, remembered that he still had his screecher in his hand, and fired it full into the Janbotti's face.

He'd never shot a living being with a screecher at close range. It wasn't a pretty sight. Both eyeballs cracked and fell to pieces, its teeth all shattered, and it tried to scream but the bones in its jaw had shattered and it could barely open its mouth.

Pretorius stood back, let the Janbotti fall to the floor, then quickly checked to make sure it was dead. He noticed a truly complex computer atop a table in a corner, then went out into the hall and, putting a couple of fingers into his mouth, emitted a loud, shrill whistle.

All five of his teammates showed up within a minute.

"Wow!" said Apollo, looking at the Kabori's corpse. "What the hell did you do to him?"

"Screecher at about five inches," answered Pretorius.

"Kind of makes you wonder why the burner is everyone's weapon of choice," said Apollo.

"I think," said Pandora, standing in the doorway and staring at the computer, "that you've uncovered the mother lode."

"Makes sense," agreed Irish. "He seems to be the only one left. My guess is that he was probably under orders to destroy the machine before he left."

"Well, you've got a machine," said Pretorius to Pandora, "and you've even got a teammate who speaks and reads Kabori."

"A little," qualified Apollo.

"More than the rest of us, which is what counts," replied Pretorius.

He turned to Apollo. "Any chance we can move this computer to the ship without damaging it?"

"I doubt it," replied Apollo.

"Then we'll leave the two of you to have the computer dope out the next leg of our mission while we keep searching the building."

He walked out the door and turned to his right, followed by Irish, Snake, and Proto, and a moment later they were back in the original room.

"You think they'll find anything?" asked Irish.

"They certainly figure to," answered Pretorius. "That's a hell of a complex, sophisticated computer, and the Janbottis thought enough of it to leave one of their own behind to guard it, and probably destroy it."

"You know," said Snake, "somehow these missions are never as smooth or easy as they sound."

Pretorius smiled. "You've noticed that, have you?"

"We never stick to the plan," continued Snake.

"The plan is to kill or kidnap Michkag. Everything else is the details, and they're what change as situations change. The plan's the same as the day we started."

"You gonna be a college professor when you quit the service?" she asked with a smile.

"I certainly hope not," said Pretorius. He looked around. "Well, we might as well keep looking while they work on the machine. Split up into pairs, and meet back here in half an hour."

When they returned to the room that housed the computer, Pandora and Apollo were waiting for them.

"Well?" asked Pretorius.

"I *think* we've found a way," said Apollo.

"It all depends on no one shooting us down as we approach the castle," added Pandora.

"And they shouldn't," said Apollo. "After all, we're flying a Kabori ship."

"And now we've got access to their codes, and I've already transferred them to the ship," said Pandora.

"Well, that all sounds encouraging," said Pretorius.

"I'm glad you agree," said Apollo. "I'm good with the language—well, passable anyway. But this lady broke the locks and safeguards on the code a hell of a lot faster than I could have."

"Okay," said Pretorius, "we've accomplished what we can. It's time to get the hell out of here. No sense sticking around to greet a punishment party." He turned to Apollo. "I hope it's as safe and easy to get into the castle as you make it sound."

"Oh, it's easier than I thought it would be," answered Apollo. "Right now, with what we learned, and approaching in a Kabori ship, I figure the odds are no more than fifteen-to-one against us."

15

"So what do we know now that we didn't know a few hours ago?" asked Pretorius, as the ship sped through the Garsype atmosphere toward the castle.

"I've found and adjusted the cloaking device," answered Apollo. "We're okay until they can see us with their eyes, as opposed to their instruments."

"And we know the codes we need to approach the castle and land without getting blown out of the sky," answered Pandora.

"And we've got a rough map of the castle," added Apollo.

"How rough?"

"It's not divided into rooms, but into sections," said Apollo.

"Explain," said Pretorius.

"We know, for example, the broad area where the military's quarters are, but not how many separate rooms they have, how many showers—always assuming they wash—and where they eat. We know where the ships land. We know the major areas set aside for commerce."

"Commerce?" said Irish.

Apollo smiled. "There's more than a billion soldiers on the planet. Every now and then I'm sure they have an urge to buy things—a shirt, a video, a better meal, whatever."

Snake shook her head. "It's just hard to picture a billion armed soldiers in that castle."

"Oh, I don't think it holds much more than half a million," said Apollo. "And even that seems crowded. As we approach it, we'll be flying over a military encampment that'll cover more ground than the biggest city on Deluros VIII."

"As well as the biggest spaceport you've ever seen, or imagined," added Pandora.

"I don't remember any humongous spaceport in Orion," said Snake, frowning.

"That's because they *lived* in Orion," answered Pandora. "They're all transients here, and once Michkag has firmly established his rule I would imagine most of them will either be going back to Orion or to the next huge piece of the galaxy he wants to take over."

Snake turned to Pretorius. "You really think we can pull this off with a *billion* armed soldiers down there ready to kill anyone who tries?"

"He had close to a billion in Orion and we pulled off the switch," answered Pretorius. "It's just a matter of doing our homework."

"And being a little bit lucky," added Pandora.

"Oh, we're gonna need more than a *little* bit of luck to pull this off," said Apollo. Suddenly he grinned. "As soon as I dope out the odds we'll discuss my fee."

"Take it off Michkag's smoldering body," said Snake. "He's richer than we are."

"Even assuming he can pull this off, *and* take another section of the galaxy when he's done here, what does he expect from it?" asked Irish, frowning. "I mean, he had no childhood, no young adulthood. Physically he was probably past the halfway point when he took his first breath. Doesn't he ever want to sit back and just enjoy everything he's got?"

"It's the getting that's the enjoyable part for beings like

Michkag," said Pretorius. "Take Earth's various emperors and dictators. They could tell you exactly what they thought they wanted—China, living space, access to the ocean, whatever—but what they really wanted, even if they didn't quite know it, was for history to acknowledge that they pulled off an accomplishment or set of accomplishments that were clearly beyond anyone else. That's why, with a few exceptions such as Rome, hardly any empires survive their founders and thrive under their successors."

"The next step is to say, 'Well, hell, Michkag's empire isn't going to outlast him by much, and it'll probably never be half as powerful, so why bother at all?'" said Apollo.

"I'd like to say the Democracy is concerned with the fate of all the enslaved billions," replied Pretorius. "But I think the truth of the matter is that if he didn't present a direct threat to us, we'd let nature and history take their joint courses, rather than lose quite a few million lives and quite a bit of treasure fighting him."

"You know," said Irish, "that's so outrageous that I'm sure it's the absolute truth."

"What does our own alien say?" asked Apollo.

"I am totally apolitical," answered Proto. "I am also without religion and deeply held convictions."

"Oh, come on," said Apollo.

"It's true," answered Proto. "In a galaxy filled with beings like yourself and Pretorius and Michkag, the average member of my race stands about fifty centimeters high and weighs no more than twenty pounds. When you have armies of billions and my entire race numbers in the thousands—not even the tens of thousands—we are a little more concerned with survival than with conquest or posterity."

"Makes sense when you put it that way," said Snake.

"Thank you."

"Then why are you here at all?" asked Apollo.

Proto's human image nodded his head in Pretorius's direction. "He owns me."

"He *what?*" demanded Apollo.

"I was serving time in jail," said Proto. "Colonel Pretorius paid my bail provided that I would join his team."

"But I gather you were part of the mission that put the clone in Michkag's place, and you helped rescue Edgar what's-his-name . . . ?"

"Nmumba," Proto prompted him.

"Yeah, Nmumba, from some prison planet in the Antares Sector. Just how many millions of credits was your bail if you're still working for him after all that?"

"It wasn't very large at all," said Proto.

"Then why—?"

"He and the others treat me with respect," replied Proto. "Do you know how rare that is for a member of my race? Whenever something, *any*thing, goes wrong, we are the easiest to blame because even if they saw the villain doing his or her foul deeds, they can never be sure it wasn't one of us."

"That's ridiculous!" said Apollo. He pulled his burner out of its holster and held it in front of him. "Here! Take this!"

"You know I can't."

"Then why doesn't everyone else know it?"

"Because only a tiny handful see us in our true form, and of that tiny handful, only a miniscule percentage realize that we are casting an image and not actually morphing into the being that they see."

"And of course there's the obvious added advantage," said Apollo.

"Oh?" said Proto with a puzzled expression.

Apollo smiled. "If someone shoots the whole Dead Enders crew, you're going to survive just fine unless they aim at your feet."

"You think it's lucky to be eighteen inches high with no physical defenses, you should try it some time," Proto shot back.

"Should I start showing you holos of what we're facing on the way there and once we're inside?" asked Pandora. "Or would you rather keep picking on Proto?"

"Much as I'm sure we all enjoy picking on Proto," said Apollo, "I suppose we should get back to business."

"We've accessed the codes we need to prove that this isn't just a ship in Michkag's navy, but that we're Kaboris and have every right to be flying it in Garsype's atmosphere," said Pandora. Suddenly the castle appeared. "Now as you can see, the damned thing's locked up tighter than a drum. No discernable windows, not even the size of portholes."

"They've got to have some," said Pretorius. "They're just well-camouflaged."

"Probably," she agreed. "But whoever took the holos didn't make any effort to spot them." Suddenly a view of the roof came up. "Given how big the damned building is, I'd have thought we'd land on the roof, but as you can see, there are no ships there, and in fact it's not as flat as it seems from afar. All sides gently slope down about ten or twelve degrees to the very center."

"So where do we land?" asked Pretorius.

She turned to Apollo. "Can you give it commands in Kabori? That'll certainly be easier than my translating Terran into Kabori on the keyboard."

"Certainly," he said, uttering a low command.

Suddenly they were looking at a section of totally flat ground with absolutely nothing growing on it, perhaps fifty meters on a side, about one hundred meters from the castle.

"It's just a flat field," said Snake, staring at the holos. "But if it's a landing field, where the hell are all the ships, plus all the ones that are stationed there?"

"Watch," said Apollo, uttering another command in Kabori.

"Son of a bitch!" exclaimed Snake as the field opened at the center, and then all the sides slid quickly and noiselessly into the surrounding ground at a depth of perhaps ten meters.

"Be hard to miss that," commented Irish.

Suddenly Apollo uttered another command and the holographic screen froze.

"Look over to your left, which is due south as far as I can tell," he said. "That dirt-covered structure is an artificial wall, unlike all the rest of the ground surrounding what I think we'll call the landing field."

"So once we land," began Pretorius, "hell, once *anybody* lands, some ground crew, or underground crew to be more accurate, tows the ship through the false wall to an enormous hangar where they've stored most of their ships."

"Also," added Apollo, "my guess is that if they know you're coming, you won't land on the soil floor. They'll have something low and flat on wheels, you'll set the ship down on that, and it'll tow you to wherever they want to store you. That way you don't take any chance of ripping your ship's belly or sides open when they tow you off the landing spot." He turned to Pandora. "Okay, all yours again."

"Well, it's obvious that once we land, Proto's got to impersonate the Kabori pilot," said Pretorius. "I wonder if he can get away with claiming he's Michkag, back from a secret mission, and that we five are his prisoners."

"Or perhaps his turncoats and coconspirators," suggested Irish.

"I suppose it depends on how fast they can contact Michkag or one of his closest advisors," said Apollo. "With a hundred thousand or so stationed in the castle, it could take a couple of hours."

"Will they hold us that long?" asked Snake.

"Not if Michkag has a temper tantrum over being delayed," said Apollo.

Pretorius shook his head. "Won't work."

"Why the hell not?" asked Apollo.

"Because Michkag can't have a tantrum without yelling. Or even speaking at normal volume," said Pretorius. "Now, only you can speak Kabori, the odds are that you've got some discernable accent that of course Michkag hasn't got, and even if not, Proto's lip movements have to match your words, and *he* doesn't know the language."

"I know a few words of Kabori," said Pandora. "After all, I've been reading their signals."

"A few words isn't enough, and your voice coming out of Michkag isn't going to convince anyone," said Pretorius.

"But except for all that it's a great idea," said Snake sardonically.

"Had to consider it for a minute," replied Pretorius. "We'll consider forty or fifty more, and hopefully one of them will be workable." He paused. "Pandora, show us some close-ups of the roof."

"We land there, we'll probably fall right through," said Snake.

"I think it's stronger than it looks," said Pretorius, "and I wouldn't be surprised if they had a ship hidden somewhere inside one of those walls or even the floor."

"Why would you think so?" asked Irish.

"He wouldn't be the first dictator who had to leave in a hurry, and he's bright enough to have an escape route already planned and set up."

"Okay," announced Pandora. "Here's the roof. I don't think the walls are thick enough to hold even a two-man ship. The floor? I don't know. It seems to have been built in sections, but I can't spot any opening or any moving parts."

"Keep looking," said Pretorius.

"But I just told you—"

"I know what you told me. Keep looking anyway."

"Damn it, Nate, if you think I'm lying . . ."

"Have I said you were lying?" replied Pretorius.

"Then why am I still looking when I told you twice that I can't see a place to dock or hide a ship?"

"Because we're not coming back to the Democracy without at least taking a shot at accomplishing our mission," said Pretorius. "If you can't find a place to hide a ship, fine. Now look for a place, probably camouflaged, where if we land on the roof the six of us can find an entrance to the castle."

"And the ship?" asked Pandora.

"It'll be our gift to them."

She frowned. "But—"

"It's a Kabori ship," said Pretorius. "It's probably never been out of the Garsype system. There's nothing in it to identify us, or even our race. Let 'em have the damned thing. We'll steal another. Or, once we've got Michkag, he'll command them to give us another."

She stared at it him a long moment.

"Well?" he said.

"I hate to admit it," she said, "but you're probably right."

"So spend the next few minutes trying to find a door or the equivalent," said Pretorius.

"Let's assume you're right and we can actually gain entrance from the roof," said Apollo. "Only one of us can be seen," he continued, jerking a thumb at Proto, "and only one of us can be understood." He tapped himself on the chest. "So what do the other four do?"

"Hide as best we can, and kill anything that's moving," said Snake.

Pretorius got to his feet. "I'm going to grab some coffee," he said, walking toward the galley.

"Me too," said Irish.

"What the hell," said Apollo, following them. "It beats looking at blank walls."

Snake stayed where she was, as did Proto, who had no interest in coffee and no way to hold or drink it even if he wanted some.

"What's Michkag like?" asked Apollo, as they sat at the table in the galley, sipping their coffee.

"Real son of a bitch," said Pretorius. "Their equivalent of . . ." He tried to come up with the right name.

"Hitler?" suggested Apollo. "Conrad Bland?"

Pretorius shook his head. "No, they were crazy as loons. Michkag's as evil a bastard as tyrants get to be, but he's not crazy, and he doesn't kill just for the fun of it."

"And we're not after Michkag anyway," added Irish. "We're after his clone, who spent his first few years in the Democracy, in the care of the military, learning a bunch of things I'm sure they wish they'd never taught him, and doubtless observing some he was never supposed to see."

"And you didn't kill the original," said Apollo, shaking his head. "That was dumb."

"They thought they could get information out of him and feed it to the clone, who was theoretically on our side," replied Pretorius. "They were wrong on both counts. The original never told them a thing, and the clone *likes* being the top gun in the Coalition."

"Who's smarter, or more dangerous?"

"Take your pick," replied Pretorius.

"Too bad. If you knew—I mean, really *knew*—that the clone was more dangerous, if our mission fails—and it's dozens-to-one that it will—they could probably have the original collude with them to eliminate the clone."

"Not a chance," said Pretorius.

"I agree," said Irish. "They miscalculated once and gave us an even more deadly Michkag. What if they miscalculated again and we wound up with two of them?"

"Even if that didn't happen, do *you* want to be the politician who has to tell the Democracy that the Michkag clone is safely locked away and buried and you'll never have to worry about him again—and, oh yes, we've just been attacked by the original and a few billion of his deadlier forces?"

"Okay," said Apollo. "I was just blue-skying."

"And red-soiling," answered Irish with a smile.

"*Hey!*" yelled Pandora from the bridge. "I got something!"

The three of them hurried back to the bridge, where Pandora had a large holograph covering half the bridge.

"This is the east end of it. Not due east, but just a couple of degrees south of that. And check about two and a half meters above the floor. Do you see it?"

"It's rectangular," said Apollo. "I don't see any handle or hinges, though, and it really blends in well with the wall."

"It's not a door," said Pretorius. "But it'll function as one."

"What do you mean?" asked Snake.

"It's a panel, made of the same material, and the reason there's no handle or hinges is because it slides inward to let people pass through into the castle—and I think it's big enough to let a ship pass through. Not a battleship with hundreds of warriors on it, but surely *this* little one."

"Will it sense the ship as we approach it and open for us?" asked Irish.

"We're probably not going to know until we get there," said Pretorius. "Only way to be sure before we put it to the test is for some other ship to arrive, one that also doesn't want to go through normal channels." He turned to Pandora. "How soon before we're there?"

"About ten minutes," she answered.

Pretorius turned to Apollo. "You're the betting man. What are the odds another ship lands there before we do?"

"No more than twenty-thousand-to-one," was the answer. "Against."

16

"**S**o how are we doing?" asked Pretorius, as the castle began to fill the screen.

"So far the cloak and the codes are working," answered Pandora. "Nobody's asked any questions or issued any orders."

"That'll change," Pretorius assured her.

"Why?" she asked. "Like I said, we've got all the codes and clearances we need."

"Not to land on the roof, we don't."

"Damn!" said Pandora. "It's been going so smoothly I forgot about that."

"You know," said Apollo, "I've been thinking . . ."

"Oh, shit!" said Snake. "Not again!"

He smiled. "I love you too, Reptile."

"Snake," she corrected him.

He shrugged. "Whatever." He turned back to Pretorius. "Like I say, I've been thinking, and I may have a way to buy us a little extra time while we're on the roof and trying to get through what we all hope is an entry panel on the wall up there."

"Let's hear it," said Pretorius.

"I noticed a trio of enclosed pods in the hold here. What if Pandora sets the controls so that the ship crashes a mile away from the castle while we float down, two apiece in the pods, to the roof?"

"You think they won't see us?" demanded Snake.

"Of course they will," answered Apollo. "But remember—this is a Kabori ship. I'm guessing their first duty will be to rescue any survivors, and also to make sure we're not carrying any nukes or other explosives, just in case the wreck is on the verge of blowing up."

"How much time would you think we'd have?" asked Pretorius.

"If it crashes a mile from the wall," answered Apollo, "it's got to take them a minute or two to understand what happened, check to see that it really is a Kabori ship, leave through an exit, and get to the ship. Got to think they can't get to it and start examining it in less than five minutes, maybe more if some ships of this type *are* carrying bombs."

"Well, we know where the damned entrance thing is," said Pretorius. "If we can't open a goddamned door in five minutes, we deserve to wind up in their brig."

"That presupposes that there's no lock on the door," said Irish.

"Even if there is, if we're alone on the roof, or even just that section of the roof, we'll blow it away."

"When we're about to release the pods, shall I radio an SOS?" asked Pandora.

"Good idea," said Pretorius. "Might as well make sure they're looking where we want them to look."

"What do we do once we're inside?" asked Snake. "Besides kill the bad guys, I mean."

"Let's hope no one has the opportunity to kill anyone before we locate Michkag," answered Pretorius. "Once we're in we'll probably be confronted with many routes we can take. We'll choose whatever seems to be the least likely. The trick is to get out of the area fast, because once they see that the ship is empty, and they remember that we came down on pods, they're going to know how we entered the castle, and they'll start their search from there."

"And if we bump into one or more of them?" asked Pandora.

"That's easy enough," said Apollo. "We hide our weapons, Proto morphs into a Kabori, he covers us with a weapon"—he turned to Proto—"and make sure it's the right one, something the Kaboris carry as part of their everyday arsenal."

"He's right," added Pretorius. "If we have to take some Kaboris out we will, but anything like that will alert Michkag, and even if he doesn't know who we are and why we're here, it's a given that he'll double or triple his personal guard if he knows he's got a bunch of armed enemies inside the castle, even if he doesn't know quite what we're all there for."

Pandora frowned. "I don't want to get too far away from Apollo. I assume I'm our escape pilot, but I can get us away a lot faster if he's translating the codes and commands for me."

"I can fly it too," said Apollo.

"Yeah," she said, "but you'll be of more use translating an occasional term I don't know and shooting the bad guys."

"Maybe we shouldn't crash this one," said Snake.

"Might as well," said Pretorius. "If it lands, we don't know where the hell they're going to stash it. Besides, there's nothing unique or special about it. It's not like it's a Democracy ship with Democracy controls and codes and food. We took it from the Kaboris; now we're giving it back."

"In pieces," added Apollo with a smile.

"They're signaling us now," announced Pandora. "They want to know why we're approaching the planet. We'll hit the atmosphere in just another minute or two. I suppose I'll tell them we're experiencing engine trouble and just want to land anywhere on the planet's surface; no sense letting them think we have any interest in the castle."

"*No!*" said Pretorius sharply.

She pulled her hand away from the controls. "What is it?"

"Don't tell them we've got engine trouble or anything remotely similar," he said. "This is a Kabori ship. They'll almost certainly send some ships out to help us and guide us down to where they'll have mechanics and ambulances waiting."

"So what do I say?" asked Pandora.

"You're following orders, you've no intention of going anywhere near the castle, and you have to follow your orders, which include radio silence."

Apollo walked over to where Pandora sat, bent over the controls, and sent the message.

"Thanks," she said. "It would have taken me two or three minutes to translate and send it, and by then they might already have been flying up to help us."

"Or shoot us down," added Snake.

"One or the other," agreed Apollo.

"How long now?" asked Pretorius.

"Maybe six minutes," answered Pandora. "Can't go anywhere near as fast now that we've entered the atmosphere."

"Okay," said Pretorius. "Apollo, I want you and Irish to go down into the hold and see if any of those two-man pods are functional. Might as well see if they work before we climb into them."

"And if we can fit," added Irish.

They went below to find the pods, and Pretorius walked over and looked at the viewscreen. "So where the hell is it?" he asked.

"We're approaching from an angle," answered Pandora. "No sense getting into their sights for any longer than necessary. As it is, they'll be able to see us in another couple of minutes."

"Good thinking."

Apollo and Irish went below and moved three pods next to an emergency exit. Apollo spent a few seconds checking and adjusting the controls, then nodded his head. "They're all functioning properly. I've programmed them to be a slave to the controls in *my* pod; that way whoever's in them doesn't have to learn Kabori in something less than two minutes."

He and Irish went back down to the hold and passed two more pods up.

A few seconds later Pandora announced, "Here it comes, sir!"

Pretorius looked at the screen and saw the castle suddenly come into view.

"Let's not waste any time," he said, turning to Irish, Apollo, Snake, and Proto. "Exit the ship as fast as you can." He turned to Pandora. "Where do you plan to crash it?"

"About a mile north of the castle," she said. "The ground's just a bit more uneven there, so it might take their land vehicles an extra seventy or eighty seconds to reach it."

"Good!" said Pretorius. "Get into a pod with Snake, and let me know how much time I've got before the last pod has to go."

Pandora took one last look at the screen before walking across the ship and joining him. "Count to twenty and then jump," she said.

Irish and Apollo were the first to go, followed by Pandora and Snake.

"Can you latch onto some part of the damned thing?" Pretorius asked Proto, as he climbed into the pod with Proto tucked under an arm, then closed the cover over them, "or do I have to hold onto you?"

"Let me hang onto your leg and I'll be all right," answered Proto.

"Okay, here we go!" shouted Pretorius. He kept his hold on Proto until the pod's engine began purring softly and it leveled out with a slightly downward angle. He made sure Proto could wrap himself around his leg, and then concentrated on guiding them to the spot on the castle's roof that they had pinpointed on the video transmission.

The ship crashed with a deafening explosion, and half a dozen vehicles—most of them ambulances, but one definitely military—raced out to access the situation and rescue any survivors.

Apollo and Irish were close to half a mile ahead of them; they adjusted their course a couple of times as they got closer to their destination and then landed very gently on the roof, about twenty meters from where the moveable panel was just barely visible. Snake and Pandora touched down next, followed by Pretorius and Proto.

"Well?" said Pandora. "What do you think? Can we open it? We've probably only got three or four minutes tops."

Pretorius approached the wall. "No marks to indicate anyone ever tried to blow it away," he said. "Nothing like a keyhole."

"We haven't used keys in five millennia," said Snake.

"Yeah, but we didn't build this door," said Pretorius.

Then, suddenly, as he walked closer to study it more thoroughly, the panel withdrew into the darkened interior of the castle.

"Well, I'll be damned!" said Apollo. "It sensed your presence. Talk about dumb!"

"It wasn't built to defend the castle against intruders," answered Pretorius. "Hell, for all we know, this place is the equivalent of Vatican City a few millennia ago."

"Well, let's get inside it before either the panel slides shut or they get curious about the people who aren't on the damned ship," suggested Apollo.

"Proto," said Pretorius, "become a Kabori. The more weapons and medals, the better. Anyone approaches us, we're your prisoners."

"Right," answered Proto, changing instantly.

"Okay," said Pretorius. "Everybody inside. Hide your weapons. Whisper now, and as soon as it gets minimally lighter, use hand signals. Remember: we're now under the same roof as Michkag and God knows how many of his troops."

"Lucky us," muttered Snake, as they began feeling their way down a winding, dimly lit corridor.

17

The corridor got darker. The air was stale but breathable, and Apollo, burner in hand, led the way. After they'd proceeded perhaps thirty meters, he stopped and fired his burner straight ahead.

"There's nothing there," whispered Irish, looking ahead.

"I know," answered Apollo.

"Then why—?"

"I want to see where we're going," he whispered back. "Clearly this door, probably the whole roof, isn't used very often."

"That'll change the second they find the pods," said Snake.

"That's why I want to get to someplace where we can see what's coming and defend ourselves."

"Less talk and more walking," said Pretorius, and they fell silent and commenced walking again.

They had proceeded another hundred meters, still in total darkness, when Pretorius spoke again. "Irish, walk along the left wall and run your hand over it while you're walking. Pandora, do the same with the right wall. For all I know, we're walking right past a number of rooms."

They walked another twenty meters and then Irish whispered: "Got something!"

"A door?" whispered Pretorius back at her.

"There's no handle."

"Push against it," he suggested.

She did so, and they heard a sudden creaking as the portal

slowly drew back from the wall, revealing a dimly lit chamber possessing a desk and two chairs.

"Get in quick!" Pretorius whispered to the others. "We don't know how soon the door might close."

They all got into the room, and the door slid shut about twenty seconds later.

"Not a damned thing but the chairs and desk," said Snake.

"True," agreed Pretorius. He looked around the room and frowned. "And puzzling."

"In what way?" asked Pandora.

"No dust," he said. "Someone's used, or at least cleaned the room recently. But there's no computer, no alarm system, nothing to imply that the room even *has* a use."

"Well, if they've got a cleaning robot, or the Kabori equivalent of a housemaid, there's probably another door," said Apollo.

"If they do, it's well camouflaged," said Irish.

"Each of you, take a wall and see what you can learn," ordered Pretorius. "Proto, I can't imagine there'll be any trap doors or trip lines, but you're low enough to the ground in your real form to find any, so that's your chore."

"And what do *you* do?" asked Snake.

"I check out the ceiling," said Pretorius.

"But we're on the top floor!" she said.

"You ever hear of an attic?" asked Pretorius. "Or a roof?"

"Okay, okay," muttered Snake, going back to examining her section of the wall.

Pretorius pulled a chair away from the desk, stuck it in a corner that seemed a logical starting point, climbed atop it, and reached his hands up to the ceiling. It felt solid where he was, and he moved the chair a couple of feet to the left and went through the same procedure.

Just about the time everyone was sure that the only entrance or exit from the room was by the route they'd used to reach it, Irish exclaimed, "Pay dirt!"

All eyes turned to her as she tapped the door once with the flat of her hand.

Nothing happened.

"You're wrong," said Pandora.

She smiled. "No, I'm not. The damned door can count!"

She tapped it twice, and it slid up a couple of inches. She leaned against it and it instantly closed.

Then she tapped it three times and it slid halfway open.

"Smart goddamned door!" said Snake, walking through to the next room.

When the rest of the team had walked through, Irish followed them, then turned and tapped the door three times from the other side, and it slid shut.

They found themselves in a dimly lit corridor lined with similar doors.

"There's got to be half a dozen spy-eyes hidden along the length of this," whispered Pretorius. "Even if we can spot them and disable them all, we've told the Kabori right where we are. Let get the hell out of this area and find someplace a little less public to plan our next step."

Apollo led the way, followed by the three women and Proto, with Pretorius bringing up the rear. They came to a cross corridor, Apollo turned to his right, and finally they came to an airlift about six feet on a side.

"What now?" asked Apollo.

"Remember where it is, but we're not taking it yet," answered Pretorius.

"Why not?"

"We know the damned castle can hold about half a million warriors," replied Pretorius. "So until we're a little more certain of what's below us, we'll stay up here and learn what we can before we move."

"Good idea except for one problem," said Irish.

"Only one?" replied Pretorius with a smile. "Okay, what is it?"

"Their defense system had to see the pods landing on the roof. Even though they were from a Kabori ship, they have to be curious as to why we haven't contacted them yet."

"Good point," agreed Pretorius, "and there's one obvious bet we've been missing." He turned to Proto. "Become a Kabori, you know the military uniform, and have a burner in your hand. If anyone sees us, you're taking us to Michkag, but since you've never been here before you don't know quite what part of the castle he's in."

"You think anyone'll buy that?" asked Apollo dubiously.

"Long enough for us to draw our weapons," answered Pretorius.

Apollo frowned. "This level is maybe two miles long and one wide. *Somebody* has to live up here."

Snake began sniffing the air. "I don't know if they sleep up here," she said, "but some of them sure as hell *eat* up here."

The other began inhaling deeply.

"It's not human food, but it's food," said Irish. "I want to say it's coming from straight ahead of us, but hell, it could be coming out of any of these rooms and then wafting down the corridor."

Pretorius turned to Proto. "Okay, back to your original size, even smaller if you can manage it. Then go down the corridor until you come to the source of the odors."

"How far should I go if they're not in the immediate vicinity?" asked Proto.

"For as long as it's a straight line."

"It's pretty dark," said Proto. "We'll lose sight of each other before I've traveled a quarter mile."

"If there's any shooting at either end, the other will see the lights," answered Pretorius. "Now go before they stumble over the pods and come looking for us."

Proto, all near-shapeless eighteen inches of him, began making his way slowly down the corridor.

"What do you think?" whispered Snake. "It can't be this deserted."

"Of course not," answered Pretorius. "Even if they're out on a raid, or in a serious battle, you don't leave your headquarters totally empty. You leave a big enough force behind to take care of business."

"I agree," said Apollo. "I'm just worried about what happens to that little bastard if he finds someone. He can't even hold a weapon."

"He can turn into you, me, or Michkag in a tenth of a second," replied Pretorius. "He doesn't need to hold a weapon. Hell, he *is* a weapon."

Suddenly, as he reached the limit of their visible range, Proto assumed the image of a human again, turned to face them, and waved them over.

"Little bastard found something after all!" said Apollo, striding forward enthusiastically.

The five Men reached Proto in about half a minute.

"What's up?" asked Apollo.

"There's some kind of room to my right, your left," whispered Proto. "I heard voices, and then I heard a door slide shut. Not here—this one's always been closed—but another one within the room."

"You see an outline anywhere on the wall here?" asked Pretorius.

"No," answered Apollo and Snake together.

Pretorius turned back to Proto. "You sure you haven't heard any voices or any noise since the other door closed?"

"None."

"Okay," said Pretorius. "We'll assume that there's a maximum of one Kabori in the room. If he's military he'll be armed, but he'll have no reason to have his burner in his hand or on a table or desk if we enter fast enough."

"We kill him, of course?" said Snake.

"If we have to. If we can overpower him without drawing any attention, I'll want to question him. But one scream and we're given away and probably pinpointed."

"How do you want to break in?" asked Apollo. "I could probably bust a hole through the door just bumping up against it half a dozen times, but that hardly keeps us a secret."

"I know," said Pretorius. "Okay, Pandora and Irish, pull your burners out, and on my count of three, fire at the most likely spot for a lock, one of you on each side. Apollo, on three you and I hurl ourselves against the door."

"What about me?" asked Snake.

"If the door gives too easily," said Pretorius, "Apollo and I are probably both going to land on the floor. If we do, kill the bastard before he can kill us."

Snake smiled. "Suddenly I like your plan a lot better!"

"Somehow I knew you would," said Pretorius. He and Apollo stood as far from the portal as they could. "Ready?" he said softly. "One . . . two . . . *three!*"

Pandora and Irish began firing while Pretorius and Apollo rammed their shoulders into the door, which gave way with a crunching sound. They fell to the floor atop it, at the feet of a Kabori in military garb, who had a screecher in his hand. Before he could aim and fire, Snake fired her burner at his head, and he fell to the floor atop Apollo, his body twitching slightly for a few seconds and then becoming absolutely still in death.

Pretorius got to his feet and shoved the body off of Apollo. "Everyone all right?"

"Yeah," said Apollo, echoed by Snake, Irish, and Pandora.

"Where the hell is Proto?" asked Pretorius.

"I'm here," came the answer, as Proto, now in his human guise again, entered the room. "That was terrifying."

"Not really," said Snake. "We had all the angles covered, unless there were half a dozen of the bastards in there."

"My only defense is the art of illusion," replied Proto. "If I can't fool an enemy, I'm gone. A five-year-old human child can kill me if I can't frighten him into thinking twice about it."

"Okay," agreed Snake. "It was terrifying. Get used to it. There's probably half a million more of these bastards between us and Michkag."

"I know," said Proto glumly.

Pretorius was kneeling beside the body, examining its uniform.

"Well, he's not an officer," he announced. "That makes it less likely that anyone's going to come looking for him. Anyone see anything in here—papers, communicators, anything?"

"No," was the answer.

"There's no bed, so it clearly wasn't his quarters. And there aren't any spy devices, so he's not looking for intruders. I wonder what the hell he was doing up here?"

"There's always the obvious," said Snake.

"Obvious?" asked Irish.

"Waiting for a lady Kabori. Or another male, depending on his preference."

"I think that's reaching," said Pretorius. "But just in case you're right, there's a possibility that his bedmate hasn't shown up yet, so let's get the hell out of here before she or he does."

"Not the way we came?" said Pandora.

"No, let's use the door that everyone uses and see where the hell it takes us."

And with that, Pretorius lightly touched the door on the far side of the room, which receded far enough to allow his party to pass through.

"I'd hide the body, but I don't know where, and I'll be damned if we're going to carry it for the next fifteen or twenty minutes looking for a suitable place to dump it," he said. "Besides, once they find the pods they'll know we're here anyway."

"They may think it's just more Kaboris," said Proto.

Pretorius shook his head. "Not a chance. Visitors to Michkag's headquarters would make their presence known before they got shot."

Proto looked as upset as a six-foot image of a man *could* look, and fell silent.

"Lot of light up ahead," noted Apollo. "More than we'd get from the door of a well-lit room being open."

"So send Proto to see what it is," said Snake.

Pretorius shook his head. "He's in no emotional condition to go there alone. Besides, if there's any talk going on, we've only got one Kabori speaker." He turned to Apollo. "Get as close as you can without being seen, and then just hold still and listen for a few minutes and let us know what they're talking about."

"Piece of cake," said Apollo confidently, walking silently down the corridor toward the light.

"Looks like it's a big room that a bunch of corridors all lead to," said Irish. "Remember, we've been walking *inward* from where we left the pods, even when we changed corridors."

Apollo began approaching the room, while his companions all stood and silently watched him. When he'd gotten to an area just beyond the lights he dropped to one knee and listened, while watching to make sure no one was about to enter the corridor where they were all standing.

He remained there for almost five minutes, then carefully, silently made his way back to his companions.

"Well?" whispered Pretorius.

"Ever hear of a race called the Quall?" asked Apollo.

"No."

"Well, you never will again," said Apollo. "Evidently one of Michkag's elite regiments just wiped out their whole planet, lock, stock, and barrel."

"Doesn't sound much like celebrating," said Snake. "No yelling, no laughing. At least, I assume none. I can't imagine it wouldn't carry down the corridor to us."

"Not that big a world," answered Apollo. "And they lost one of their top officers. No one's sure yet what killed him."

"You mean he might have been shot by a Kabori?" asked Pandora.

Apollo shook his head. "No, but he may have stepped on some planted Kabori explosives or been too damned close to a bomb that was dropped on some of the Quall army."

"Are they going to be there much longer?" asked Pretorius. "I don't want us to spend the whole night out in the open in this damned corridor."

Apollo shrugged. "I don't think so . . . but I couldn't get close enough to take a look and see just how much drinkin' stuff they've got left."

"Okay," said Pretorius. "At least *this* corridor has real doors, not like the one we had to burn and bash our way through. Let's start trying them. If anyone's in a room and not ready to shoot, we'll take him prisoner and find out where the hell Michkag's quarters are."

"You think we can walk right up to him once you know?" said Snake sardonically.

"No, of course not," said Pretorius. "But even *you* would get tired of fighting your way into and out of five or ten thousand wrong rooms."

"True," she admitted. "Okay, let's go beat the info out of someone."

"Let's find someone who doesn't require killing first," said Apollo, starting back down the corridor.

"Wait!" whispered Pretorius.

"You can yell," said Apollo. "We can't hear them from here, so they almost certainly can't hear us."

"I'm not worried about them," said Pretorius. "It's whoever might be behind these doors," he concluded, indicating the closest doors on both sides of the corridor.

"Damn!" said Apollo, frowning. "They've been so quiet I forgot about them." He paused. "Okay, what did you stop me for?"

"I don't want you to go first."

"Why the hell not?" he said. "If we have to break a door or some bones, I'm the biggest."

"And if we walk into a room and someone's got a burner trained on us, you're the one guy we can't spare," said Pretorius. "At least, not until we get another Kabori speaker on our side."

"I hadn't thought of that," admitted Apollo.

"I know," said Pretorius. He turned to Snake. "You go first."

"Right," she said, burner in hand, as she began walking down the corridor.

She tested the first three doors they came to, and each opened onto an empty, and seemingly unused, room.

The fourth door was locked.

"Well?" she said. "Clearly *this* one's not empty. Bust it in or hope he sleeps the rest of the night through?"

"Neither," said Pretorius. "Apollo, come over here."

"Yeah?" said Apollo, walking over. "You want *me* to bust it open?"

"No," said Pretorius. "We don't need another broken door and another dead Kabori."

"Then what . . . ?"

"You speak the language. Use it."

Pretorius knocked on the door with the handle of his screecher. A moment later a voice responded. Apollo replied, they exchanged two more sentences, and then the door slid open and they found themselves facing a Kabori. He was armed, his weapons were in their holsters, and Pretorius and Apollo threw him onto his back and disarmed him before he could make use of them.

The rest of the team entered the room, and Irish touched the control that closed the door.

"He wants to know what we want," said Apollo.

"Tell him we're old friends of Michkag's," answered Pretorius. "We want to see him, we have vital information for him, but since he's at war with the Democracy we felt we couldn't approach the planet and the castle directly."

Apollo passed the message on, listened to the reply, and then turned to Pretorius. "He's not buying it."

"Big surprise," said Pretorius. "Tell him he leaves this room as our guide and ally, or he never leaves this room again."

Apollo spoke, the Kabori spoke, and Apollo turned to Pretorius with the strangest expression on his face.

"Well?" said Pretorius.

"He doesn't want to be a traitor to his leader, and he doesn't want us to kill him, so he's proposed a third course of action."

"What is it?"

"He'll give us a detailed map of the castle," said Apollo, "and while he doesn't know Michkag's exact location, he knows which section he lives in when he's not off fighting wars."

"And he's got the map right here in this room?" asked Pretorius.

Apollo shook his head. "He doesn't have a map . . . *yet*. But any computer in the castle can produce one."

"I hope to hell he doesn't think we're going to send him out of this room all alone to get one made," said Pretorius.

Apollo and the Kabori exchanged words very quickly.

"Okay," said Apollo, looking up. "He knows that won't work. He's willing to tell us where there are three or four nearby rooms with computers. He can't guarantee any of them will be empty at any given moment. It'll be our job to gain entrance, give the computer its orders in Kabori—which I can do, of course, and probably so can Pandora—and then get the printout."

"Will anyone but you and Pandora be able to read it?" asked Pretorius.

"Not a problem," answered Apollo. "Once it's done, I can translate it into Terran."

"Tell him he's got a deal," said Pretorius.

Apollo spoke briefly to the Kabori, the Kabori answered, and then he got to his feet.

"His name's Suttorz, by the way," said Apollo.

"Might as well start now," said Pretorius. "No telling how crowded the corridor will get once the party breaks up."

"My thought exactly," said Apollo. He opened the door and prodded Suttorz with his burner. "Let's get this show on the road."

18

Suttorz led the group down the corridor, then stopped at the third door on the right.

"Okay," said Pretorius. "How do you open it without breaking it down and making a racket?"

Suttorz traced a five-pointed star on it at eye level, and the door slid back noiselessly. He stepped inside the room, pointed to a desk with a computer sitting atop it, then stood aside as Apollo and Pretorius walked passed him.

"Is it working?" asked Snake.

"It's working," said Apollo.

"Okay," said Pretorius. "Tell him he kept his end of the bargain, and we'll keep ours. No harm will come to him, but he's got to go back to his room and stay there until we say otherwise."

Apollo looked dubious. "What do you think will keep him there once we've gone off to find Michkag?"

Pretorius turned to Irish. "You go with him and keep your burner trained on him until we get back. If he tries to leave the room, kill him."

"In cold blood?" she asked, frowning.

"I have no idea what temperature his blood is," said Pretorius. "Just do it."

"I've never killed anyone like that," said Irish.

"There's an alternative, of course," said Pretorius.

"Oh?"

Pretorius nodded. "He kills you."

She nodded her head. "Yes, sir."

"Apollo, sit down and see about finding the map," ordered Pretorius.

Apollo sat at the desk and began issuing orders to the computer.

"What the hell are you saying?" asked Snake, frowning.

Apollo smiled. "It's easier to talk code to it than punch in all the correct keywords. Pandora, is it making sense to you?"

"Pretty much," she replied. "I don't understand a couple of the words, but I'd have no trouble if I was sitting there and using the symbols."

He spoke to the machine for another thirty seconds, and then a six-level holographic map appeared in the middle of the floor. He uttered one more command, and a room on the sixth floor began flashing.

"That's us?" asked Snake.

"Right."

"Where's Michkag?" she asked.

Apollo shrugged. "Who the hell knows?" He uttered a few more commands, and a room near the center of the second level turned a brilliant red. "That's where he sleeps, at least in theory. But we don't know for a fact that he's in the castle or even on the planet—and if he's in the castle, there's half a dozen places he could be eating, and who the hell knows if he's taken a fancy to one of his female warriors and is camped out in her quarters?"

"So much for maps," said Snake.

"It's a starting point," replied Apollo.

"Okay," said Pretorius, "how do we get down to the second level, preferably without being seen?"

"There's a major airlift *here*," said Apollo, uttering a command. An empty shaft started blinking on and off in yellow.

"No good," said Pretorius. "It's right in the middle of the castle, and it's five times the size of the smaller airlift over there against the north wall. Too damned public." He paused, staring at the map. "In fact, airlifts in general are too public. They're silent, which is good, but they don't have doors, so anyone can see you as you ascend or descend past their level. What we could use is an out-of-the-way staircase."

"I'll look, but don't get your hopes up," said Apollo. "Stairways never caught on once we left Sol's system. Too many faster and easier ways to go up and down." He manipulated the map for another few minutes, then looked up. "Nothing inside but airlifts."

"What about outside?" asked Proto.

Apollo grimaced. "There are a couple of ramps that circle the building top to bottom, with an entrance every five hundred meters or so."

"Then why make a face?" asked Snake.

"Because they've got about ten thousand armed guards surrounding the building," said Pretorius. "You can see some of them when you look out of any window in the place. I assume they're mostly for show—I mean, hell, who besides us is crazy enough to go after Michkag in his home quarters?—but that doesn't mean their weapons aren't all loaded and primed."

"Don't they have anything like, I don't know, a laundry chute?" asked Pandora.

"I can't find any," answered Apollo.

"Don't forget," added Pretorius, "this place wasn't built for humans. For all we know, the guys who built it before the Kaboris took over were all naked. We've seen enough shaggy races that were sentient but didn't need clothes for protection against the elements."

"So how do we get down?" asked Pandora.

"I guess we do it the hard way," said Pretorius. He turned to Proto. "You're a Kabori."

Proto instantly appeared as one.

"You've got a burner in each hand."

"Wouldn't one be more what I'd likely hold on you?" asked Proto.

"If you know who and how they salute, fine," answered Pretorius. "Otherwise, this gives you an excuse for not saluting."

"Okay, we're his prisoners," said Snake. "Then what?"

"Then he takes us down to the third level."

"The third, not the second?"

"He's not going to march us right by Michkag's quarters without passing, I don't know, maybe a couple of hundred guards," explained Pretorius. "Someone's bound to talk to him, question him, slap him on the back, do *something* that will give him and us away. We know where Michkag's rooms are, so maybe we can blast into them faster and easier than walk past his bodyguards into them."

"Okay, makes sense," said Apollo.

"And it gives our map-readers a little more time."

"I thought we found what you wanted," said Pandora.

"You found part of it—Michkag's quarters," said Pretorius. "Now I want you to find something else. See if they've got a prison wing in this damned building."

"Why didn't you ask when I was on the computer a minute ago?" asked Apollo.

"I wanted to make sure no one would come looking for us," answered Pretorius. "They might not have pinpointed this room, but they'd have the whole place on alert if they thought anything was wrong."

"Okay," said Apollo, activating the computer. He uttered a number of Kabori commands, then watched the screen. "Levels three through six are all okay," he said. "No way they'd put a prison on the same level as Michkag's quarters, or on the ground level either."

"So that's it?" asked Proto.

"Not quite," said Pretorius. "See if there's a basement."

Apollo gave two more orders, then looked up and smiled. "Bingo!" he said.

"Dumb word," said Snake.

"They tell me it used to be some kind of game," said Apollo.

"For five-year-olds, probably," she said contemptuously.

"Fine. Let me amend that: Success!" Apollo stared at her. "Any better?"

"How big is the jail?" asked Pretorius.

Apollo voiced a few more sharp commands. "Maybe forty cells. I have a feeling each cell holds more than one prisoner, but I can't certify it here."

"You mean each cell *can* hold more, or each cell *does* hold more?"

Apollo shrugged. "You guess is as good as mine."

"Why are we so interested in prison cells?" asked Proto.

"If we need some allies, that's the likeliest place to find 'em," answered Pretorius. He turned to Apollo. "Okay, turn the damned machine off."

Apollo deactivated the computer and go to his feet. "Third level?" he asked.

"Right," said Pretorius. "Get us to the nearest airlift."

Apollo frowned. "Uh . . . I have a suggestion."

"Yes?"

"I know we've made some progress, but we're still closer to the outer wall than the center. It won't make much difference up at this level, as long as we avoid that party up ahead, but that's a long way to walk—all of it out in the open—on the third level, which figures to be a lot more populated."

"And your suggestion?"

"Let's go down to the basement and lead the jailbreak. We can go after Michkag in the confusion."

Pretorius shook his head. "First thing that'll happen is they'll triple the guard around Michkag. And if we're not all dead in ten minutes, they'll fly him off the planet and not return until they *know* we're all dead."

Apollo grimaced. "Okay then, let's start walking."

"Stop," said Pretorius. The others turned to him questioningly. "Apollo's idea is good in principle, just not in particulars. We'll go to the fourth level, make our way closer until we're above Michkag's quarters, and examine our options once we get there."

"The fourth, not the third?" asked Pandora.

"Right," answered Pretorius. "Who the hell knows what they may have treated the ceiling with—anything from alarms to explosives that only fire up, not down." He turned to Proto. "You're still a Kabori, and we're still your prisoners."

"Right," said Proto.

"Okay," said Pretorius to the others. "Hide your weapons, and follow Apollo."

"Why him?" asked Snake.

"If you know where the airlifts are, we'll follow you instead," said Pretorius.

Snake looked embarrassed. "Just asking."

"All right," said Pretorius. "Let's go."

Apollo stepped out into the corridor, followed by the others, with Proto and his image bringing up the rear.

"Coming to a branch," said Apollo. "Bear right."

"That takes us nearer the outside wall and away from the center," noted Pandora, who had read at least some of the map.

"It also avoids that celebration that's not yet winding down," said Apollo.

"Oh, right," she replied.

They walked for another hundred meters, then came to a pair of side-by-side airlifts. Apollo entered the nearer one and immediately began ascending.

"Shit!" he muttered as he vanished from sight.

His companions held still, and a moment later he appeared in the adjoining shaft and stepped out onto the floor.

"Only one goes up, only one goes down," he explained. "I never saw that before."

"Okay," said Pretorius, "everyone into the farther one. Proto, go third, right after Snake. It wouldn't look right for you to let her and Apollo too far ahead of you."

"Right, Nate," said Proto.

They entered the airlift at began descending one at a time, gathering again on the fourth level. Apollo was leading them down the corridor again when a voice rang out: "Halt!"

They stopped, and two armed Kabori approached them from around a turn in the corridor.

"You are under arrest!" said one, and Apollo translated.

Shit! thought Pretorius. *The logical thing is for Proto to say he's already arrested us, but he can't speak the language.*

"Tell them we're emissaries from the Democracy, here to make peace," said Pretorius.

"Looking like this?" said Apollo.

"I'm just buying time, not trying to sign a pan-galactic treaty," said Pretorius.

Apollo shrugged, turned back to the Kaboris, and translated the message. One of them threw back his head and laughed. The other walked over and glared at Pretorius, his face maybe six inches away.

The laugher said something, and Apollo translated again. "He says you're a coward and a liar."

Pretorius answered, "Tell him at least I'm not an ugly coward and liar."

"You sure?" asked Apollo.

"You heard me. Translate it."

Apollo spoke, and an instant later the Kabori knocked Pretorius to the ground with a roundhouse left.

Pretorius rolled over against Snake's leg, then knelt unsteadily.

"Bend over and give me a hand up," he said in pain-filled tones. Snake bent down to help him, and he whispered, "And grab your burner while you're at it."

He reached into his boot with the hand that his body shielded from the Kabori's vision. He and Snake both stood up, firing as they did so, and the result was two dead Kaboris about three seconds later.

"Okay," said Pretorius, "we can't leave them here. Snake, burn 'em each again to cauterize the wounds and make sure they don't bleed. Apollo, choose a door, open it, and let's pull 'em out of the corridor where people will trip over them. Pandora, get your weapon out in case someone's in the room he chooses."

Apollo traced the star they had seen on the sixth-level door, and it worked on this one as well. There was a Kabori asleep on what passed for a bed, and Pandora killed him before he even woke up. Then Apollo and Pretorius dragged the two corpses into the room, walked out into the corridor, and Pandora ordered the door to close behind them.

"Open it again," ordered Pretorius.

She did so, with a questioning look.

"No reason making it too easy to find the bodies," he explained. He stood in the doorway, faced the metal latch that would catch and lock the door, aimed his burner at it, and kept his finger on the trigger for eight, ten, and finally twelve seconds.

"Okay," he said when he was done. "Close it."

Apollo ordered the door to close. "What was that all about?" he asked.

"I melted the metal in the lock," explained Pretorius. "When it hardens around the metal in the door, you won't be able to get into this room without breaking the door down, and they might not do that for another day or two. Why make it too easy for our enemies?"

"A telling point," said Apollo with a grim chuckle.

"Okay, Boss," said Snake, "we've killed three bad guys, Irish is keeping another one safe on the sixth level, we're probably not even halfway to Michkag yet, always assuming he's even here in the castle, and you got to figure we've done the easy part so far. So what's next?"

"I'm working on it," replied Pretorius.

19

"Let's begin by getting to the same spot as Michkag's room two levels down," said Pretorius after a moment's thought.

"Okay," said Apollo, heading off. "Then what?"

"Let's see what it looks like before we plan too far ahead."

They walked down the corridor, weapons hidden, while Proto followed them with his nonexistent weapon in his nonexistent hand.

"They can't just be endless rooms," complained Snake. "After all, this is a castle, goddamnit!"

"You want huge rooms that serve other functions, go down to the first or second levels," answered Apollo. "I don't know who built this castle originally, but whoever it was had a ton of money, which means he had a ton of enemies, which means he had or hired a ton of soldiers and bodyguards, and unless he wanted them punching a timeclock and going home each night he had to provide living space for them." He turned to Snake and smiled. "We're in it."

"Then where *are* they all?" she demanded.

"We just killed three of them," said Apollo. "Wasn't that enough for you?"

"You know what I mean," said Snake irritably. "If the castle is home to half a million warriors, where they hell are they?"

"Probably half are on duty, thirty percent are sleeping, and twenty percent are in lower-level function rooms or getting some fresh air away from the castle," said Pretorius. "Now stop complaining and—"

Suddenly he stopped, and within a couple of seconds the others had followed suit.

"What is it?" asked Pandora.

Pretorius looked up at the ceiling. "Correct me if I'm wrong, but isn't that a vent over here, just next to the top of the wall?"

"Looks like one," said Apollo. "Why?"

"Let me show you one of the reasons I put up with all of Snake's bullshit," said Pretorius. He turned to her. "Snake?"

He cupped his hands at knee level, she placed a foot in them, and he boosted her until she could reach the grate that covered the vent.

"Need any tools?" he asked.

"No, it'll come off with a good yank," she said, and indeed it came away in her hands a few seconds later.

"Okay," said Pretorius, boosting her higher. "You should be able to see through the vents. Keep in touch with your communicator, remember to whisper in case sound travels and gets amplified in that vent, and see what's up ahead."

"You got it," said Snake, as she pulled herself the rest of the way into the vent. "And any time it branches off, I'll follow the branch to the right. It's got to beat looking into three hundred bedrooms in a row."

"Wait!" said Pretorius.

She stuck her head back down. "What is it?"

"Stick this grate back in place," he said. "No sense telling every soldier who walks down this corridor that we've got someone sneaking around up there."

"Right," she said, grabbing it from him and fitting it into place. "Okay, I'm outta here."

And with that she vanished from their sight. They stood still for a moment, and then Apollo turned to Pretorius.

"I'm glad she told us where she's going," he said. "She's as silent as . . . well . . . a snake."

"I don't know if you're aware of it, but she's also one hell of a contortionist," said Pretorius.

"Makes you wonder why the hell she ever joined the military when she could make a handsome living as a thief."

Pretorius chuckled. "She's not military."

"Oh?"

"It's a matter of work for me or serve her full jail sentence."

"Well, I'll be damned!" said Apollo with a laugh. He turned to Pandora. "You serving time here too?"

She shook her head. "No, but I'm not military either. I just have some talents for sale, and Nate and General Cooper decided to buy them." She smiled. "Well, *rent* them, anyway."

"Son of a bitch!" said Apollo, still grinning. "I'm on a team with fellow mercenaries."

"Hey, Snake!" called Pretorius.

"Yeah?" came her voice from above, and perhaps forty feet distant.

"Keep tapping very lightly on the ceiling—well, our ceiling, your floor—every fifteen feet or so unless you're over a room, and we'll follow you. And if you hear any voices, any noise at all, just hold still until it passes."

"Gotcha!" said Snake, tapping twice where she was and then continuing her progress while her four companions followed the tapping from below.

"Speaking of not knowing where we are," said Proto, "I hope one of you can find your way back to the room Irish is in."

"Not a problem," replied Pandora, holding up her communicator. "We'll just home in on her signal. All we need to remember is that she's on the sixth level."

They followed Snake's tapping down the corridor until it came to a three-way branch, and she moved from the left side to the right.

"Why not the middle one?" mused Apollo. "It'll get us to the center of things."

Pretorius shrugged. "Could be a blockage. Could be some other reason."

"You trust her?"

"Yeah."

"Okay," said Apollo, "that's good enough for me."

They followed the tapping down the new corridor for a few minutes, then stopped when it went silent.

"What's going on?" whispered Pandora.

"Beats me," said Apollo.

Pretorius walked down the corridor, looking up every time he came to a vent. Finally he came to a stop.

"You okay?" he asked softly.

"Yeah," said Snake, loosening the screen over the vent. "Here, catch this."

She dropped the screen into Pretorius's hands, then lowered herself through the vent until she was hanging by her fingertips.

"I got you," said Apollo, grabbing her legs.

"I didn't need any help," she said as he lowered her to the floor.

"You're welcome," he replied with a smile.

"What's the problem?" asked Pretorius, then added, "Quietly."

"Hard to breathe," she said.

"Oh?"

She nodded. "Big room not too far up ahead," she said softly. "Got a bunch more vents. I can see the light through them. The real Michkag and the clone Michkag are the only two Kaboris we've had much association with. They're nonsmokers, but evidently a lot of these bastards smoke something that smells a lot worse and a lot stronger than pot or cigars, and there are some small fans right next to their overhead vents that suck the smoke up and then blow it down the way I was coming. Been making me sick for a few minutes."

"Why the hell did you wait?" asked Apollo. "You should have bailed out of the vent the second you smelled it."

She shrugged. "I thought the worst it could do was make me high," she responded. "I never counted on getting weak or sick."

"Put the screen back," Pretorius whispered to Apollo, "while I figure out what we're going to do about this roomful of smokers."

Apollo reached up and adjusted the screen as best he could. When he was finished, they waited a few minutes until Snake said she was ready to proceed, and they began walking cautiously down the corridor.

"Shit!" muttered Snake after a couple of minutes. "There it is again!"

"But the meeting room or whatever it is is still seventy or eighty feet away," said Apollo.

"Don't take *my* word for it," snapped Snake. "Take a deep breath."

They all inhaled deeply.

"I don't know what the hell it is," said Apollo, "but it's sure as hell not cigar smoke, not even from alien cigars. There's too damned much of it; they should be setting off fire alarms by now."

Pretorius had been frowning since the odor first hit them. Finally he turned to Snake. "You healthy enough to do a little work?" he asked.

"I suppose so," she said unenthusiastically.

"You're the best lock-pick on our team," said Pretorius. "Open that room." He indicated a door that was perhaps fifteen feet ahead of them, on the right wall.

She walked over, reached into a small pouch that hung down from her belt, pulled out a pair of odd-looking metal instruments, and twenty seconds later the door slid back.

"Everyone back up!" ordered Pretorius. "Apollo, take a deep breath, walk into the room, and see where the hell that smell is coming from. If anyone's it in, kill them."

Apollo took a breath, made a face when the same odor that was in the vents floated out of the room, quickly walked inside, took a quick look, then exited and, speaking in Kabori, ordered the door to close after him.

"Well?" said Pretorius as Apollo bent over and took three or four deep breaths of the stale but odorless air in the corridor.

"Couldn't see much. Along with everything else, that air is foggy." He finally straightened up and turned to Pretorius. "You knew, didn't you?"

"Knew *what*?" demanded Snake.

"Let's say I had a pretty strong suspicion," answered Pretorius.

"What the hell are you talking about?" asked Snake.

"That's not cigar smoke," said Pretorius. "Nobody can stay in a room that ejects smoke and odors like that."

"So what was it?" persisted Snake.

"I don't know the race, but it's what passes for their atmosphere," answered Pretorius. "That's why I had Apollo check out one of their sleeping rooms."

"Got to figure they're here for a peace conference, or as mercenaries," said Pandora.

"Probably not mercenaries," said Pretorius.

"Why one and not the other?" asked Pandora. "Hell, we don't even know what race they are."

"We'll know their race the minute we get you to a computer," said Pretorius.

"Fine, but you didn't answer my question," she replied. "Why allies or potential allies of the Kaboris rather than mercenaries?"

"Because of that shit they breathe," answered Pretorius. "Sooner or later it's going to get into every corner or every room of the damned castle. If they're here for a peace conference, or even a trading deal, they'll pull out in four or five days tops, the Kabori will fumigate the fourth level and anywhere else where the odor of their air lingers, and that'll be that. Whereas if they're mercenaries, they're here permanently, and Michkag would be crazy not to build them their own quarters with a machine that generates their own air, somewhere other than within the castle. I know Michkag, and he's a lot of things good and bad, but crazy isn't one of them."

"Okay," said Snake. "So what do we do now?"

"Oh, I think maybe one of us," began Pretorius, "maybe one who's so small and so abusive they she'd never be missed, will see if there's a way around whatever room they're all meeting in without getting so sick or drunk that she can't go on."

"I don't know anyone who fits that description," said Snake.

"Well, truth to tell, neither do I," said Pretorius. "So why don't *you* go reconnoiter and see if there's a way to get past their meeting room without getting sick or drunk or whatever."

"And if there isn't?" asked Pandora.

"Then we go back to where we started and try a different route, or we go down to the third level and hope our luck holds out."

Snake left without another word, proceeded cautiously down the absolute center of the corridor as if that would stop her from encountering the alien air. She made it to the meeting room, then knelt in the fog and the shadows and pressed against the wall as a door slid open and two bark-skinned aliens, each larger than her but smaller than Pretorius, walked out into the corridor. Each had a pair of hand weapons tucked into holsters at belt level, and one of them had some strange mechanism, which may or may not have been a weapon, attached to his shoulder.

They spoke softly, laughed loudly and gratingly, and arm-in-arm turned left, away from where Snake was crouching, and proceeded down the corridor.

Snake stuck around for another couple of minutes, until three more aliens left, one alone and two in tandem. All proceeded in the same direction as the first one.

She quickly made her way back to Pretorius and told him what little she'd been able to see.

"No sense going that way," he said when she had finished. "Sounds like they'll be coming and going on no set schedule for hours. It's not worth getting seen by them, and if enough of them are opening doors from time to time, we're either going to get drunk or pass out breathing that shit."

"So what's our next step?" asked Apollo.

"Grab a room with air we can breathe, and work out the step after *that* one," said Pretorius.

20

They tried two empty rooms, hated the residual fumes, and finally came to a room that had not been inhabited—at least recently—by the aliens.

"So what's our next step?" asked Proto.

"The next step is to find out how the fumes affect *you*," replied Pretorius. "We don't have any special breathing gear with us, and I need to know if any of us can be in their company for any length of time."

"I must confess that I found the odors mildly distasteful, but not to the extent that you four seem to have."

"Well, that's something, anyway," said Pandora. "Now if only you could hold a weapon . . ."

"We don't want to start our battle on the fourth level of a castle that's almost as big as some megalopolis on old Earth," answered Apollo.

Pretorius grimaced. "We may have to," he said. "It's going to be pretty hard to hide all five of us while we're looking for an airlift or even a stairwell if one exists."

"Perhaps not," said Apollo.

"Oh?"

Apollo smiled. "Outside of Michkag, how many of these bastards have actually seen a human?"

"Back at the fortress in Orion, maybe a dozen," said Pretorius. "In battle, who the hell knows?"

"And since none of us has ever heard of these foul-smelling aliens, maybe—just maybe—they've never seen a Man either."

"You doing this because you like to talk?" asked Pretorius. "Or have you got some point?"

"What's to stop us from walking straight to an airlift, taking it down to the second level, and marching right up to Michkag?" said Apollo. "If anyone questions us, we say we're here to volunteer to fight for his side."

Pretorius smiled and shook his head. "It'd make a great video adventure, but we'd all be dead or incarcerated before we got halfway to him."

"Why?" asked Apollo.

"Because he is the most powerful tyrant in the goddamned galaxy," answered Pretorius, "and that means he's the best-protected. Remember, this castle can hold a million beings. Even if it's half full, they're still not going to let strangers from a race they've either never seen or else been to war with walk unhindered up to Michkag. If we wear our weapons, they'll mow us down the second they see us. If we don't, they may not shoot immediately, but we'll sure as hell be incarcerated until someone cracks or Michkag himself gets a look at us. Don't forget: he was in our company for a month while we flew to Orion and waited for the opportune time to make the switch."

"What the hell," said Apollo with a shrug. "It was an idea."

"Oh, it's time to do *something*," agreed Pretorius. "I'd just prefer to live through whatever it is."

"Sounds like every other colonel I ever knew," replied Apollo with a chuckle.

"And the first thing we have to do is capture one of these foul-smelling aliens," continued Pretorius.

"He'll breathe on us and we'll pass out," said Pandora. "If just being near him doesn't do the trick."

Snake studied Pretorius's face. "You know a way, don't you?"

Pretorius nodded. "Yeah, I do."

Snake smiled. "That's why he's the king and we're all peasants."

"I wouldn't put it quite that way," said Pretorius.

"Why the hell not?" demanded Snake.

"Because I'm modest to a fault," he answered.

"Okay," said Apollo. "What's your foolproof plan for getting near one of them?"

"Any of you seen any garbage in the corridors?" asked Pretorius.

"No," said Pandora, frowning. "Is garbage part of your plan?"

"Not exactly," he replied. He walked over to the room's sole window and looked out. "Nice view."

"Okay, it's a nice view," said Apollo. "So what?"

"So it wouldn't be a nice view if the window hadn't been cleaned recently," said Pretorius.

"I hope you're not suggesting that we get some janitor to do our dirty work for us," said Snake.

Pretorius chuckled. "You find one, I'll ask him. But in the meantime . . ."

"In the meantime?" she said.

"It should be obvious," said Pretorius. "The corridors are clean. Walls and ceilings are spotless. Windows have been washed."

He waited for one of them to leap to what he thought was the obvious conclusion, and finally Apollo spoke up. "Oh, shit!" he bellowed. "Of course!"

"What do you know that I haven't figured out yet?" demanded Snake.

"The odors are totally confined to the meeting rooms and the bedrooms," said Apollo. "We know that. But we also know everything has been cleaned, and not by one of these foul-smelling aliens, or the corridors, the windows, everything, would smell like they do. So clearly some Kaboris are on this level's maintenance staff. And since they breathe pretty much the same air as we do, and none of them are dead in the corridors or throwing up all over themselves in the rooms, it's only reasonable to assume they've got some protective gear that lets them breathe pretty much the same air that we do."

"Not identical," added Pretorius. "We know that from Orion. But pretty close."

"So the trick . . ." began Apollo.

"Is to find the protection the maintenance staff uses and adapt it to our own needs and structures," concluded Pandora.

"That's my job, I suppose," said Snake.

"No," answered Pretorius. "It's Apollo's."

"Why the hell isn't it me?" she demanded in hurt tones.

"This isn't going to require any crawling or slithering in small spaces," said Pretorius. "Apollo can pick any lock you can pick. And he's got to be two and a half times your size."

"So what?"

"So if he enters the wrong room or closet or corridor and the aliens have been there, the smell won't knock him out as quickly as it will you."

She thought about it for a moment, then nodded her head. "Okay," she said. "It makes sense."

"Okay," said Apollo, "I might as well start now. Anyone from either race tries to stop me, they're dead meat."

He stepped out into the corridor, and the door slid shut behind him.

"And we're deader," commented Pretorius.

"Really?" asked Proto.

"They're not going to find a thing of interest on him, including whatever phony ID he carries, so they'll have to assume he's not alone."

"You're always looking at the bleak side," complained Snake.

"If you don't anticipate it, you can't react properly to it," answered Pretorius.

Pandora walked over to a computer that sat on a small desk in a corner. "While we're waiting, I can contact Irish, give her a progress report, and see how she's doing."

Pretorius shook his head. "I've got to think that if Michkag's got spy devices anywhere, they're in his headquarters. Besides, we haven't made any progress to speak of. That doesn't begin until we're beyond all these foul-smelling bastards."

"What race are they, I wonder?" asked Pandora.

"It lacks a certain dignity, but we might as well call them Stinkers until we know what they call themselves." Snake chuckled. "On second thought, better not. Who knows what their translating devices will make of that?"

They sat silently on the mildly uncomfortable Kabori furniture for fifteen minutes, then ten more.

And then the door burst open and a grinning Apollo entered the door, a large sack slung over his shoulder.

"Don't get too close to me for another couple of minutes," were his words of greeting.

"You found some breathing mechanisms?" asked Pretorius.

Apollo nodded his shaggy head. "I found more than that—or, rather, *it* found *me*."

He set the sack down on the floor. "They're never going to strap onto your heads or fit comfortably, but you can hold them in place with one hand until we're past the worst of the smell." He grinned. "I also found out what they look like, close up. And he found what a Man looks like, close up. Only one of us was going to survive that meeting." He reached into the sack and tossed a small device to Pandora. "Here," he said, "see what you can make of this."

"What's it supposed to be?"

"A t-pack."

She began studying it. "A translating mechanism?"

He nodded. "And I guarantee it works. He growled something, the t-pack translated it into Terran, I cursed at him, and I could tell he understood what I was saying. Don't put it too close to your nose or mouth for more than, oh, I dunno, maybe half a minute. At least, not until some of the smell has dissipated."

Suddenly Pandora set the device down as if it was about to bite her. "Thanks," she said. "I was so fascinated that I forgot about the odor." She blinked her eyes. "I smell it now."

"So how many breathing devices did you bring back, and what do they look like?" asked Pretorius.

"Five, though I'll be damned if I know how the hell Proto can wear one when he's pretending to be a Man or a Kabori."

"Five?" said Pandora. "What about Irish?"

"I assume we're picking her up on the way, assuming we live that long," answered Apollo. "And under those circumstances she'll never need it."

"It's no problem," said Proto. "You're quite right. I can't wear or even hold anything that's more than eighteen inches above the ground, so save it for her, just in case."

Apollo reached into the sack, withdrew four strangely shaped facemasks, and passed them out.

"Where's the oxygen or whatever they're attached to?" asked Pretorius.

"You're gonna have a hard time believing this, but there isn't any," answered Apollo.

"Well, they're no good without an air source," said Pretorius. "You're gonna have to go back and—"

He was interrupted by Apollo's raucous laughter.

"Okay," he said. "What am I missing?"

"The Kaboris have a hell of a scientist working for them," said Apollo. "At least one." He held up the facemask. "You see a little thing, the size of a fingernail, over the left cheek?"

"Yes," said Snake. "What about it?"

"That keeps the odor out."

"But if you're wearing it, and you're blocking the odor, what the hell do you breathe?" continued Snake.

"It lets the air in, and we breathe pretty much the same stuff as the Kaboris do. It just keeps the sick-making aerosols away." He reached into the bag, held up a handful of small tubes, then tossed them back in. "And that's what you spray on yourself, your clothes, your boots, anything the odor might have clung to, once you're back in breathable territory."

"The dead alien," said Pretorius. "What's his race like?"

"A little bigger than Snake. Two arms, two legs, two eyes, two ears, two noses, only one mouth. No hair at all. I suppose it has something to do with that stink; can't spread it to your friends if half of it gets caught in your hair."

"And it spoke?"

"Well, kind of guttural, but yes, it spoke, and yes, it was translated into Terran, which makes that a damned fine t-pack since I don't recall ever seeing or hearing about a race like this."

"Weapons?"

Apollo shrugged. "They're not natives, and they're in Michkag's headquarters. They couldn't have come this far without weapons and space flight and a lot of other things, but the one that attacked me—well, let's say the one that *found* me; we attacked each other—wasn't carrying any weapons: no guns, no blades, nothing, though his harness was built to accommodate them."

"Doesn't tell us much," said Proto.

"It tells us everything we need to know," replied Pretorius.

"It does?" said Snake.

"Yeah," said Pretorius. "Consider what Apollo just told you. The Kaboris need breathing devices around these aliens. There's a sack of them on the floor. And of course the aliens are almost certainly here to sell their military services to Michkag."

Snake frowned. "How do you figure that?"

"Because their odor makes the Kaboris as sick as it makes us, or they wouldn't have the masks. Now, if they were a permanent part of Michkag's empire, they'd be living elsewhere, where his own warriors wouldn't have to worry about getting sick walking through their own headquarters. And they have no fear of the Kaboris, who massively outnumber them in the castle, or they'd be armed at all times."

"I hadn't thought about it," admitted Apollo, "but that makes sense."

"So we don't have to go to war with them," continued Pretorius. "We enlist them or we ignore them—and by *ignore* I mean we avoid them as opposed to fighting with them."

"Hell, if you're right, they should be out of here any day now," said Apollo. "Either he hires them and sends them off to the front, wherever the hell *that* is, or he doesn't hire them and they all go home. Or to Deluros VIII, to sell their services to the Democracy."

"Okay," said Pretorius, "that pretty much sums up the situation. Time to proceed to the next step."

"And what is that?" asked Pandora.

"We either make friends with one of the foul-smelling aliens, or possibly even hire him, and find out exactly where in this enclosed city Michkag is . . . or else we capture one and use whatever means we can to find out where Michkag is and what his plans are."

"*Can* we do it?" asked Proto.

"If Apollo could kill one, don't you think four of us can subdue one?" asked Pretorius.

Which ended the discussion.

"And you," he said, turning to Proto, "any time you appear as a Man, create the illusion that you're wearing one of these masks unless we've reached the point where we no longer need them."

"Yes, Nate," said Proto.

"Okay," said Pretorius, turning to Apollo, "let's you and me go out and find us a Stinker."

21

"I dunno," said Apollo, when they'd proceeded some fifty feet from the room. "If I hold it to my face I'll be fine as far as the odor goes, but I'll only have one hand to fight with."

"Yeah, I know," said Pretorius, removing his belt and wrapping it around that section of the makeshift mask that covered his mouth and nose. "Now the worst that'll happen is that my pants will fall down in the middle of the fight."

"Not to worry," said Apollo. "Once he sees us without our pants, he'll probably faint from envy." He paused. "Did Snake give us any description of these things?"

Pretorius shrugged. "Bipedal. Humanoid. Two eyes, two arms. Not much more."

"Sounds like four-fifths of the Democracy," said Apollo with a chuckle. "What the hell is it about being humanoid and bipedal that makes 'em want to go to war with us?"

"Probably the same thing that made us conquer space in the first place."

"Yeah, I suppose so," said Apollo. "Put two kids together, or two teens, or two of damned near any humanoid, and sooner or later they fight."

Pretorius held up his left hand and stopped walking, and Apollo instantly followed suit. They could hear footsteps approaching, a little louder every few seconds, but they couldn't tell how many feet were making them.

Then, suddenly, a strange-looking alien came around a corner.

It was bipedal, but nowhere near as humanoid as Snake had led them to believe. Its legs were unencumbered by boots, shoes, or pants, and resembled nothing more than a pair of double-jointed tree trunks, complete with bark. Its torso was rectangular, with a pair of arms, also heavily barked, coming out of its shoulders. It had an extra set of hands at the end of each arm.

Its head was oblong, narrowing at the chin, quite broad across the forehead, with ears sticking out a few inches on each side like miniature trumpets. The eyes were large but seemed normal until Pretorius saw that they had haws—inner lids—just like a dog's, to protect them.

"We mean you no harm," said Pretorius, moving toward where the corridor turned so the alien couldn't make a quick retreat. The t-pack garbled his voice beyond recognition.

"Do these damned things still work?" asked Apollo, indicating the t-packs.

The alien growled something unintelligible back at them. "Yes," said the t-pack in Terran, "they work. Who are you and what do you want of me?"

"We mean you no harm," said Pretorius.

"Then stop pointing your weapons at me," said the alien.

"We will shortly," said Pretorius.

"Probably," added Apollo.

"What do you call yourself?" asked Pretorius.

"I am Xhankor," was the answer.

"And your race?"

"I am Xhankor of the Jebarnogusti."

Apollo and Pretorius exchanged looks which seemed to say, *Hell of a name for a race.*

"I am Pretorius, and this is Apollo," he said. "We are of the race of Man."

"Ah!" said Xhankor. "So *you* are the enemy!"

"Why are we the enemy? We have never seen you before this instant."

"Oh, you are not *my* enemy, or the enemy of the Jebarnogusti," replied Xhankor. "*Yet.*"

"We're both pleased and willing to be Michkag's enemy," said Pretorius. "What is the Jebarnogustis relationship to him?"

Xhankor offered its version of smile, which would probably have sent small children screaming in the opposite direction. "Let us say that it is indefinite at this moment."

"I knew it!" said Pretorius. "You're mercenaries, offering to hire out to Michkag and his Coalition."

"That pretty much sums it up," said Xhankor. "That is why I have not resisted you, or tried to kill you. It has not yet been determined whose side we are on. Would Man and his Democracy like to make an offer? I would be happy to take you to my leaders."

"We are merely an advance guard, hoping to peel off some of Michkag's mercenaries and bring them over to our side," said Pretorius. "I am afraid I do not have the authority, or access to the money you will doubtless require, to fight for the Democracy. The best I can do is offer a peace while we're in the Cassiopeia Sector, and guarantee you safe passage to some higher-ups who *can* hire and pay you."

Xhankor was silent for a moment, and his face was so alien that neither Pretorius nor Apollo could tell what he was thinking.

Finally he spoke. "We have come all this way. I suppose we at least have to hear Michkag's offer."

"Is there any way, short of violence, that we can dissuade you?" asked Pretorius.

"Me, perhaps," replied Xhankor. "But I am not our leader, and I have no authority to agree to your terms."

"So we seem to have two options," said Pretorius. "Kill you now, or hope that your leader will agree to our offer."

Xhankor's expression changed again, into almost a smile. "There are more options than that," he answered. "First, I may not be as easy to kill as you seem to think. Second, it is entirely possible that my leader will be impressed by your boldness—just two humans invading Michkag's castle—and decide to accept your offer. But there are other options as well. For example, *we* may offer to hire *you* to fight for us."

Apollo chuckled.

"Your partner is choking," said Xhankor.

"He's laughing," replied Pretorius. "There's not all that much difference. It's painless and harmless."

"Well?" said Xhankor. "I await your decision."

"We'll have to discuss it."

"Go right ahead," said Xhankor. "Turn off your translating devices, and I won't be able to overhear you."

"There are more of us to discuss it."

"Oh?" said Xhankor. "How many more?"

"A few," said Pretorius. "Let us make a temporary peace treaty right now."

"That seems reasonable."

"No Man will attack any Jebarnogusti within the palace until your leader and I meet in person, and no Jebarnogusti will attack or expose the presence of any Man."

"So they don't know you're here!" said Xhankor with another alien smile. "I thought as much!"

"One more thing," said Pretorius. "We're still on the move, but clearly you have permanent quarters here, at least until you make a deal with Michkag or fail to. Where can I find your leader?"

"I hope your translating device can work it out, since we possess different words for all directions and distances," said Xhankor. He proceeded to rattle off a long set of alien words. The t-pack captured it, announced that it would be working on it for the next half-minute, and then, after thirty seconds, offered an incredibly complex list of directions.

"What the hell is that all about?" asked Apollo.

"Three back, five forward, one left, two back, one right, one forward," said Pretorius, reading a transcription on the t-pack's screen. "We'll simplify it later."

"But why do it this way at all?"

"To confuse the hell out of any enemy who picks this up off a computer. We read it far enough, I'll bet it'll have three leaps to the left, and slither forward one body length, enough shit like that to confuse any machine or anyone who gets his hands on it and doesn't know what to chop out."

"Is there a problem?" asked Xhankor.

"No, everything's fine. What's your leader's name?"

"She is Graalzhan."

"She?" said Apollo. "That's a step in the right direction."

"Do you know if or when she is scheduled to meet with Michkag?" asked Pretorius.

"She has already met with him once, or we would not have access to the castle." Suddenly his alien eyes narrowed, and he stared at the two Men. "*You* have not met him. Therefore, he has no idea you are here."

"That's correct," said Pretorius as the tension returned to his body.

"*That*, too, is a step in the right direction," said Xhankor.

"Let us share that little secret with no one," said Pretorius.

"I will tell no one but Graalzhan."

"Fair enough."

"Is there anything else we need say to each other before going our separate ways."

"Yeah, there is," said Pretorius. Xhankor looked at him questioningly. "Are you aware of the effect your physical presence has on Kaboris?"

"Yes," said Xhankor. "That is why we are restricted to this wing of the fourth level of the castle. It is why we do not interact with the Kaboris. And," he added, pointing to Pretorius and Apollo's masks, "why we will stay away from you unless you are prepared—and equipped—to meet in person with us."

"Okay," said Pretorius. "I would shake your hand, but . . ."

"Why?" asked Xhankor. "It does not come off—and I thought we were going to be friends, or at least hoping to be."

"Shaking hands is a sign of friendship among Men," explained Pretorius.

"Ah!" said Xhankor. "Barbaric and cruel among some races, like the Tharr and the Beondothi, but friendship among Men." He offered his equivalent of a smile. "Interesting galaxy, isn't it?"

Then he turned and went back around the corner and down the corridor from which he had come.

"What did you think of him?" asked Pretorius.

"Ugly as hell," answered Apollo, "but he seemed a nice enough guy. You did forget to ask him one important question, though."

"Oh?"

"Yeah," said Apollo. "How many of them are in the building?"

"Too many for us to beat, and not enough to kill Michkag," replied Pretorius.

"What the hell kind of answer is that?"

"The only one that matters. We're going to stay on good terms with them, because we know from Snake and him that they've got at least a couple of dozen armed men—well, armed Things—in the castle, and there's only five of us."

"Six," said Apollo.

Pretorius shook his head. "Proto can scare the hell out of them, but he can't hold a weapon or deliver a punch." He paused. "And since they don't have enough to kill Michkag, they're going to look at us and count up to five—well, six—and decide they don't like the odds. So we'll stay friendly if we can, remote if we have to, but we won't fight them and we won't try to enlist their aid. I just hope they stay up here so that odor doesn't sicken us at a critical moment."

"Okay," said Apollo. "So now what?"

Pretorius shrugged. "Now we go back to the room, get the garbage out of the translation, tell them we have met the semi-enemy and that he is semi-ours."

"And then?"

"Same as usual. We keep honing plans to kill or kidnap Michkag."

"If he's that much of a monster, why kidnap him at all?" asked Apollo. "The Democracy will never put a price on his head."

"No, of course not," said Pretorius. "But," he added with a small smile, "I'll bet they'd love to have a shot at finding out what's *inside* that head."

22

"**W**ell?" said Snake, as the two men entered the room.

"We made contact," said Pretorius.

"Kill anyone?" asked Snake.

"I hate to disappoint you, but no," said Pretorius.

"Did you make contact with the Kaboris or the Stinkers?"

"The Stinkers," answered Pretorius, "and from this day forward, they are known as the Jebarnogusti."

"So are they allies, or Michkag's mercenaries, or what?" asked Pandora.

"That has yet to be determined," replied Pretorius. "They *are* mercenaries, but they haven't finalized anything with Michkag yet."

"Do they view us as rivals, or intruders, or . . . ?" said Pandora.

"That's yet to be determined. They evinced no hostility toward Apollo and me—or, rather, *he* evinced none."

"There was only one?" said Snake.

"Oh, come on now, Snake," said Pretorius. "You know there are a batch of them. We confronted a single warrior in one of the corridors."

"Get to the meat of it," said Apollo with a grin.

"The meat of it is that we're trying to set up a meeting with their leader to see if they'd like to sell their services to the Democracy rather than the Coalition."

"Are there enough of them to make a difference?" asked Proto.

"Everything depends on conditions," answered Pretorius.

Proto frowned. "Conditions?"

"Stand right next to one and tell me you don't understand what effect conditions can have," said Pretorius with an amused smile.

"Let's go back to square one," said Pandora. "They're here to offer their services to Michkag. You want them to sell out to us. Michkag is protected by maybe a million warriors right here in the castle, a few million more on the planet, and more than ten billion in ships and on Coalition worlds. What can we possibly offer them that gets them to join four Men plus Proto to overthrow Michkag on his home territory?"

"Five," said Pretorius.

"Okay, five if Irish is still alive," said Pandora. "That doesn't make much of a dent in the odds."

"We'll explain that we've beaten these odds before, that this is *our* Michkag, and that this time we don't even want to sneak him away safely, we want to kill him."

"Oh, they're gonna love you for that, Nate," said Snake. "*We* created this monster. Help us kill him when he's offering you money to fight *for* him."

"I know I'm not really a member of the Dead Enders . . ." began Apollo.

"The hell you're not!" said Pretorius.

"All right. I think we appeal to their self-interest," said Apollo.

"Their self-interest is staying alive," said Snake.

"It's more than that," replied Apollo. "There may be a couple of hundred of them, if that many, in the castle. If they join him, there'll be certain worlds and certain enemies where their particular physical attributes will carry the day, but when all is said and done they'll be something like 0.0001 of Michkag's forces. That limits their pay, their freedom to choose their assignments, and just about everything else. If and when *we* meet with them, Nate can lay out a scenario where they operate pretty much on their own, where they can choose reasonable, beatable targets rather than something like five billion Kaboris, and whatever Michkag's offering them. I assume we can double or triple it?"

"If there are as few in this castle as we think, we can more than triple it," answered Pretorius.

"It's really a matter of making a difference, and basing your income on that," continued Apollo. "Here they're just a few more foot soldiers to add to a billion or more—with the disadvantage that their greatest weapon—proximity—prevents them from interacting with the Kabori or rising in the ranks. Whereas if they'll help us, it'll be a billion versus a handful, and clearly killing Michkag will make an enormous difference. Once word gets out, they'll have offers from every government, as well as every tin-pot dictator in the galaxy."

"And what if we meet with them and they decide they don't like the odds, or they don't think you can deliver on your offer?" asked Snake. "All they have to do is pull your mask off, or even just rip your shirt off, stay in the room with you for a few hours, and you'll probably be dead. Then they show our bodies to Michkag—and *this* Michkag knows who we are except for Irish and Apollo—and he'll heap riches on them, because of all the goddamned Kaboris on this planet, he is the one who knows for sure what we're capable of."

"It's a chance we'll have to take," said Apollo. He turned to Pretorius. "Unless the boss can think of something better."

"I'm working on it," replied Pretorius. He tossed his t-pack to Pandora. "In the meantime, get this translated, just in case we have to use it."

"What is it?" she asked.

"Directions to the leader of the Jebarnogusti."

She stared at it dubiously. "T-packs are pretty good, but if it's never come into contact with one of them before . . ."

"It worked when we spoke to him," said Pretorius.

"Not a problem," added Apollo. "I've worked on some of the more esoteric ones. They not only examine words and sentence structures, but inflections, pauses, and if you've got that tiny spy-eye activated, even posture."

Pandora shrugged. "Here goes."

She began working the t-pack. Suddenly she stopped and grinned.

"What is it?" asked Apollo.

"You knew what you were talking about," she said. "Our Jebarnogusti friend is giving directions based on how many paces to this turn or that fork . . . and it's trying to determine the average length of his pace to that of a Man's."

Apollo frowned and turned to Pretorius. "What would you say, Nate? About the same?"

Pretorius shook his head. "They have longer legs and shorter torsos." He lowered his head in thought for a moment, then turned to Pandora. "Take six inches off each Jebarnogusti stride and that should come awfully close to being right."

"Okay," said Pandora. "Right and left are the same, I assume?"

"Can't imagine they wouldn't be," said Apollo.

"Okay," said Pandora. She looked up a moment later. "I've instructed the computer to print it out so there'll be no misunderstanding. I'd say you should reach the room or suite in question if you're not stopped."

"We'll be stopped," said Pretorius. "If they're not *that* efficient, they're not worth Michkag's time *or* ours."

"So what's our next step?" asked Snake.

"I'll need a few minutes to consider all the possibilities," said Pretorius. "In the meantime, I imagine Irish must be feeling pretty sleepy and pretty deserted. Apollo, get back up to the sixth level and being her back."

"And her prisoner?"

"If he seems reasonable, bring him along."

"And if not?"

"Kill him," said Pretorius.

"You know," said Apollo thoughtfully, "if I kill him where he is, someone has to notice right away, and it won't be hard to put two and two together. But if I take him down to four and knock him out, proximity to all those Stinkers could put him out of his misery and our hair."

"Okay, makes sense," said Pretorius, "And make an effort to call them Jebarnogusti, not Stinkers. They have t-packs too, you know."

"Got it," said Apollo, walking to the door and exiting.

"I haven't thought of her since we left her behind," said Pandora. "I hope she's okay."

"She's pretty capable," said Pretorius. "I wouldn't worry."

She smiled. "I thought it was your job to worry. So what *are* you worrying about?"

"Same as since we got here," replied Pretorius. "We're planning on assassinating the most powerful tyrant in the known galaxy, while surrounded by a few million of his warriors, in a section of the galaxy where we probably don't have a single friend or ally."

"I hadn't thought of it in those terms," admitted Pandora. "I envy you," replied Pretorius with a bittersweet smile.

23

"I think Apollo or I will check that section of the corridor every hour or two," said Pretorius. "Assuming Xhankor gets his leader's permission for us to talk to him, he has no idea how to contact us—or we him."

"I can go too," said Snake.

Pretorius shook his head. "He hasn't seen you. He'll assume you're with us, but until he *knows* it, he'll never expose his team to possible discovery."

"What if you can't find this Xhankor?" asked Proto.

"We'll keep looking." Pretorius offered him a bemused smile. "If Michkag or we live an extra day or two, it probably won't have that much effect on the history of the galaxy."

"It *could*," said Snake. "He's killed some mighty important people. Who the hell knows who's next on his list?"

"Try not to be so cheerful," said Pretorius, attaching his jury-rigged facemask and walking to the door. It sensed him and pulled away, allowing him to pass through into the corridor. "I'm off to hunt for Xhankor. I'll be back within half an hour."

"I'll come with you," said Snake, donning a mask. "There's nothing to do in this room, and you never know when you might need some help."

Pretorius stared at her for a moment, then nodded his head curtly. "Okay, let's go."

She followed him out into the corridor. He turned right and began walking, and she fell into step beside him.

"This is the direction you were going when you met the Stinker?"

"Yes," said Pretorius. "And if you can't remember to call him Xhankor or the Jebarnogusti, call him the alien. He'll have a t-pack, and I don't want you insulting him before I've had a chance to talk to his leader."

"Okay," she said, then lowered her voice to a stage whisper. "But they *are* stinkers."

Pretorius made no reply, and the two of them walked another hundred meters, stopping every few steps to listen for sounds behind the doors or above and below the corridor.

"You sure you met him in this area?" said Snake. "It's pretty dull and unmemorable."

"You've seen a lot of corridors that aren't, have you?" he shot back.

"This is a castle, not a ship," she replied. "It ought to have paintings or engravings along the walls."

"It's the size of a small city," said Pretorius. "You ever see a city with paintings and sculptures on every wall or building?"

"You're being very unpleasant, you know that?" complained Snake.

"I'm searching for someone who might be the key to our achieving our objective, and you're bitching about the décor."

"Okay, okay," she said. "I was just making conversation."

He froze and held his hand up to signal her to stop.

"What is it?" she whispered, pulling out her burner.

He pointed down the corridor, then noticed her burner. "Don't shoot," he whispered.

"What if it's a Kabori?"

"Then we'll have a prisoner we can question."

He crouched down, and Snake did the same, her entire body hidden behind his larger one.

Suddenly he stood up and waved at a Jebarnogusti who had turned into the corridor some thirty meters ahead of them.

"Xhankor?" said Pretorius.

The Jebarnogusti pulled out its t-pack and spoke into it. The translation came out of Pretorius's device. "No, but I am a member of Xhankor's unit, and he and his leader have sent me here five times already, searching for you. You are Pretorius."

"Yes."

"And you," he added, indicating Snake, "are Apollo."

"She is Snake, another member of my team," answered Pretorius. "May I ask why you have been searching for me?"

"Xhankor is under the impression that you wish to form an alliance with us," said the Jebarnogusti. "Was he mistaken?"

"No, he was not mistaken. May I ask your name?"

"I am Czizmar."

He reached his hand straight forward, with six fingers pointing toward the ceiling. Pretorius assumed he was supposed to respond in kind, did so, and was immediately hugged by Czizmar's free arm.

"Graalzhan—my leader—is waiting," said Czizmar. "Will you follow me, please?" He turned to Snake. "You too, of course."

He turned and headed back the way he had come, with Pretorius and Snake falling into step behind him. They came to two forks in the corridor, bore to the right both times, and finally came to a stop.

Czizmar turned to them. "May I have your weapons?"

"Hell, no!" responded Snake immediately.

"I really cannot let you in unless you are disarmed."

Snake was about to make another retort, but Pretorius laid a hand on her shoulder and nodded his head. "It's okay, Snake," he said.

"But they're here to fight for the son of a bitch we want to kill!" she said.

"That's what we're here to discuss," said Pretorius. "Who they're fighting for and who they're fighting against."

He handed his burner and his screecher to Czizmar, and she reluctantly followed suit.

"And the blade," said Pretorius.

She glared at him, but withdrew a wicked-looking knife from her boot and handed it to Czizmar.

Czizmar uttered a command that sounded remarkably like a carnivore's growl, and the door dilated to let them through.

They found themselves not in a small, relatively featureless room like the one they had just left, but in a large suite, luxurious by the primitive standards of the castle, with at least two other rooms that Pretorius could see. A quintet of armed Jebarnogustis were posted about the room but made no threatening motions.

"Follow me," said Czizmar, leading them to the room on their left, and from there into a far larger room, this one with eight armed warriors and a tall, slender representative of the species sitting on a tall wooden chair.

"Graalzhan, may I present the Man Pretorius that I told you about, accompanied by the Man Snake."

"Greetings," said Graalzhan's voice as it came through Pretorius's t-pack. "Xhankor tells me that we may possibly have a goal in common."

"It is entirely possible," affirmed Pretorius.

"I understand you are here to kill Michkag." There was a brief pause. "Let me assure you that anything you say here will remain here."

"All right," said Pretorius. "Yes, we're here to assassinate Michkag."

"It might be amusing," said Graalzhan. "I wonder if he has ever even seen a Man before."

"He has," Pretorius assured her.

"Still, you might approach him by presenting yourself as an ambassador seeking to negotiate a treaty for certain worlds, now that he has moved from Orion to Cassiopeia."

Pretorius shook his head. "Won't work."

"Oh?" said Graalzhan. "You think he is that perceptive?"

"Perception's got nothing to do with it," answered Pretorius. "He knows all but two of my team's members."

Graalzhan stared at him for a long moment, then spoke: "Now I *am* impressed."

"Then perhaps we can work together," said Pretorius.

"Anything is possible," said Graalzhan. "Tell me of your previous encounter—or is it encounters—with him."

"Let me think for a minute," said Pretorius.

"Suddenly I sense more than a failed assassination attempt in which both sides survived," said Graalzhan.

"You're very perceptive," said Pretorius.

There was another moment of silence.

"Well?" she persisted.

"All right," said Pretorius. "What the hell. It can't change anything, not at this late date."

"This becomes more and more intriguing," remarked Graalzhan, leaning forward on her chair.

"To begin with," said Pretorius, "Michkag—the true original Michkag—sits in a prison deep in the Democracy."

Czizmar uttered an untranslatable shout. Graalzhan turned to him, held up a hand, and ordered him to keep silent and listen.

"If you have Michkag in captivity," said Graalzhan, "then who sits on this castle's throne down on level two?"

Pretorius smiled grimly. "Michkag."

"Hah!" cried Czizmar. "I knew it!"

"There is a flaw here somewhere," said Graalzhan. "I thought you said he was in jail within the Democracy."

"He is," answered Pretorius. "I saw him not too long ago."

"But now you say he is in command of the castle in Cassiopeia," continued Graalzhan. "How can this be?"

Pretorius sighed, and wished he had brought along a smokeless cigarette. "A few years ago a Kabori medic managed to get a skin scraping and a blood-soaked bandage from Michkag after a battle. He was sickened by the wars and the lack of freedom on so many Coalition planets, so he defected to the Democracy and brought the scraping and the bandage with him." He paused. "Do you see where this is leading?"

"You created a Michkag clone!" exclaimed Graalzhan excitedly.

"Yes, and the defector schooled him in everything he would have to know to replace the original Michkag."

"And I assume he did?"

Pretorius nodded. "Maybe a year and a half a ago." He waited until the t-pack converted that into Jebarnogusti measurements.

"And no one knew or suspected?"

"No," said Pretorius. "We assumed at first that it was because we had schooled him so well. He knew the original's favorite foods, expressions, moods, females. He knew how the original would plot a campaign, how he would deploy his forces, everything he had to know to fool those closest to him. And then it happened."

"*What* happened?" asked Graalzhan, listening to the story with a single-minded intensity.

Pretorius grimaced. "He decided that he *liked* being Michkag and running the Coalition and winning wars of conquest. And in truth he's more effective than the original was because he's had the advantage not only of being schooled down to the last detail in being Michkag, but also because his first few years of existence were as the property of the Democracy's military, and he learned a lot of things that the original could never know."

"So you killed the original and replaced him with a clone!" said Graalzhan. "Truly remarkable!"

"Not quite," said Pretorius. "We—that is to say, my team—didn't want to kill the original. If even a trace of his DNA were found, that could expose the whole ruse and cost the clone his life—back when we thought he was on our side."

"So you kidnapped the original and brought him home with you!" said Graalzhan. "That is the most remarkable achievement I have ever heard of!" She leaned forward. "I assume you plan to kill this one."

"He's shown his true colors, so to speak," answered Pretorius. "No sense taking a chance."

"What will the Democracy pay for him?"

Pretorius frowned. "Nothing. My team are all members of the military, under the command of General Wilbur Cooper."

"I have heard of him," replied Graalzhan.

"A lot of people have."

"And you, of course, are totally loyal to him?"

Pretorius nodded his head. "Totally."

"That is a shame. I would love to add your incredible team to my current force, but I can't picture you helping us kill Michkag with the foreknowledge that you will not make a credit for it."

"Don't be so fast to decide," said Pretorius. "Whether we join you or work alone, we're not going to get the reward either way."

"Well, then, it's all settled and your team will work alongside mine as allies." There was a pause, and Graalzhan frowned. "Possibly."

"Possibly?" said Pretorius.

"We each have a vital decision to make, do we not?"

Pretorius stared at her for a long moment. "I guess so."

"What decision?" asked Snake, speaking up for the first time.

"My soldiers and I were invited here to *join* Michkag," answered Graalzhan. "We are not only highly trained warriors, but we also have an added dimension that no other warrior race possesses."

"Your odor, right," said Snake, nodding her head.

"That makes us more valuable than the average battle-hardened mercenaries. I must weigh the rewards of joining Michkag with those of killing him." She paused and flashed her equivalent of a smile. "There is no set fee for assassinating him, of course, but there are major rewards on some twenty-three worlds. I plan to find out what Michkag is offering, and compare it with the risk and rewards for killing him. And you . . ." She let the words hang.

"It's not a choice between joining him and killing him," replied Pretorius. "With us, it's a choice between killing him, if I think we can get away with it, or, since the odds just inside the castle are a million-to-six against us, leaving and awaiting a more favorable opportunity."

"I find that difficult to envision," said Graalzhan.

"We're not suicidal," said Pretorius. "I lost two Dead Enders on our last mission, which was nowhere near as dangerous as this one."

"Shall we think about it for a day, and then speak again?" suggested Graalzhan.

"Sounds good," he said. "As long as you remain here. I made some very light markings on the corridor walls as Czizmar led us here."

"I will not leave this room—well, this suite of rooms—until we have spoken again." She finally stood up. "We each have two very viable alternatives to consider."

"Actually, we have three," said Pretorius, as Graalzhan walked him and Snake to the door through which they had entered.

"Three?" asked Graalzhan, frowning.

"Yes," answered Pretorius. Suddenly he grinned. "I'm wondering if it's worth the effort to kidnap this one instead of kill him."

24

"Guess what?" said Snake, when she and Pretorius returned to the room. "We're gonna put the snatch on this one, just like we did on the original."

"The hell we are," said Pretorius.

"But you said—"

"That was just to impress her with our skills," answered Pretorius. "First, we have nothing to learn from *this* Michkag. And more to the point, they'd know in two seconds that we were stealing him. Remember, to this day none of them knew that we kidnapped the original, because we replaced him with a perfectly trained genetic duplicate."

"Damn!" muttered Snake. "It would have been fun."

"Think about it for a couple of minutes and you'll see what it would have been was deadly." He looked around. "Irish and Apollo aren't back yet?"

"You see 'em anywhere?" responded Pandora.

"Shit!" said Pretorius. "I hope they haven't run into trouble."

He sat down by the computer. After a moment he looked at one of the screens. "Ah, here they come!" he announced.

"Is the Kabori with them?" asked Pandora.

"No, just the two of them," answered Pretorius. "The Kabori's dead."

"What makes you think so?"

"Because Apollo knows enough not to leave a live one behind, one who can alert Michkag and his lieutenants to our presence."

"He'd *better* know enough!" said Snake.

The door opened a few seconds later, and Irish and Apollo entered the room just before it snapped shut.

"Well?" said Pretorius.

"Well, here we are," said Apollo.

"You killed the Kabori, of course?"

"Of course."

"It's a shame," added Irish. "He wasn't a bad sort. Been drafted, just like most foot-soldiers on each side."

"Snake and I ran into more aliens while you were gone," said Pretorius.

"Xhankor's friends and relations?" asked Apollo.

Pretorius nodded. "Yeah," he confirmed. "Met their commanding officer."

"And?"

"Made an informal peace treaty," said Pretorius. "They have no interest in harming us, we have no interest in harming them."

"Well, *that's* solved!" said Apollo with a smile.

"Partially."

"Oh?"

"They don't plan to harm us. They *may* want to hinder us." He paused. "On the other hand, they may want to join forces with us."

Apollo frowned. "Did this meeting last more than thirty seconds?"

Pretorius nodded his head. "They're here to join him or kill him. If they join him, we're the enemy."

"There's a million or more Kaboris and only five of us," said Apollo. "Easy call."

"*Six* of us," muttered Proto.

"Okay, six," said Apollo with an amused smile. "Clearly that makes all the difference."

"They're measuring the odds against the reward," said Pretorius. "Michkag's wanted all over the galaxy, and the price on his head varies with the economy of the planet or group of planets that's offering it. I explained to them that this isn't the original Michkag they're after, that we kidnapped *him* with a team of six. So now they're weighing their options and doping out the odds and comparing them to the payoff."

"You *told* her that?" said Apollo, frowning. "*Why?*"

"It's a longshot, but it was worth telling her that if we can get her on our side. Besides, the knowledge is of absolutely no use to her otherwise. What's her life expectancy if she tells Michkag that she's going to reveal it? Two seconds? Three?"

"If she's got any brains," added Irish, "she'll realize that there's no upside. Why would Michkag pay to shut her up? He'd be better off going in front of his people and saying, 'Yeah, it's true, I'm a clone of Michkag, better in every way because I know everything the original knew plus everything I learned while living among Men in the Democracy.'"

"He was a blank slate when he was born," said Proto.

"So what?" replied Irish. "Who, in his audience of Kaboris, is going to stand up and correct him? Hell, he's probably the only Kabori, including the original, who knows it."

"Lady's got a point," agreed Apollo.

"Well, I meet Graalzhan—their leader—again tomorrow, and then we'll know if we've got an ally, an observer, or another enemy." He turned to Irish. "You had the Kabori for over a day. Learn anything from him?"

She shook her head. "Just that he—and most of them—practically worship Michkag. They don't know why he moved here from Orion, but the mere fact that he did it makes it a great idea." She paused. "I tried to make sure where the prison block is, in case we could set some free and create a distraction, but he either didn't know or wouldn't tell."

"How could he not know?" asked Snake.

"Easily enough," answered Pretorius. "There's a million Kaboris here, and they've been here less than a year, fighting wars of conquest all along. Do you think every one of the million knows where everything is? Well," he added, "everything besides the armory anyway?"

"Okay, okay," said Snake in annoyed tones. "You've got a point."

"You're the brains of the operation," said Apollo to Pretorius. "What do we do if this Graalzhan says yes, and what do we do if she says no?"

"Either way we have to play it by ear," said Pretorius. "She hasn't had an audience with Michkag yet, so that's probably first on her agenda."

"That's really stupid!" said Apollo. "They sicken and kill people just by their proximity. Why let 'em stay in the castle for weeks or even days? If you're half as smart as the original, you make a deal or refuse to make one, and get them the hell out of here before your troops start dropping over."

"I find that encouraging," answered Pretorius. "Clearly this Michkag isn't as bright about some things as the original."

"As a clone, he's got every bit as much potential brainpower," said Pandora. "But clearly he's never been up against a situation like this, with a potential ally whose mere presence presents a mortal danger. Hell, I'll bet the original Michkag wouldn't have been any brighter about it."

"Probably not," admitted Pretorius.

"So do we just sit around until you go off to meet Graalzhan tomorrow?" asked Apollo.

"Most of us do," said Pretorius. He turned to Snake. "But not you."

"Oh?"

"You're the best sneak thief on the team. You've got about twenty hours to steal us some facemasks. The Kabori who are stationed on the fourth level have to be equipped with them. Get us five, plus whatever will fit Proto, and give us enough time to customize them for Men."

"Right now?"

"Now, after dinner, whenever. Just have 'em back a few hours before we need 'em so we can work on them."

"I hope that doesn't precipitate a search of the entire castle for them," said Irish.

"It won't," replied Pretorius. "Snake's not going to swipe any of them from within a couple of hundred feet of the next. Besides, it's not like stealing weapons. If it's reported at all, and I half-suspect that it won't be, they'll figure a Kabori or two got a whiff of one of these Jebarnogustis and wanted to play it extra safe while they're stationed on the same level."

"I might as well get started," said Snake, walking to the door. "There are no windows, at least not in the corridors of any of the rooms I've been in, so there's not that much difference between day and night here."

"I'll bet that right about now you wish you'd have become a ballerina after all," said Apollo with a smile.

"I never wanted to be a ballerina," answered Snake. "I always wanted to be a big-game hunter on untamed alien worlds." Suddenly she smiled. "Then I found out how much more fun it was to rob the residents."

She walked out into the corridor, and the room was sealed again a couple of seconds later.

"Where the hell did you find her?" asked Apollo.

"In the course of duty," said Pretorius with a smile.

"She joined the service willingly?" said Apollo, frowning. "I find that difficult to believe."

Pretorius shook his head. "She's not a member at all. View her as a freelancer." He smiled wryly. "Hell, they're *all* freelancers except for me."

"She's a remarkable lady," said Apollo.

"She also the best contortionist you ever saw," added Pandora. "You wouldn't believe the things she can fit into."

"I'm surprised you pay her enough to keep her," said Apollo.

"We don't. Whenever we need her, I pay her bail and she sticks with us until the task is over. And because she likes a challenge, it's not long before they arrest her again because they'll come to a crime scene where only she could have pulled it off." Pretorius paused and smiled. "I've bailed her out seven times in nine years—and I don't believe she was ever caught in the act. Cops come in, take one look, conclude that only Sally Kowalski—that's her real name—could have pulled it off, and arrest her." Another grin. "They've never guessed wrong yet."

"Fascinating!" said Apollo with a chuckle. "So she's even got a professional name."

"Except for me, they all do," replied Pretorius.

"Iris Fitzhugh at your service," said Irish.

"And I'm Toni Levi," added Pandora.

"But they'll only answer to Snake, Irish, and Pandora," said Pretorius.

"How about Proto?" asked Apollo.

"He'll have to tell you. None of us can pronounce it."

Apollo turned to the alien. "Well?"

"Gzychurlyx," was his answer.

Apollo chuckled. "Count me among the ones who can't pronounce it."

"Shall we have some lunch or dinner while we're waiting?" suggested Irish.

"Might as well," agreed Apollo. "She won't be back for a couple of hours."

"Don't bet on it," said Pandora.

They went to the alcove that was doubling as a small kitchen, opened unnourishing packets of alien vegetables and fruits, and sat down to eat.

"I really resented the ship's food," said Apollo, "until we started feeding ourselves on this dirtball."

They ate in silence, as usual—no one was enjoying the meal enough to lengthen it by conversing—and just as they were returning to the main room Snake entered, loaded down with breathing masks, and handed one out to each member of the party. When she came to Proto, she knelt down and placed a very oddly shaped mask on the floor.

"I don't know if this'll fit," she said, "but if not, I'm sure we can jury-rig something."

"Not a problem," said Proto. "It doesn't affect me quite as much as it affects Men."

Snake walked over to Pretorius. "I saw half a dozen Stinkers coming up the airlift from a lower level," she said. "I *think* Graalzhan was leading them."

"So she's had her preliminary talk with Michkag," said Pretorius. "We'll give her a couple of hours to think about it, then pay her a visit."

"*All* of us?" said Pandora. "What if she's already joined Michkag?"

"If she's told Michkag about us," added Irish, "we *could* be her first assignment."

"Then I guess all of us won't go," said Pretorius. "Just the two she's seen—Snake and me."

"You don't think anything's going to happen—at the meeting, I mean?" said Pandora.

"At my meeting with her?" repeated Pretorius. "Yeah, I think we're either going to make a deal or depart as friends. I really don't think they'll come after us."

"Why the hell not?" asked Apollo.

"Because," said Pretorius with a smile, "they don't know anything about us except what I've told them. They know that six of us kidnapped the original. They know that six of us are in the most heavily guarded building in the galaxy and not a single Kabori knows it."

"Not a single *living* one," Snake corrected him.

"They seem an honorable race," he continued. "Well, for a race of mercenaries—and when you're a mercenary, keeping your word is every bit as important as your ability to fight." He exhaled deeply. "Yeah, I think we'll be okay during the meeting, and if she's joined Michkag, then I think she'll give us a chance to leave the planet in one piece."

"That's a lot of faith to place in one smelly alien," said Apollo.

"If I guess wrong, you get to lead the next mission," said Pretorius with a hint of a smile.

"The Ghost Brigade, right," said Apollo with an amused chuckle.

25

They relaxed for a few hours and finished another meal, and then Pretorius got to his feet.

"Time to find out where we stand," he said. "Snake, you come with me."

"I'll come too," said Apollo.

Pretorius shook his head. "Graalzhan knows her. She's never seen you. I want her to be at her ease—well, as much at ease as possible given the circumstances." He turned to Snake. "You ready?"

"Let's go," she said, commanding the door to open.

They walked into the corridor, then headed off in the direction of Graalzhan's room. They were about halfway there when doors opened on each side of them and armed Jebarnogustis came out into the corridor.

A voice from within the room on the left said, "They're okay. I know them." And a moment later Czizmar stepped out into the corridor.

"You're coming to talk to Graalzhan, right?" he said.

"Right," replied Pretorius.

"Good! She's been waiting for you. Follow me."

He headed off toward Graalzhan's room, and Pretorius and Snake fell into step behind him, followed by the two other Jebarnogustis, who had holstered their weapons.

They walked in silence until they reached their destination. The door opened, Czizmar led them in and nodded to the two guards, who saluted and began making their way back to their quarters.

"I'll let her know you're here," said Czizmar, heading off to an interior room and almost bumping into Graalzhan.

"I already know it," said Graalzhan. "I am pleased to see you again, Pretorius, you and the little one."

"The name's Snake," she replied.

"I meant no offense, Snake," said Graalzhan. "Come into my room and sit, both of you."

She turned and led them, and a moment later the three of them were seated at a table.

"You too, Czizmar," said Graalzhan, and Czizmar joined them.

"Well?" said Pretorius. "Have you considered my proposition?"

"It is a very enticing one," replied Graalzhan. "I have done a little research on you, Nathan Pretorius. You have a record to be proud of." She turned to Snake. "You I could find no record of."

"That's because you looked in military files rather than police," Snake answered with a smile.

"Oh?" said Graalzhan. "Now I *am* impressed."

"So," said Pretorius, "will we be forming an alliance?"

"Let me preface my answer by saying that I consider you friends and allies, and whatever happens, you will remain so."

Pretorius stared at her for a moment. "If I interpret your remark correctly, even if you join Michkag's army you will ignore our presence here and will not hinder us if we try to leave. Is that correct?"

Graalzhan's face contorted into the Jebarnogusti equivalent of a smile.

"Half correct. We will ignore your presence here, whether you wish to join us or not, and we will not hinder you if you try to leave the planet."

"So you're going to hire out to him," said Pretorius. "You're making a mistake."

Graalzhan smiled again. "No, my friend, it is *you* who are making the mistake."

"Explain, please?"

"The reason we are not prepared to leave with you is not that we plan to *join* Michkag, but rather that we plan to kill him."

"I think you're making an even bigger mistake," said Pretorius.

"You risked even greater odds and succeeded," Graalzhan pointed out.

"We had a major advantage," replied Pretorius. "He knows you're on the planet. He had no idea we were there."

"But he also knows we have come to enlist in his cause."

"I think his experience with us will have made him doubly cautious. He *knows* that a heavily guarded Michkag can be kidnapped or killed. It's not just theory anymore."

"There's a huge risk involved, no question about it," admitted Graalzhan. "But there is a huge reward as well." She leaned forward. "Do you know how much the *new* Commonwealth will pay, just to make sure that he never tries to reacquire what is now theirs?"

"Okay, how much?"

"Three hundred billion credits in any currency we demand."

"That's a nice tidy sum," said Pretorius. "My considered opinion is that none of you will live to spend it."

"*You* did," said Graalzhan.

"We did it for our regular pay. But more to the point, we did it first, and by doing it right, we were not hunted down day and night for kidnapping Michkag, because there was a genetically identical

Michkag, who had been schooled to behave and think exactly like the original, sitting in his place less than a minute later."

"I know," said Graalzhan. "The odds against your success were enormous, and the odds of mine dwarf yours." She paused and stared across the table at Pretorius for a long moment. "May I speak to you as a friend? I realize we've only met once before, but what I have to say I cannot say in front of any of my warriors except for Czizmar, who has served with me for twenty revolutions of our planet around our sun."

"We call them years," said Snake.

"Yes, years," responded Graalzhan. "Well, may I?"

"Speak frankly?" repeated Pretorius. "Yes." He turned to Snake. "Go into the next room until I call for you."

She seemed about to protest, then shrugged, got to her feet, and walked out.

"You, too," said Pretorius to Czizmar.

Czizmar looked questioningly at Graalzhan, who signaled her agreement.

"All right," said Pretorius, when they were alone. "What did you want to say?"

"I am a loyal Jebarnogusti—to my world, to my race, to all the things I was raised to be loyal to," said Graalzhan. "And I am not a fool. I know the odds of actually killing Michkag are astronomical, as are the odds of escaping if I *do* manage to kill him." She paused and exhaled deeply. "But my family is not among those favored in our society, and the only way to secure their future is with far more money and more prestige than I can accumulate in my allotted span of years. So if I kill him and it costs me my life, I will consider that an advantageous trade."

"Provided there's a survivor to carry the word back to whoever's offering the reward," said Pretorius.

"Actually, there are six different rewards, totaling the figure I named. And I have determined to do the deed myself so some of my warriors can take the truth with them when they return to our home system."

"Alone?" said Pretorius.

"Yes."

"Let me suggest that Michkag won't need any bodyguards. The average Kabori outweighs you by fifty percent, and it's all muscle—and Michkag is that much bigger and stronger than the average Kabori."

"I know."

"Then why not get some of your warriors to help?" asked Pretorius.

"Because if enough help, the military will demand the reward, and if not enough help and it costs them their lives, they'll have died for no purpose except a selfish effort on my part to acquire the reward."

"There's an alternative," said Pretorius.

"Oh?"

"Ask *my* team to help. That's the reason we're here, and since my superiors haven't mentioned any reward, and in truth couldn't care less about it, it need never be mentioned to them."

"That is an interesting proposition, Pretorius," said Graalzhan, "and under almost any other circumstance I would happily accept it, but I will not be responsible for the deaths of a team that has shown only consideration toward me."

"You're making a big mistake," said Pretorius. "We have not come unprepared for what must be done."

"I am sorry, but—"

Pretorius help up his hand, palm facing the Jebarnogusti.

"Will you agree to wait until tomorrow, so you have more time to at least consider it?"

Graalzhan stared at him for a long moment. Finally she nodded her consent. "I will consider it," she said.

"Good," said Pretorius rising from the table. "Snake!" he called. "Time to go." They walked to the door, and then he turned to Graalzhan. "I'll see you tomorrow. Same time."

Graalzhan nodded her head, and then they were on their way to rejoin the rest of the Dead Enders.

26

There was a gentle knocking at the door. Irish answered it.

"Nate," she said. "It's for you."

Pretorius walked over and found himself confronting Czizmar.

"It's pretty early in the day," he said. "Is there a problem?"

"A major one," said Czizmar.

Pretorius frowned. "She tried to do it herself."

"Yes," confirmed Czizmar.

"Stupid," said Pretorius. "I assume she's dead?"

"Her head is already on display just outside Michkag's private quarters."

"And the rest of you?"

"We're out of here, before they decide we had something to do with it."

"Did you?"

Czizmar shook his head. "We wanted to, but she was our commander. She knew the odds and didn't want us—or you—to take the risk. I must leave now. It will only be a short time before they come for us."

"You shouldn't have come by here," said Pretorius. "We'd have figured it out."

"I bring you a present from Graalzhan," he said, pulling a folded paper out of his military harness and handing it to Pretorius.

"What is this?"

"A rough map plan to the center of the second level of the castle."

"I thank you," said Pretorius. "Stay safe, my friend." He stepped back as the door closed, then turned to his team. "I suppose you all heard that?"

"We're alone again," said Pandora.

"Hell, we were alone at the start of it," said Snake. "Nothing's changed."

"Not quite nothing," said Pretorius. "A potential ally has been killed."

"And we've got a map," added Apollo.

Pretorius opened it up. "Correction: we've got a map that none of us can read."

"Well, let's assume it's accurate and that we just have to translate it," said Irish.

"You know," said Pandora, "it's possible this Kabori computer here can read it."

"You really think so?" asked Apollo.

She shrugged. "It depends how long they've been here, and how much they've spoken to Michkag's people via the computer."

"Run it through and see what it comes up with," said Pretorius.

She inserted one end of the map into the computer and the machine slowly pulled it through.

"No good," said Apollo, picking up the map as the last of it came out of the computer. "Looks just like it did before."

Pandora smiled. "It *is* what we saw before. Give me a minute." She uttered a few commands into her t-pack, waited for it to translate them into Kabori, then sat back. "Give it a minute, maybe ninety seconds, and we'll see what's what."

And eighty seconds later, the computer disgorged a new map.

"Not bad," said Pretorius. "Not all of the words seem to have a Terran equivalent, but at least we won't get lost using it."

He spread it out at the end of the table that held the computer.

"Okay," he said. "Here's the largest meeting room, these are four smaller rooms attached to it. Over here is a huge galley or restaurant—I can't tell which, but it doesn't really matter. Here's the armory. This looks like a sick bay or a small hospital." He studied the map further. "Ah!" he said. "And here, not close to anything, looks to be Michkag's quarters."

"Look at the size of them!" said Apollo. "He sure lives like a king."

"Why is he so far from the other stuff—the meeting rooms, the armory, things like that?" asked Snake.

"Our presence notwithstanding," answered Pretorius, "he's probably the best-protected being in the whole sector. Why not sleep and relax where it's quiet? I guarantee you that suite of rooms is in contact with everything he needs to be in contact with, in and out of the castle, on and off the planet."

"Still, it makes our job a little easier," said Apollo.

"Minimally," said Pretorius.

"Well, what's first?" asked Snake.

"Seriously?" said Pretorius. "First we kill a Kabori, preferably an officer."

"Why?"

"Would you rather go down to the second level as five Men looking for something or, more likely, *someone*, or would you rather go as a Kabori's prisoners?"

"What does one have to do with the other?" she asked.

He pointed at Proto. "There's the most valuable member of

the team at this point. If we can find out how he should appear, he can display his uniform, replete with a few dozen medals, point his imaginary burner at us, and march us straight down to Michkag's quarters."

"He may not have the whole damned army there," said Irish, "but he's got to have a fair number of them protecting his quarters."

"All the more reason why we want an officer of high enough rank that no one will challenge him," replied Pretorius. "Preferably one of Michkag's bodyguards."

"Hell, he can be a five-star general, and they're still not going to let him—and us—into Michkag's quarters alone."

"True," agreed Pretorius. "But if they hold it to maybe a dozen elite guards, and we can each pull a couple or burners or screechers on a second's notice, that's about the best odds we'll face start to finish."

"Okay," said Apollo, "let's go find us a general, or a high-ranking bodyguard."

"Would you know one if you saw one?" asked Pretorius.

"No," admitted Apollo. "Would you?"

"Not yet," said Pretorius. He turned to Pandora. "Give me a few hard copies of a general's insignia."

She nodded, spoke into her t-pack, which spoke into the computer, and a moment later it cast a holograph into the center of the room: six smaller holos of generals in full regalia, and finally detailed close-ups of the insignia that told onlookers that they *were* generals.

"Okay," said Pretorius. "You better give us the equivalent on captain, major, and colonel as well. I mean, how the hell many generals are likely to be roaming the fourth level, especially before they get rid of those odors?"

"More now than tomorrow," said Irish.

They all turned to her.

"*We* know our foul-smelling friends are gone," she continued. "But *they* don't."

Pretorius nodded his head. "You've got a point." He stared at Apollo for a moment, then turned to Snake. "Okay, you're elected."

"I thought *I* was going!" growled Apollo.

"It's my experience that generals don't walk alone," said Pretorius. "That means our assassin is going to have to stay hidden *until* one is alone long enough to kill him without alerting everyone else. Snake probably weighs a hundred pounds, and as I told you, she's a contortionist. I put you at close to three hundred, all muscle, and you contort about as well as an iron rod."

"But—"

"I promise there'll be work to do and Kaboris to kill before we're done," said Pretorius. "But our first job is to get off the starting line." He turned to Snake. "You had enough time to study those drawings?"

She nodded.

"Okay, no sense wasting any more time," said Pretorius, stepping away from the door, "On your way, and good luck."

"No problem," she said, walking to the door. Suddenly she stopped and smiled. "When I find our general, I'll just pretend he's Apollo."

Then she was gone.

"Should have sent me," said Apollo. "She awfully damned small to take on a Kabori."

Pretorius smiled. "You'd be surprised at some of the things she's taken on."

"I asked once before: how the hell did you find her?"

"She was robbing my ship one night when I came back from an assignment. If she didn't have a taste for butterscotch I'd never have caught her, but she loves the stuff, and since it was a Man's ship, she wasted about fifteen extra minutes hunting for some."

"Interesting story," said Apollo. "But killing a Kabori . . ."

"She's killed bigger."

"Oh, well, might as well eat," said Apollo. "Hopefully there won't be too many more meals of this . . . this whatever-it-is."

"There won't be," said Irish.

"Oh?"

"If we kill Michkag in the next day or two, we're out of here," she said, "and if they catch us, they'll probably kill us before the next mealtime."

"I love traveling with optimists!" said Apollo with a laugh.

"Realists," said Pretorius. "We think we'll do it, but we know the odds are against us."

Apollo opened his field kit, pulled out a brilliant red alien fruit, and took a bite of it. "Hell, Michkag himself can't taste any worse than this," he remarked.

"If all goes well, you can take one bite of his corpse before we leave," said Pretorius.

Apollo chuckled, then took another mouthful and made a face.

"Don't say it," said Irish. "Believe me, you won't dine any better on a Dead Ender's pay."

"I find that hard to believe," said Apollo.

"Good," said Irish with an amused smile. "We can use another atheist on the team."

Pandora tried to bring some pleasant, restful music into the room, but all she could get was something that resembled an atonal screeching.

"And they relax to *that*," said Irish.

"Could be worse," said Apollo. "Could be louder."

Suddenly the music, such as it was, stopped, and the door opened.

"What's going on?" asked Proto.

Pandora pointed to a screen above her head. "We're about to welcome a friend," she said.

And no sooner had the words left her mouth than Snake entered, carrying a large, medal-filled Kabori jacket.

"Good job!" said Pretorius. "He cause you any trouble?"

"Not as much as I caused her," answered Snake.

"*Her?*"

Snake chuckled. "You think we're not as deadly as you guys?"

"Oh, I know that you are," answered Pretorius. "But I don't see any sexual differences between male and female Kaboris."

"They're not mammals, so that takes care of one difference," replied Snake.

"How do you know that?" asked Apollo.

"Well, I *did* take her uniform off," said Snake.

"Shit!" muttered Apollo. "I can solve differential equations in my head, and I can create computer systems that make this one look like a retarded infant." He frowned. "So why can I never see the obvious?"

They all laughed at that. Then Snake tossed a very small object to Pandora.

"What's this?" asked Pandora.

"A holo of the late unlamented," answered Snake. "In case Proto decides to become her."

"Okay, Proto," said Pretorius. "Study it until you know it as well as your own face and body—and when you're ready we'll get this show on the road."

"Right," said Proto, moving over to study the uniform.

Pretorius turned to Pandora. "While he's studying that, *you* study the map. I need to know the least-populated way to get where we're going, and the fastest way to get from there to the ship."

"I'm on it," she said, map in hand.

She spent the next half hour conversing in low tones with the computer, asking about possible routes to and from Michkag's quarters, while Proto stood still as a statue, his eyes glued to the uniform.

"Final touch," said Pandora, taking Proto's t-pack out of his kit and hanging it around what she assumed was his neck. "We're going to be in close quarters. It'll be better if no one sees me whispering into my t-pack a couple of seconds before you move your lips."

When Proto, now appearing to be a Kabori officer, announced that he was ready, Pretorius walked to the door.

"Okay," he said. "It's time to go to work."

And with that, he stepped out into the corridor.

27

"**T**his way," said Pandora, pointing to her left as they came to a fork in the corridor. "Then—"

"Stop!" whispered Pretorius.

She turned to him with a questioning expression.

"We're prisoners," he continued. "We don't know one corridor from another. *Proto* is the Kabori. Assume he's told us or is telling us where to go. Just proceed as if you're under his orders to go exactly where you plan to go."

She nodded her head, then continued walking.

They continued for another hundred meters, and then she took a sharp left turn, walked down past three normal doors to an extra-large one, and stopped. It sensed their presence and dilated, revealing an airlift that ran from the top level to below the ground. When they were all inside it, she ordered it to stop at the second level.

When it stopped, Pandora ordered the door to remain shut.

"What's the problem?" asked Pretorius.

"I need to be able to speak," she said.

"Go ahead, and make it fast in case someone's waiting to use the airlift."

"All right," she said. "This is as close as we can get to Michkag's quarters without having to walk through public areas that are probably loaded with his guards. Even from this remote spot, and using what seems to be the least-populated approach, we're still going to be seen. And there are a *lot* of twists and turns along the way."

"Your point?" asked Pretorius.

"There's no way we're not going to be seen by at least *some* of his officers. And if we're seen, and we're not marching in a straight line for the duration of that sighting, *I* can't give directions. Proto will look to be in charge, but he can't speak Kabori."

"Not a problem," said Pretorius. "Proto, you've been wounded. Half your lower jaw has been shattered. You're bandaged there."

Proto instantly created the illusions of bandages covering his mouth and jaw.

"Looks legit," said Apollo approvingly.

"Yeah, but it won't *sound* legit," said Snake. "He doesn't speak Kabori."

"He's got the t-pack Pandora gave him," said Pretorius.

"We still have a problem," said Pandora.

"Oh?" said Pretorius.

"It's *our* t-pack. They'll recognize it."

"I doubt it," answered Pretorius. "This is the home guard, charged with protecting Michkag and the castle. They'll have no reason to have handled or examined alien t-packs." He paused for a moment, considering their situation. "Okay, from this point on, Snake and Apollo can take turns leading. Then Irish and me. Then Pandora directly ahead of Proto, so you can whisper orders. Irish and I will pass them up to Apollo and Snake, and Proto will utter them into the t-pack, which will translate them into Kabori for the benefit of anyone who happens to overhear him. And if his sentence structure is a bit awkward, no one will figure out that there's a t-pack involved; they'll write it off to a busted jaw and words he can't pronounce with it."

"Why don't I just keep the t-pack and give the directions myself?" asked Pandora. "It'll still come out in Kabori."

Pretorius shook his head. "At some point we may come across some enthusiastic guards who want to examine the five Men for hidden weapons before we can confront Michkag. The odds are that they won't feel compelled to examine a fellow Kabori, especially one who just got busted up capturing us. Okay, let's get moving before some guard notices that we're a stationary blip on his spy screen."

They began marching again, Twice they skirted large areas filled with Kabori troops, but no one stopped them.

So far, so good, thought Pretorius, as they headed into another winding corridor. *We can't stay this lucky all the way to Michkag's quarters.*

They began marching without further incident for another two hundred meters, then came to an empty room with its door open. A Kabori soldier was standing in front of a mirror, adjusting his uniform.

Apollo turned to Pretorius, a questioning look on his face. Pretorius ran his hand across his throat in a slicing motion. Apollo nodded, entered the room silently, reached the soldier in two steps, and dropped him with a sledge-like blow to the head. He then knelt down, pulled a knife, and was about to slit the unconscious Kabori's throat.

"*No!*" hissed Pretorius in a whisper.

The rest of the team entered the room, and Pandora ordered the door to shut behind them.

"I thought you wanted him dead," said Apollo, still kneeling next to the Kabori.

"I thought better of it," said Pretorius. "They find him like this, it could be a stroke, a heart attack, any number of things. They find him with his throat slit, and they know they've got enemies prowling around Michkag's level of the castle."

Apollo shrugged. "Makes sense." He found a couple of pieces of cloth nearby, stuffed them into the soldier's mouth, and clasped his hand over his nose. The soldier began jerking spasmodically for perhaps thirty seconds, then lay still. Apollo removed the cloths and dumped them in a trash atomizer. "That buys us all the time you want," he announced, "and stops him waking up at an awkward time."

"Okay," said Pretorius, turning to Pandora. "How close are we getting, and where are the bulk of his troops stationed? The ones on this level of the castle, I mean."

"The guards are all the hell over," answered Pandora. "There are three main halls, or arenas, that look like they could each accommodate thirty thousand Kabori, maybe even a bit more. We'll be near one of them as we approach Michkag's quarters, but we won't actually enter it or walk through it."

"So how far are we from Michkag?" persisted Pretorius.

Pandora shrugged. "Maybe a hundred and fifty meters on a straight line."

"*Is* there a straight line approach to him?"

"Not unless you want to introduce yourself to a few thousand Kabori," she said. "There's a somewhat sweeping semicircle that'll get us damned close. From the map, it looks like we could just walk in, but of course we can't."

"If we follow that route," continued Pretorius, "how close can we get before you figure we're an open target?"

"I haven't seen the disposition of their troops," answered Pandora, "but I'd guess about sixty meters."

"Could be worse," said Pretorius.

"You're kidding!" said Snake.

"Am I smiling?" replied Pretorius.

"We're going to run a gauntlet of hundreds, maybe thousands, of armed Kabori for more than fifty meters?" demanded Snake.

"No, of course not," said Pretorius. Suddenly he smiled. "We're going to *walk* it."

"*What?*"

"Calmly, coolly, with our hands up," he replied. "As Proto's prisoners."

"That might work back where we climbed out of the airlift, but not as we get close to Michkag," said Snake.

"I'm open to suggestions," said Pretorius. "You got a better one?"

Snake muttered an obscenity.

"Anyone else have an alternative?" he continued.

Nobody spoke.

"Then before anyone comes looking for our dead friend here," said Pretorius, gesturing toward the Kabori corpse, "let's study the map so we don't need instructions to get the last fifty or sixty meters, and then it's about time to do what we came here to do."

28

They walked single file, with Proto appearing as the Kabori guard and holding a wicked-looking-but-nonexistent burner at the ready.

"I can't believe it!" whispered Pretorius. "Why the hell isn't someone guarding the place?"

Pandora stood before the door, which sensed her presence and dilated. All six of them walked through it and found themselves not in a room or suite of rooms but a huge circular area, perhaps fifty meters in circumference, filled with artwork, alien flowers, strange-looking furniture that would fit neither Man nor Kabori, and other trophies of conquest.

"Okay," said Pretorius softly. "Which way now?"

Pandora shrugged helplessly. "I don't know. This doesn't agree with the map."

"Figures," said Apollo. "The castle is probably a couple of thousand years old. Michkag's only been here a little more than a year. Any changes he's made wouldn't show up on ninety-nine percent of the maps in existence."

"Well, we can't just stand around waiting for him to come or go from wherever he does come and go," said Pretorius. "Let's find something a little less out in the open while we dope out our next step."

He went to the first door he came to, and it slid back to reveal a storage room about one-tenth filled with food, some frozen, some refrigerated, some stored dry in small bins. "Clearly it's not enough to feed half his men a single meal, so it must be just his favorites, which leads us to two conclusions."

"It does?" asked Snake.

He nodded. "First, he doesn't eat with his men, and second, someone will be by before too long to put together his next meal."

"We can't all of us hide in here when his cook comes by," said Snake. "You want some of us to hunt up another room?"

Pretorius shook his head. "No. We're safe here. Who the hell knows how safe any other room is. And before too long someone's going to come by to pick up the makings for Michkag's next meal. When that happens, we've got some questions to ask him."

"Fine," said Snake. Then: "How often do the Kaboris eat?"

"Beats the hell out of me," answered Pretorius. He smiled. "Have you got something better to do than wait for him to get hungry?"

Snake glared at him and sat down, her back propped up against some boxes.

"I should have brought a deck of cards with me," said Apollo.

"You're in the service now," said Pretorius. "You can't afford to bet on cards anymore."

Apollo chuckled. "Well, I was never much good at it anyway. It's really strange. I can solve the most complicated differential equations in my head, but I absolutely cannot draw to an inside straight."

"Sure you can," said Irish. "You just can't draw the card you need."

"I stand corrected," said Apollo.

"I wonder if this stuff tastes any better than the stuff in our field kits?" mused Snake.

"You can try it if you want," said Pretorius. "But our job is eliminating Michkag. We won't wait for you or come back for you if you get sick from experimenting with alien food."

She made a face. "I love you too."

"Of course you do," said Pandora with a smile. "He's the guy who keeps bailing you out of jail."

They all chuckled, and then Apollo, who was standing by the door, waved them to silence.

"What is it?" whispered Pretorius.

"Someone's coming this way."

"Can you tell how many?"

Apollo shook his head. "No. He or they will be entering or passing by in maybe ten seconds. Be ready."

Six seconds passed, then seven, then eight. The steps didn't slow down, so Pandora had the door iris. Apollo reached out and grabbed a Kabori by his uniform and literally threw him into the room as Pandora ordered the door to snap shut.

Apollo reached down and removed the stunned guard's burner, gesturing him to remain sprawled out on the floor.

"Pandora, get that t-pack working," said Pretorius.

"It is."

"Okay, now translate anything I say and any reply he makes."

"Ready," she confirmed.

"Stay on the floor," said Pretorius. "If you get up, or even try to get to your feet, we will kill you. Do you understand?"

The Kabori nodded his head.

"Let me hear you say it," said Pretorius. "I may not understand your head movements."

"I understand," said the Kabori.

"We have business with Michkag. I know he's on this level, and not far from here. How do we get to his quarters?"

"You are in his quarters," was the reply.

"I mean his private quarters. It is essential that we speak to him."

"You wish to do more than speak to him, or you would have come through normal channels."

"Nevertheless, you are going to tell us what we want to know."

"You can kill me if you want, but I will not betray my leader."

"Don't you mean your general or your commander?" asked Pretorius.

"Semantics," spat the Kabori. "I will not betray him."

"Sure you will," said Apollo, kneeling down next to him.

The Kabori uttered something unintelligible and spat at Apollo.

Apollo grabbed the Kabori's nearer hand and broke each finger, which created a number of snapping noises. The Kabori howled in pain.

"You're still not interested in talking?" he asked.

"No."

Apollo grabbed the Kabori's other hand and repeated the procedure.

"All we want to know is how to reach him."

The Kabori finished screaming and cursed again.

"I'm sure a doctor will be able to fix your fingers if we let you live," said Apollo to the Kabori, as he pulled a knife out of his pocket. "But I'll be damned if I know where he's going to find another eye of the same shape, size, and color."

He leaned forward, holding the eye open with one hand as he brought the knife down to it with the other.

"All right!" cried the Kabori. "I will tell you what you want to know."

"Good," said Apollo. "And should it turn out to be a lie, I'll be back for both of your eyes."

The Kabori uttered some very simple directions. Apollo looked over to Pandora, who checked her t-pack and nodded that it had been translated and captured.

Apollo pulled something like a billy club out of yet another pocket and cracked it against the Kabori's head, instantly knocking him out.

"Would you really have cut his eye out?" asked Irish.

Apollo shrugged. "Beats me. So far the threat as always been enough, at least against races that are visually oriented. I'd probably have to threaten to cut off a nose if I was presented with the alien equivalent of a bloodhound."

Pretorius turned to Pandora. "Well?"

"We should make it in two minutes at the outside." She cast her map on a wall. "This door here seems to be the main entrance, This little one over here, I don't know. Maid's area, maybe. But *this* one," she added, pointing to it, "leads right into the kitchen."

"That's the one we'll use," said Pretorius. "No one's come by for food, so there doesn't figure to be anyone cooking right now. And I guarantee someone as powerful and self-centered as Michkag doesn't do his own cooking. Also, if he's got bodyguards in there with him, they're much more likely to be in the main entry room than anywhere else, and if someone's always on duty, some noncombatant who could nevertheless warn him of our presence, it's more likely to be in the maid's area or whatever the hell else it is than in the kitchen."

"So what now?" asked Apollo.

Pretorius walked to the door. "Now we take care of business and go home."

29

They ordered the door to open, walked through it, and found themselves in a large reception room, with about half a dozen doors leading off it.

"Stop right there!" said a harsh voice, and they turned to see a heavy-set Kabori officer staring at them. He pulled his weapon and began approaching.

"Go away!" said Proto, mouthing the words into his t-pack. "Can't you see they're my captives?"

The officer did a double-take. "I . . . I didn't see you, sir," he stammered.

"Well, you see me now! Go away!"

"Yes, sir! I'm sorry, sir!" Then, "Are you all right, sir?"

"Of course I'm all right."

"You sound . . . *different*," said the officer.

"I said to go away!" growled Proto. "I'm still waiting, or do you intend to disobey my order?"

"No, sir," said the Kabori, saluting and walking out through the nearest door.

"Proto, you'd better stay out in this area," said Pretorius. "They won't obey anyone else."

"Should we three split up?" asked Apollo, indicating himself, Snake, and Pretorius.

"Will you know Michkag if you see him?" asked Pretorius.

"They all look pretty much alike to me," answered Apollo, "but I assume he'll have the most hardware on his uniform—medals, weapons, everything."

Pretorius frowned. "Okay, but never be more than a room or two away from me, just in case you run into the second- or third-best decorated warrior in this castle." He turned to Snake. "If you find him first, take no chances."

"Don't you have any questions to ask him?" she said.

"Not over your dead body. If you can find him and get the drop on him, fine, march him out here. If not, kill him where he stands."

"You're the boss," she said with a shrug.

Pretorius smiled. "It took you seven missions to admit it."

"Shall we start?" asked Apollo.

"Yes, with a caveat," said Pretorius. "There's got to be more than six or seven rooms here, given the size of the one we're in. Don't get more than two rooms from where you can retreat or call for help. And if you see something that just seems to cry out that it's Michkag's room and he's not in it, contact us if you can, and get the hell back here if you can't."

"Right," said Apollo. "I'll start at the left."

"I'll take the center," said Snake. "That's where *I'd* stay if I was the boss."

"The commander," said Pretorius.

"Same thing," she said, and headed off toward the central door.

Pretorius watched them until they'd passed through the doorways, and then headed off to his right. The door sensed his presence and irised, and a moment later he found himself in a wide corridor with doors on each side of it, set at twelve-meter intervals. The first five were open, displaying empty rooms—not dormitories but rooms with tables, rooms with computers, and one room was a small armory, holding perhaps fifty weapons.

He checked the weapons, found they were in good repair, and

concluded that they were there just in case an invading enemy reached the chamber where he had left Proto and the two women. He walked a little farther and came to a closed door. He drew his burner, then approached the door. Unlike the others, this one didn't slide back, which meant either that it was locked, or that it was only programmed to allow Kaboris to pass through, and probably only Kaboris it recognized.

He reached out, touching the door lightly, hoping to find some small or hidden latch. There was none, but suddenly the door began to glow, which could mean anything from a "Keep Out" message to an intruder warning.

A few seconds later it opened, and he found himself facing a Kabori who took one look at him, growled something he couldn't understand, and launched himself at him. Pretorius fired his burner at point-blank range, an expression of absolute surprise crossed the Kabori's face, and a second later he had fallen to the floor, twitching slightly.

Pretorius entered the room, pulled the Kabori out of the way, and looked around to determine what was so special about it that it had been kept shut and locked. It was when he saw the untidy sleeping mat in a corner that he had to conclude the door was closed solely because its occupant had been sleeping.

He spent another minute rummaging through the room, hoping to find something, *anything*, of value, came up negative, and left the room. The door did not close automatically behind him, so he tried a few words and gestures to get it to move. When nothing happened, he took another minute to hide the Kabori under his bedding.

He then stepped out into the hall again, walked by the room in both directions, decided that there was nothing to attract the curious other than the open door, about which he could do nothing, and continued on his way.

He proceeded to the end of the corridor, turned back, came to a fork, went off in a new direction, and spent the next half hour following forks and finding nothing of use.

Finally he decided to go back to the point where they had started to see if any of the others had experienced anything more useful, and found Snake waiting for him.

"Apollo?" he asked softly.

She shrugged. "Not a word."

"Let's hope he's found something."

"Well, if he hasn't, *I* have," said Snake.

"Oh?"

She nodded her head and smiled. "If it's not his private quarters, then it belongs to the most decorated Kabori in history. If you had to choose knowing only that, which would you pick?"

"Got a lot of medals and decorations around it?"

"Let me put it this way," said Snake. "If they weren't using some alien hardwood for the door frame, it would have collapsed a long time ago. Or if it *is* Michkag's, a couple of months ago."

"Okay," said Pretorius. "You wait here for Apollo."

"Where are *you* going?" she demanded.

"To get Proto, Irish, and Pandora," he answered. "I hope you're right, but even if you're not, they've been standing out there long enough. See you in a couple of minutes."

Pretorius made his way back, opened the door, silently caught Irish's attention, and waved them over. Once they began walking, he pressed a forefinger to his lips, and they remained silent.

He led them to where Snake awaited them. A moment later, Apollo came back down his corridor and rejoined them.

"You've found him!" he said, when he saw that Pretorius had reassembled the team.

"Perhaps," was his answer. "Snake found something interesting enough for us all to check it out, and we couldn't leave half the team exposed for much longer."

Apollo looked dubious. "That's not half the team. That's two-fifths of it plus a Kabori officer."

"Only until he starts to speak and says a wrong thing," answered Pretorius. "It's better—and safer—this way."

"So what did Snake find?" asked Apollo.

"That's what we're going to find out." Pretorius turned to Snake. "Lead the way, and signal me when we're getting close."

"Right," said Snake, heading back the way she had come. A glowing ceiling illuminated the corridor.

They had proceeded for about thirty meters when Pretorius noticed a camera lens embedded in a wall. He froze, staring at it.

"Not to worry," said Snake, as the rest of the team also saw it.

"I assume you have a reason?"

She withdrew a small device out of as pocket. "From my less-interesting but better-paying job," she said, pointing it at the camera lens. A blindingly brilliant beam of light came out and hit the lens. "It didn't do anything this time, of course," she explained, "but the first time blinded it permanently."

"It also means we're on the right track," said Apollo. "I never saw a camera the direction I went."

"Ditto," confirmed Pretorius. "Okay, Snake, let's keep going."

She led them in a straight line for another twenty meters, then turned sharply left, then right, and suddenly they came to a door of hand-carved, sculpted bronze, with various medallions lining each side of it.

Pretorius positioned himself directly in front of it to see if it would respond to his presence by opening. It didn't. He then touched it lightly, prepared to pull his weapon if it sounded an alarm, hoping it would vanish into the wall. It did neither.

He turned to Snake. "How the hell did you open it before?"

"I didn't," she replied. She knelt down and examined the door minutely, pressing here and there, but nothing happened.

"Well, it's not visual and it's not tactile," she said softly. "The only thing left is music."

"And words," said Pretorius.

She turned to him. "Okay, there's got to be fifty million songs, and probably ten times that many words. Where do you want to start?"

"By using our brains," answered Pretorius. He turned to the team. "Think of a word, a term, *something* that'll have special meaning to Michkag."

"I think I've got it," said Pandora. "If he's got one friend, one ally that he can trust who's not part of his empire, one intruder he doesn't want killed, who is it?"

"The original Michkag?" asked Snake.

"Hell, no," said Pandora. "He's masquerading as the original, has taken over his empire. He'd want the original dead before he could talk to anyone."

"Oh, shit!" said Pretorius. "Of course!"

"You know?" said Snake.

"So do you," answered Pretorius. "Would it help if I told you that Proto also knows, but Irish and Apollo don't?"

"You gonna play games or you gonna tell me who it is?" demanded Snake irritably.

"I'll tell you, of course," said Pretorius, "and I'll bet the damned door opens when I do."

"Okay, I'm waiting."

"Who's the one friend we know Michkag has in the Democracy?" said Pretorius. "Who's the Kabori who brought us the DNA we needed to clone him, and who spent years training him to impersonate the original Michkag?"

"I feel like an idiot," said Snake. "I know who you mean, and I can't remember his name."

"Try Djibmet," said Pretorius—and as he uttered the word, the door receded into the wall.

The room that was revealed was circular, roughly fifteen meters in diameter—and four Kabori who had been sitting on chairs jumped to their feet and went for their weapons.

They were too late. Apollo and Irish already had theirs in hand, and Snake had hers out and firing a fraction of a second later. It was decided more by the element of surprise than superior marksmanship, but in another second all four Kabori lay dead on the floor.

"What now?" said Irish wearily. "More killing?"

"They *were* the enemy," said Pretorius.

"I know, and the rest of you have been doing this for years. But this is only my second assignment as a Dead Ender, and all this blood takes getting used to."

"Just be glad it's *their* blood," said Snake.

"It won't be long," said Pretorius. "There are three doors plus the one we came in through. If we're lucky, Michkag'll come bursting through one of them any minute now." He gestured Apollo to one door, Snake to the other, and he positioned himself by the one in the middle. "Proto, you're Michkag now."

Proto promptly changed his image to become Michkag's duplicate.

"And if it's not Michkag coming through one of the doors?" asked Pandora.

"Then having Proto standing in our midst will give us a momentary advantage," said Pretorius. "Either way there's no sense hiding your weapons."

They stood, tense, silent, and motionless for almost a minute, and then Michkag burst out of the central door, a huge laser pistol in his hand.

"Hi, Michkag," said Pretorius, turning his burner on Michkag's hand until the Kabori screamed and dropped his pistol to the floor. "Remember us?"

"You're as good as dead, all of you!" snarled Michkag.

"No," said Pretorius, stepping aside so Michkag could see the four dead guards. *"They're* as good as dead."

"You don't think you can get out of the best protected castle in the galaxy, do you?" demanded Michkag.

"Why not?" said Apollo with a smile. "We got *in*, didn't we?"

"You should have stayed where we put you," said Pretorius. "A ready-made empire, and all you had to do was play ball with us."

"Ball?" repeated Michkag, frowning. "What is ball?"

"A colloquial expression," answered Pretorius. "You think about it, while I think about what to do with you."

"There are only six of you," said Michkag, "and this one"—he indicated Proto—"may look like me for the moment, but he is actually the size of a pillow. You are surrounded by more than a million Kaboris. Surrender now, and I promise your deaths will be quick and relatively painless."

"I've always wanted a quick, painless death," said Apollo. "But not for another half century or so. Or do you think you can deliver it personally?"

For an answer Michkag lunged at Apollo, who fell back against a wall. Even as Michkag was reaching for his throat, he delivered a powerful blow to what passed for the Kabori's solar plexus and followed it up with a karate kick to Michkag's knee. Michkag howled in agony, and suddenly he had a curved blade in his hand. He tried to slash Apollo's neck open with it, but Apollo was turning, and he practically cut the man's arm off instead.

"That's cheating!" snapped Snake.

Michkag turned to her, a look of total loathing crossed his face, and he began advancing on her, blade still in hand.

"Of course," said Snake, drawing her screecher, "if you can cheat, so can I."

She pressed the firing mechanism with a forefinger, and the room was filled with a low humming sound from the sonic weapon—everywhere but between Michkag's ears, where the sound began scrambling his brain, and finally turned it to something resembling glass and shattered it.

"You okay, he-man?" she asked of Apollo.

"Nothing that a transfusion and fifteen or twenty stitches won't solve," he said through clenched jaws.

"Can you hang on until we treat it?" asked Pretorius.

"I think so."

"Good."

"Why don't we do *something* for him now?" asked Irish,

ripping off a sleeve of Michkag's uniform and tightly binding Apollo's arm.

"First, because I suspect we weren't as quiet as we think, and second, if Czizmar's diagram is right, we're not that far from Michkag's ship, which surely has an infirmary or the equivalent." He paused and looked around. "First things first. There's no trash atomizer here, at least none than I can see, so we're going to have to hide the body. Irish, you're bigger than Snake and Pandora. Give me a hand. Let's drag him back to where he came from."

Irish walked over, they each grabbed a foot, and they began pulling the corpse into the next room.

"More like a study than a bedroom," noted Irish.

"Still, it's got a closet; that's all we need."

They stuffed the body awkwardly into the closet. Then, before they closed the door, something caught Pretorius's eye, and he reached in and pulled it out into the open.

"Just what I wanted," he said. "Get Proto in here."

Irish left the room and came back a few seconds later with Proto.

"Take a look," said Pretorius, indicating the full-dress uniform, replete with dozens of medals, that he had pulled out of the closet.

"Impressive," acknowledged Proto.

"You're going to be Michkag from here to the ship. Can you duplicate it?"

"Give me a minute to study it," he said, and Pretorius and Irish moved back out of his way. After some forty seconds had passed he said, "All right, I think I've got it," and turned to face them.

"Perfect!" exclaimed Pretorius, staring at the false Michkag in the false uniform.

They went back into the main room.

"He looks like the real thing!" said Apollo, clutching his arm.

"Good," said Pretorius. "Because if anyone questions it, and we don't make it to Michkag's ship unseen, he'll explain that we're from a rebel colony populated by human stock, we were offering to sell him our vast supply of fissionable materials, you got a little obstreperous, he had to discipline you, and since he wants those materials, he's taking us back to our planet so he can negotiate— which clearly means make his demands—in person."

"Will they buy it?" asked Pandora. "That he'd go without bodyguards?"

"If we just keep moving, they might question him, but I don't think anyone'll have the guts to stop or disobey him."

"I don't know . . ."

"You've seen the way his empire runs," replied Pretorius, "both in Orion and here in Cassiopeia. If you were an underling, and he was walking in full dress uniform with some prisoners and a duplicate of that laser weapon in his hand, would *you* challenge him?"

"Point taken," she said.

"I think I'll display a minor wound or two," suggested Proto. "If we do run into any Kaboris, it will show them that nothing hinders me when I make up my mind."

"All right, give it a try," said Pretorius, and Proto instantly displayed a couple of minor flesh wounds on his torso. "Pandora, you're the one who studied the map. Lead us to wherever the hell he stashes his getaway ship. Apollo, you and Proto bring up the rear. I'll be just ahead of you if you have to lean on me at some point. Now let's get lined up properly."

Snake walked to the door Pandora indicated and then looked back at Pretorius.

"Now?" she asked.

"Now," he said.

30

They made it to a large area leading to Michkag's private hangar in less than five minutes and were confronted by a group of Kabori soldiers when they arrived.

"Stand aside," said Proto into the hidden t-pack.

They did so, and then one of them cried, "You're hurt, Michkag!"

"A scratch," muttered Proto. "You want *hurt*, try *him*." Proto pointed at Apollo.

"Let *us* take him off your hands," said another. "We know how to handle Men." His voice dripped with contempt at the mention of Men.

"I promised I would return him to his world," said Proto into his hidden t-pack. "If they do not give me what I demanded for him, I will kill him there."

"We will accompany you!"

Proto stared coldly at them. "Have I asked you?" he said at last.

"But you are wounded, and traveling with five Men!"

"No mere Man can hurt me," said Proto. "I can kill them all right here if I choose to, but I promised the enemy their safe return."

"What do we get for returning them?" asked a soldier.

Proto smiled. "More than any Man, any hundred Men, can possibly be worth." He gestured with his nonexistent weapon, and they all began moving again. "Fear not for me," he said into the t-pack as the two groups parted, "but for those who sought to harm me." He turned to Pandora and Snake. "Move, you two, before I lose my temper, which is growing shorter by the moment."

The Kaboris stepped aside and Pandora led them down a narrow passageway to the actual hanger, which had no roof above it.

"Nothing but sky," said Snake, looking up.

"Do you think they bought it?" Irish asked Pretorius.

"They're not following us," he replied.

Word seemed to have gotten out that Michkag was taking his prisoners to some other world, and doing it alone. Though there were a handful of soldiers in the hangar, not one spoke to Proto or approached him, though all saluted.

"How are you holding up?" Pretorius asked Apollo.

"I'm good for another five minutes, maybe ten."

"You're too damned big to carry," said Snake. "If you pass out before we reach and board the ship, I suppose we'll just drag you by your feet."

"Just as well I can't feel the love coming from you guys," muttered Apollo. "It'd just be a distraction."

"Maybe we should let him rest a few minutes," said Irish.

"He needs treatment more than rest," replied Pretorius, "and he can't get that until we're on the ship. And there's another consideration, just as serious and just as pressing."

"Oh?"

"How long do you think it'll be before someone finds Michkag's body?"

"The man's right," muttered Apollo. "Let's go."

They approached the ship, and suddenly an armed Kabori stepped out from behind it.

"Stop where you are!" he growled, burner in hand.

They stopped.

"Where do you think you're going?"

"That is none of your business," said the t-pack as Proto mouthed the words.

"I apologize, sir!" said the guard. "I didn't see you. May I ask what these aliens—these *Men*—are doing up here?"

"I am taking them to a meeting I have with their leader."

"In the *Democracy?*" demanded the guard.

"It's none of your business, but no, to a neutral world. I am trading them for weaponry that will make us even stronger"— Proto pointed at Apollo, who was clearly in pain—"and the deal will fall apart if he dies before I can return him."

"I'll summon help, sir!" said the guard.

"I haven't time," said Proto.

"Your voice seems somehow strange, sir," said the guard. "Meaning no offense."

"Catch three or four blows to the throat while you're battling as burly an enemy as this one here," said Proto, indicating Apollo, "and *your* voice won't sound right for a day or two. Now help us or leave us."

The guard quickly moved over and helped Pretorius half-drag and half-carry Apollo to the ship and load him into it.

Proto chose not to risk any more doubts about his voice and simply saluted the guard, who returned the salute and then left the ship.

"So far so good," said Snake.

A booming voice came over the intercom and the speaker system.

"Attention! Attention!" was the t-pack's translation.

"Shit!" muttered Pretorius, sitting in the pilot's seat. "They found him. Pandora, sit next to me and translate."

He started the motor and pulled out onto the huge open section of the roof. They were airborne seconds later.

"Michkag has been killed!" said the voice. "Michkag is dead! No ship lands, no ship leaves."

Suddenly the sky turned dark with dozens of pursuing ships.

"This had better be the fastest ship in the fleet!" muttered Apollo.

"Don't worry about that," said Snake. "It's Michkag's ship. We can outrun them." She frowned, "What we can't outrun is a shot from a laser cannon."

"We're not even going to try," said Pretorius. He had the ship going at near light speeds while it was still in the atmosphere, soon shot through the stratosphere, and before any member of the Kabori fleet could adjust to his speed and fire a fatal shot, he plunged the ship into the nearest wormhole he could find.

"This one's never been charted," said Pandora, reading her computer. "I've no idea where it'll let us out."

"I don't know about you," muttered Apollo from where he sat on the deck while Snake and Irish were tending to his wound, "but anyplace sounds better than Garsype right about now."

Pretorius turned to reply and saw that Apollo had passed out.

"Good!" said Snake. "I was gonna give him my last bottle of Cygian cognac to ease the pain." She smiled. "Now I'll give him a sip when he's recovered."

"Anyone following us?" asked Proto.

"In a wormhole, who knows?" said Pretorius. "The main thing is to get out of it within reach of something—a planet, another wormhole, even a ship, but *something.*"

They emerged in the midst of an ancient solar system with a dying sun some eighty-three minutes later.

"What now?" asked Irish.

"Now we figure out where the hell we are," answered Pretorius, "and then we head for home."

31

I t took them eleven days to make it back to the Democracy. Apollo's wound was as bad as it looked, but he was in excellent shape and possessed remarkable recuperative powers. Within a week he was walking gingerly around the ship, a feat Pretorius would have wagered was impossible when they first got him onto the ship and saw the severity of the wound.

"I'm sorry it's taking so long to get where we're going," said Pandora at one point, when Apollo winced in pain from a tiny vibration of the ship.

"If we'd gone a direct route Michkag's forces would have caught us within a day," answered Apollo. "This is not the best-armed vessel I've ever been aboard. Just get us there in one piece while *I'm* still in one piece."

"That was one hell of a wormhole," remarked Pretorius. "In something like an hour and a half it stuck us way the hell out in the galaxy, beyond any political or military entity we have on record. And just about every enemy the Democracy has now or has ever had was between us and home. At least we found some charted wormholes on the way back, or we could all have died of old age long before we got halfway home." He smiled. "I'm told that for a long time Man thought the key to exploring the galaxy was to reach the speed of light. We didn't seem to realize that if you cross the galaxy at the speed of light, the journey will take a bit more than one hundred thousand years."

"Hell, I could be healed in half that time," said Apollo, and they all laughed with him.

They did make it to port in eleven days. Pretorius dismissed Snake, Pandora, and Proto, as he did after every assignment, and had Irish return to her unit. He waited until the base hospital patched Apollo's wound and pronounced him on the mend, then took him to the most heavily guarded wing of the prison and introduced him to the original Michkag.

"You'll be pleased to know that you're unique again," said Pretorius to their most important prisoner.

"There is only one Michkag," replied the Kabori.

"Well, now there is," said Apollo. "I think the other one was better-looking, though."

Michkag growled a Kaborian obscenity, turned his back, and refused to say another word.

Finally Pretorius began leading Apollo back the way they had come.

"Where to now?" asked Apollo.

"I thought you ought to meet the boss."

"*Your* boss, not mine," said Apollo.

"True enough," agreed Pretorius. "I thought you ought to meet him anyway."

A few minutes later they were admitted to Wilbur Cooper's office.

"Nice job, Nate," said the general. "I told you that a few days ago, but it bears repeating. You and your Dead Enders are something very special." He stared at Apollo. "And who have we here?"

"This is Apollo," said Pretorius. "I told you about him."

"Ah, yes! Your government thanks you for your help, Mr. . . . ?"

"Just Apollo," replied Apollo.

"And are you now one of Nate's Dead Enders?" asked Cooper.

"I'm willing to negotiate it."

"There's nothing to negotiate," said Cooper. "The pay is not inconsiderable, but we only pay you when we use you."

"There's more to negotiate than money," replied Apollo.

"Oh?"

"If the Democracy will grant me amnesty for all prior crimes, I'll be happy to join Nate's team."

"Not a problem," replied Cooper. "But I checked your record when Nate first mentioned you, and you have made a healthy living as a smuggler and a black market dealer, among other less admirable occupations. You will never make remotely that much as a Dead Ender."

"Yeah, that sounds right," agreed Apollo.

"Then may I ask why you are willing to make this commitment? With no offense intended, you do not exactly strike me as a patriot."

"I'm not."

"Then why?" persisted Cooper.

Apollo smiled. "Anyone can be a smuggler, just as anyone can be a patriot. But how many men can dethrone the Coalition's most important leader and help save the notorious Dead Enders in the process? If I decide I can't live on my pay, to hell with smuggling. I'll write my memoirs and get *really* rich."

"General," said Pretorius, "I think we just added another member to my team."

"He certainly seems to fit," answered Cooper. "God help us all."

"Wrong."

Cooper frowned. "Wrong?" he repeated.

Pretorius waved his right hand, encompassing half the galaxy. "God help *them* all."

APPENDIX 1

THE ORIGIN OF THE BIRTHRIGHT UNIVERSE

It happened in the 1970s. Carol and I were watching a truly awful movie at a local theater, and about halfway through it I muttered, "Why am I wasting my time here when I could be doing something really interesting, like, say, writing the entire history of the human race from now until its extinction?" And she whispered back, "So why don't you?" We got up immediately, walked out of the theater, and that night I outlined a novel called *Birthright: The Book of Man*, which would tell the story of the human race from its attainment of faster-than-light flight until its death eighteen thousand years from now.

It was a long book to write. I divided the future into five political eras—Republic, Democracy, Oligarchy, Monarchy, and Anarchy—and wrote twenty-six connected stories ("demonstrations," *Analog* called them, and rightly so), displaying every facet of the human race, both admirable and not so admirable. Since each is set a few centuries from the last, there are no continuing characters in the book (unless you consider Man, with a capital M, the main character, in which case you could make an argument—or at least, *I* could—that it's really a character study).

I sold it to Signet, along with another novel titled *The Soul Eater*. My editor there, Sheila Gilbert, loved the "Birthright Universe" and asked me if I would be willing to make a few changes to *The Soul Eater* so that it was set in that future. I agreed, and the changes actually took less than a day. She made the same request— in advance, this time—for the four-book Tales of the Galactic Midway series, the four-book Tales of the Velvet Comet series, and *Walpurgis III*. Looking back, I see that only two of the thirteen novels I wrote for Signet were *not* set there.

When I moved to Tor Books, my editor there, Beth Meacham, had a fondness for the Birthright Universe, and most of my books for her—not all, but most—were set in it: *Santiago, Ivory, The Dark Lady, Paradise, Purgatory, Inferno, A Miracle of Rare Design, A Hunger in the Soul, The Outpost*, and *The Return of Santiago*.

When Ace agreed to buy *Soothsayer, Oracle*, and *Prophet* from me, my editor, Ginjer Buchanan, assumed that of course they'd be set in the Birthright Universe—and of course they were, because as I learned a little more about my eighteen-thousand-year, two-million-world future, I felt a lot more comfortable writing about it.

In fact, I started setting short stories in the Birthright Universe. Two of my Hugo winners—"Seven Views of Olduvai Gorge" and "The 43 Antarean Dynasties"—are set there, and so are perhaps fifteen others.

When Bantam agreed to take the Widowmaker trilogy from me, it was a foregone conclusion that Janna Silverstein, who purchased the books (but moved to another company before they came out) would want them to take place in the Birthright Universe. She did indeed request it, and I did indeed agree.

A decade later I sold another Widowmaker book to Meisha Merlin, set—where else?—in the Birthright Universe.

And when it came time to suggest an initial series of books to Lou Anders for the brand-new Pyr line of science fiction, I don't think I ever considered any ideas or stories that *weren't* set in the Birthright Universe. He bought the five Starship books, and, after some fantasies and Weird Western excursions, he—and his successor, the wonderful Rene Sears—commissioned the Dead Enders series to be set there as well.

I've gotten so much of my career from the Birthright Universe that I wish I could remember the name of that turkey we walked out of all those years ago so I could write the producers and thank them.

APPENDIX 2
THE LAYOUT OF THE BIRTHRIGHT UNIVERSE

The most heavily populated (by both stars and inhabitants) section of the Birthright Universe is always referred to by its political identity, which evolves from Republic to Democracy to Oligarchy to Monarchy. It encompasses millions of inhabited and habitable worlds. Earth is too small and too far out of the mainstream of galactic commerce to remain Man's capital world, and within a couple of thousand years the capital has been moved lock, stock, and barrel halfway across the galaxy to Deluros VIII, a huge world with about ten times Earth's surface area, and near-identical atmosphere and gravity. By the middle of the Democracy, perhaps four thousand years from now, the entire planet is covered by one huge sprawling city. By the time of the Oligarchy, even Deluros VIII isn't big enough for our billions of empire-running bureaucrats, and Deluros VI, another large world, is broken up into forty-eight planetoids, each housing a major department of the government (with four planetoids given over entirely to the military).

Earth itself is way out in the boonies, on the Spiral Arm. I don't believe I've set more than parts of a couple of novels on the Arm.

At the outer edge of the galaxy is the Rim, where worlds are spread out and underpopulated. There's so little of value or military interest on the Rim that one ship, such as the *Theodore Roosevelt* of the Starship series, can patrol a couple of hundred worlds by itself. In later eras, the Rim will be dominated by feuding warlords, but it's so far away from the center of things that the governments, for the most part, just ignore it.

Then there are the Inner and Outer Frontiers. The Outer Frontier is that vast but sparsely populated area between the outer edge of the Republic/Democracy/Oligarchy/Monarchy and the Rim. The Inner Frontier is that somewhat smaller (but still huge) area between the inner reaches of the Republic/etc. and the black hole at the core of the galaxy.

It's on the Inner Frontier that I've chosen to set more than half of my novels. Years ago, the brilliant R. A. Lafferty wrote, "Will there be a mythology of the future, they used to ask, after all has become science? Will high deeds be told in epic, or only in computer code?" I decided that I'd like to spend at least a part of my career trying to create those myths of the future, and it seems to me that myths, with their bigger-than-life characters and colorful settings, work best on frontiers where there aren't too many people around to chronicle them accurately, or too many authority figures around to prevent them from playing out to their inevitable conclusions. So I arbitrarily decided that the Inner Frontier was where *my* myths would take place, and I populated it with people bearing names like Catastrophe Baker, the Widowmaker, the Cyborg de Milo, the ageless Forever Kid, and the like. It not only allows me to tell my heroic (and sometimes antiheroic) myths, but lets me tell more realistic stories occurring at the very same time a few thousand light-years away in the Republic or Democracy or whatever happens to exist at that moment.

Over the years I've fleshed out the galaxy. There are the star clusters—the Albion Cluster, the Quinellus Cluster, a few others There are the individual worlds, some important enough to appear as the title of a book, such as Walpurgis III, some reappearing throughout the time periods and stories, such as Deluros VIII, Antares III, Binder X, Keepsake, Spica II, some others, and hundreds (maybe thousands by now) of worlds (and races, now that I think about it) mentioned once and never again.

Then there are, if not the bad guys, at least what I think of as the Disloyal Opposition. Some, like the Sett Empire, get into one war with humanity and that's the end of it. Some, like the Canphor Twins (Canphor VI and Canphor VII) have been a thorn in Man's side for the better part of ten millennia. Some, like Lodin XI, vary almost daily in their loyalties, depending on the political situation.

I've been building this universe, politically and geographically, for a third of a century now, and with each passing book and story it feels a little more real to me. Give me another thirty years, and I'll probably believe every word I've written about it.

CHRONOLOGY OF THE UNIVERSE CREATED IN BIRTHRIGHT: THE BOOK OF MAN

YEAR	ERA	STORY OR NOVEL
1885 A.D.		"The Hunter" (IVORY)
1898 A.D.		"Himself" (IVORY)
1982 A.D.		SIDESHOW
1983 A.D.		THE THREE-LEGGED HOOTCH DANCER
1985 A.D.		THE WILD ALIEN TAMER
1987 A.D.		THE BEST ROOTIN' TOOTIN' SHOOTIN' GUNSLINGER IN THE WHOLE DAMNED GALAXY
2057 A.D.		"The Politician" (IVORY)
2403 A.D.		"Shaka II"
2908 A.D.		1 G.E.
16 G.E.	Republic	"The Curator" (IVORY)
103 G.E.	Republic	"The Homecoming"
264 G.E.	Republic	"The Pioneers" (BIRTHRIGHT)
332 G.E.	Republic	"The Cartographers" (BIRTHRIGHT)
346 G.E.	Republic	WALPURGIS III

367 G.E.	Republic	EROS ASCENDING
396 G.E.	Republic	"The Miners" (BIRTHRIGHT)
401 G.E.	Republic	EROS AT ZENITH
442 G.E.	Republic	EROS DESCENDING
465 G.E.	Republic	EROS AT NADIR
522 G.E.	Republic	"All the Things You Are"
588 G.E.	Republic	"The Psychologists" (BIRTHRIGHT)
616 G.E.	Republic	A MIRACLE OF RARE DESIGN
882 G.E.	Republic	"The Potentate" (IVORY)
962 G.E.	Republic	"The Merchants" (BIRTHRIGHT)
1150 G.E.	Republic	"Cobbling Together a Solution"
1151 G.E.	Republic	"Nowhere in Particular"
1152 G.E.	Republic	"The God Biz"
1394 G.E.	Republic	"Keepsakes"
1701 G.E.	Republic	"The Artist" (IVORY)
1813 G.E.	Republic	"Dawn" (PARADISE)
1826 G.E.	Republic	PURGATORY
1859 G.E.	Republic	"Noon" (PARADISE)
1888 G.E.	Republic	"Midafternoon" (PARADISE)
1902 G.E.	Republic	"Dusk" (PARADISE)
1921 G.E.	Republic	INFERNO
1966 G.E.	Republic	STARSHIP: MUTINY
1967 G.E.	Republic	STARSHIP: PIRATE
1968 G.E.	Republic	STARSHIP: MERCENARY
1969 G.E.	Republic	STARSHIP: REBEL
1970 G.E.	Republic	STARSHIP: FLAGSHIP
2122 G.E.	Democracy	"The 43 Antarean Dynasties"
2154 G.E.	Democracy	"The Diplomats" (BIRTHRIGHT)

2239 G.E.	Democracy	"Monuments of Flesh and Stone"
2275 G.E.	Democracy	"The Olympians" (BIRTHRIGHT)
2469 G.E.	Democracy	"The Barristers" (BIRTHRIGHT)
2885 G.E.	Democracy	"Robots Don't Cry"
2911 G.E.	Democracy	"The Medics" (BIRTHRIGHT)
3004 G.E.	Democracy	"The Politicians" (BIRTHRIGHT)
3042 G.E.	Democracy	"The Gambler" (IVORY)
3286 G.E.	Democracy	SANTIAGO
3322 G.E.	Democracy	A HUNGER IN THE SOUL
3324 G.E.	Democracy	THE SOUL EATER
3324 G.E.	Democracy	"Nicobar Lane: The Soul Eater's Story"
3407 G.E.	Democracy	THE RETURN OF SANTIAGO
3427 G.E.	Democracy	SOOTHSAYER
3441 G.E.	Democracy	ORACLE
3447 G.E.	Democracy	PROPHET
3502 G.E.	Democracy	"Guardian Angel"
3504 G.E.	Democracy	"A Locked-Planet Mystery"
3504 G.E.	Democracy	"Honorable Enemies"
3505 G.E.	Democracy	"If the Frame Fits . . ."
3719 G.E.	Democracy	"Hunting the Snark"
4026 G.E.	Democracy	THE FORTRESS IN ORION
4027 G.E.	Democracy	THE PRISON IN ANTARES
4028 G.E.	Democracy	THE CASTLE IN CASSIOPEIA
4375 G.E.	Democracy	"The Graverobber" (IVORY)
4822 G.E.	Oligarchy	"The Administrators" (BIRTHRIGHT)
4839 G.E.	Oligarchy	THE DARK LADY
5101 G.E.	Oligarchy	THE WIDOWMAKER

5103 G.E.	Oligarchy	THE WIDOWMAKER REBORN
5106 G.E.	Oligarchy	THE WIDOWMAKER UNLEASHED
5108 G.E.	Oligarchy	A GATHERING OF WIDOWMAKERS
5461 G.E.	Oligarchy	"The Media" (BIRTHRIGHT)
5492 G.E.	Oligarchy	"The Artists" (BIRTHRIGHT)
5521 G.E.	Oligarchy	"The Warlord" (IVORY)
5655 G.E.	Oligarchy	"The Biochemists" (BIRTHRIGHT)
5912 G.E.	Oligarchy	"The Warlords" (BIRTHRIGHT)
5993 G.E.	Oligarchy	"The Conspirators" (BIRTHRIGHT)
6304 G.E.	Monarchy	IVORY
6321 G.E.	Monarchy	"The Rulers" (BIRTHRIGHT)
6400 G.E.	Monarchy	"The Symbiotics" (BIRTHRIGHT)
6521 G.E.	Monarchy	"Catastrophe Baker and the Cold Equations"
6523 G.E.	Monarchy	THE OUTPOST
6524 G.E.	Monarchy	"Catastrophe Baker and a Canticle for Leibowitz"
6599 G.E.	Monarchy	"The Philosophers" (BIRTHRIGHT)
6746 G.E.	Monarchy	"The Architects" (BIRTHRIGHT)
6962 G.E.	Monarchy	"The Collectors" (BIRTHRIGHT)
7019 G.E.	Monarchy	"The Rebels" (BIRTHRIGHT)
16201 G.E.	Anarchy	"The Archaeologists" (BIRTHRIGHT)
16673 G.E.	Anarchy	"The Priests" (BIRTHRIGHT)
16888 G.E.	Anarchy	"The Pacifists" (BIRTHRIGHT)
17001 G.E.	Anarchy	"The Destroyers" (BIRTHRIGHT)
21703 G.E.		"Seven Views of Olduvai Gorge"

NOVELS NOT SET IN THIS FUTURE

ADVENTURES (1922–1926 A.D.)

EXPLOITS (1926–1931 A.D.)

ENCOUNTERS (1931–1934 A.D.)

HAZARDS (1934–1938 A.D.)

VOYAGES (1938–1941 A.D.)

STALKING THE UNICORN ("Tonight")

STALKING THE VAMPIRE ("Tonight")

STALKING THE DRAGON ("Tonight")

STALKING THE ZOMBIE ("Tonight")

THE BRANCH (2047–2051 A.D.)

SECOND CONTACT (2065 A.D.)

BULLY! (1910–1912 A.D.)

KIRINYAGA (2123–2137 A.D.)

KILIMANJARO (2234–2241 A.D.)

LADY WITH AN ALIEN (1490 A.D.)

DRAGON AMERICA (1779–1780 A.D.)

A CLUB IN MONTMARTRE (1890–1901 A.D.)

THE WORLD BEHIND THE DOOR (1928 A.D.)

THE OTHER TEDDY ROOSEVELTS (1888–1919 A.D.)

THE BUNTLINE SPECIAL (1881 A.D.)

THE DOCTOR AND THE KID (1882 A.D.)

THE DOCTOR AND THE ROUGH RIDER (1884 A.D.)

THE DOCTOR AND THE DINOSAURS (1885 A.D.)

ABOUT THE AUTHOR

Mike Resnick has won an impressive five Hugos and has been nominated for thirty-two more. The author of the Starship series, the John Justin Mallory series, the Eli Paxton Mysteries, and four Weird West Tales, he has sold seventy-six science fiction novels and more than two hundred eighty short stories and has edited forty-two anthologies. His Kirinyaga series, with sixty-seven major and minor awards and nominations to date, is the most honored series of stories in the history of science fiction.

Photo by Hugette

"Resnick is able to write deftly and poignantly
about a broad spectrum of characters,
exploring vast and colorful landscapes,
all wrapped up in a highly entertaining story."

KEVIN J. ANDERSON

New York Times–bestselling author of *The Dark between the Stars*

"This is space opera at its best—simultaneously pulse
pounding and mind expanding. Resnick is our E. E. 'Doc'
Smith, our Edgar Rice Burroughs: he is the twenty-first
century's master of excitement and adventure. Enjoy!"

ROBERT J. SAWYER

Hugo Award–winning author of *Red Planet Blues*

"Fun . . . like you used to see all the time in science
fiction but is all too rare these days."

ADVENTURES FANTASTIC

"If you're a fan of old school military science fiction,
this might be the series for you."

CCLAP

(Chicago Center for Literature and Photography)

WWW.PYRSF.COM

Available in trade paperback and ebook editions wherever books are sold.